Anne Allen lives in De daughter and grand meant a number of Guernsey for fourteen years and the people. She contrive a valid reason for frequent London, ideal for her city breaks. By profession a psychotherapist, Anne has now published four novels. Find her website at www.anneallen.co.uk

Praise for Dangerous Waters

'A wonderfully crafted story with a perfect balance of intrigue and romance.' *The Wishing Shelf Awards, 22 July 2013 – Dangerous Waters*

'The island of Guernsey is so vividly evoked one feels as if one is walking its byways. An atmospheric and tantalising read.' *Elizabeth Bailey, author of The Gilded Shroud*

Praise for Finding Mother

'A sensitive, heart-felt novel about family relationships, identity, adoption, second chances at love... With romance, weddings, boat trips, lovely gardens and more, Finding Mother is a dazzle of a book, a perfect holiday read.' *Lindsay Townsend, author of The Snow Bride*

Praise for Guernsey Retreat

'I enjoyed the descriptive tour while following the lives of strangers as their worlds collide, when the discovery of a body and the death of a relative draw them into links with the past. A most pleasurable, intriguing read.' *Glynis Smy, author of Maggie's Child.*

Praise for The Family Divided

'The search for a hidden family truth is the catalyst for this touching love story.' *Gilli Allan, author of Fly or Fall*

Also by Anne Allen

Dangerous Waters

Finding Mother

Guernsey Retreat

Anne Allen

The Family Divided

The Guernsey Novels – Book 4

Sarnia Press
London

Sarnia Press
Unit 1, 1 Sans Walk
London EC1R 0LT

A CIP catalogue record for this book is available
From the British Library
ISBN 978 0 9927112 3 8

Typeset in 11pt Cambria by Sarnia Press
This book is a work of fiction. Names, characters,
businesses, organisations, places and events are
either the product of the author's imagination
or are used fictitiously. Any resemblance to
actual persons, living or dead, events or
locales is entirely coincidental

To my mother, Janet Williams, with love

"A house divided against itself
Cannot stand"
Abraham Lincoln

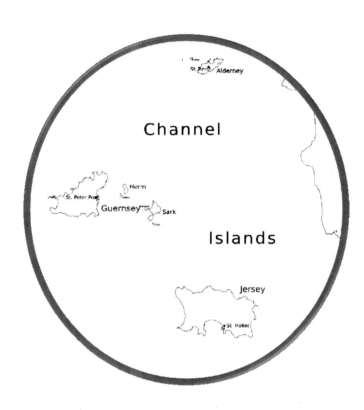

chapter one

2009

The small boat bobbed up and down as the waves splashed gently against the sides and the two men on board adjusted their rods.

'I heard your cousin Dave is up for assault again, hurting the other guy pretty bad, so they say,' Jim Batiste remarked, fitting a chunk of bread on his line. 'He could go down again for it.'

The familiar anger coursed through Andy's veins. 'Dave's always been a waste of space. He brings the family name into more disrepute than my grandfather ever did. And *he* was innocent,' he growled, the image of his cousin's grinning face overlaying his father's in front of him. He had history with Dave, the cocky grandson of his great uncle. When they met as boys Dave had been quick to remind him how he was the one from the wealthy side of the family and Andy was a nobody. The taunts had inevitably led to fights which Dave, bigger and heavier and playing dirty, always won. As the image faded Andy watched his father throw out the line with an expert flick. Something he had never managed as well, in spite of hours of Jim's patient tuition.

His father screwed up his eyes against the sun, checking the float was where he had meant it to be. Satisfied, he turned to his son.

'You're right about Dave. It's a good thing his father didn't live to see how he turned out. The trouble is that mother of his has spoiled him rotten. Never had a firm hand. Not like you,' he said, grinning.

'Right there, Dad! I never got away with anything. And Mum was just as strict,' Andy said, straight-faced.

They both laughed. His mother, Yvette, was a pussy cat where her only child was concerned.

Andy threw his own line over the side of the boat and, for once, the rod made a graceful arc over the water. Settling back on his canvas stool, he allowed himself a moment to admire the sandy bay of Moulin Huet basking in the warm September sun. He liked this spot where his father's boat was anchored; just in from the Mouillière rock. When he was a boy his parents had often picnicked on the beach and he loved to swim out to the rock to prove how strong a swimmer he was.

'Don't suppose you've seen Dave in a while, have you?' His father's voice brought him back from his happy memories.

'I'm not likely to, am I? Not only does he spend much of his time incarcerated in Les Nicolles with the other island reprobates, but when he's out he wouldn't speak to me any more than I would him. I despise his family for what they did to my grandmother and...and you and Mum,' he said, aware of a hot tide of anger flowing to his head. That bloody family! Somehow they had swindled his father out of the Batiste estate, and hadn't even acknowledged him as one of the family. Under Guernsey law at the time, as the eldest son, Jim's father Edmund would have inherited the whole lot after old man Neville died if he hadn't been killed so young. After his death Jim was the natural successor, not Dave's grandfather Harold, the younger brother.

Forcing himself to take a deep breath, he studied his father, now engrossed in lighting his pipe. A wiry sixty-four-year-old, with hands calloused from years of hauling fishing nets, his face bore more lines than usual. He looked tired and Andy wondered if his back was bad again and wrecking his sleep. He should never have had to work so bloody hard! If it wasn't for that bastard Harold...Feeling his chest tighten again, he took another deep breath before saying, 'Dad, I wish you'd explain why you weren't acknowledged as the natural heir when you arrived from France and–'

Jim's eyes flashed. 'How many times do I have to tell you I'm not prepared to discuss it! Ever. It's history and not your business.'

'But it is my business! Apart from the fact I'd have liked to see you and Mum enjoying the comfortable lifestyle you were entitled to, I'd have not had to endure the taunts of being poor from the boys at school, including that...that toerag Dave.' Andy fought hard to control his temper. He didn't want to fall out with his father, particularly when they were fishing together, always something he enjoyed.

Jim seemed to shrink in front of his eyes. 'I'm sorry, lad, for what you had to put up with. It's not what I wanted or expected when your mother and I came over here. But can we put it aside for now and concentrate on the fishing? I'd been looking forward to coming out with you today,' he said, a pleading look in his eyes.

Andy nodded, reluctantly accepting once again the subject was closed. For now. But perhaps one day...

A strong pull on his rod announced he had caught something.

'Dad, I've got the first bite! And I reckon it's a big one.' He managed a smile as he reeled in the line, the anger easing with the chance of a catch.

'Good on you, lad. We might have fish for supper after all,' Jim said, puffing on his pipe.

Andy had to hold on tight as the fish fought to free itself but slowly he won the battle and reeled in a dark grey slithering fish, grabbing it quickly as it landed on deck.

'Black bream. A good weight too. About 3lbs, I reckon. Make a good supper, it will.'

Andy grinned at his father as he expertly pulled the hook from the fish's mouth and dropped it in the water bucket.

'Do you want it for you and Mum? Or are you planning on catching your own supper?' he asked, his grin broadening.

Jim was saved from answering as his own line gave a quick pull and he braced himself to reel in his catch. The fish flashed silver in the sun as it was dragged through the water.

'Grey mullet, about 4lbs,' muttered Jim as he finally grabbed the fish and, after removing the hook, dropped it in the bucket with the bream.

'So neither of us will go hungry tonight, Dad. Happy to stay a bit longer and stock up the freezer?'

Jim nodded. 'Not too long, though. My back's been playing up lately. I don't want to have to pay a visit to the osteopath again. He charges an arm and a leg and I'm not convinced it does me much good.'

Andy knew his father did not have much spare cash; his only income was the State Pension and his wife's meagre earnings. And he was too proud to accept financial help from his son.

'I've an idea, Dad. I'm on good terms with the people running the health spa in Torteval. If you remember, I was the architect for the renovation and extension. How about if I ask if someone could take a look at your back? As a bit of a favour to me. I've heard good reports about the therapies they offer,' Andy said, keeping his fingers crossed his father would agree. If there was a charge, he would pay it without his father knowing.

'I don't know,' Jim said, frowning. 'Sounds a big favour to me. And what if I needed more than one treatment? You can't expect them to keep seeing people for nothing.'

'No, but it wouldn't hurt to let me ask, would it? You never know, one session might be all you need if the right person takes a look at you.'

'Suppose not. It would be good not to be in pain as much.'

'Right it's agreed, then. I'll give Paul a ring and see what he says. Now, shall we have a little bet on who catches the most fish?' Andy said, pleased his father had agreed. Sort of.

'Cheeky devil! You know I'm a better fisherman than you, any day. You'll be throwing your money away, I warn you,' Jim said, with a grin.

They settled down to their fishing and, two hours later, Jim was the undoubted winner at five fish to Andy's three. After handing over the sum of two pounds to settle the bet, Andy helped his father to clear their gear away before Jim took the wheel and started the engine. Andy sat quietly in the stern while his father steered the boat around the coast towards Bordeaux Harbour in the north of the island. Guernsey's south coast was rocky and the cliffs loomed above them as they motored onwards.

Andy felt the remnants of his recent anger rise again as they approached Telegraph Bay. The place where, sixty years ago during the German Occupation, his grandfather, Edmund, having been branded a traitor by his brother Harold, had been pushed to his death.

chapter two

As the plane started the descent into Guernsey, Charlotte gazed out of the window, eager to spot any familiar landmarks. Not that she knew the island very well, having only spent a mere few weeks here in the early spring. She was just relieved to be arriving on the island with the prospect of being amongst friends. The past few months had not been easy and she hoped the change of scene and the pampering at the retreat would bring much needed clarity. A chance to look forward and not back. Catching a glimpse of what could be La Folie, she smiled.

'You look happy, dear. Returning home are you?' asked her neighbour, an older woman clad in layers of woolly jumpers in spite of the mild September weather.

'No I'm not, actually. But I've been here before and loved it. I'm staying at the new retreat, La Folie.'

'My! I've heard it's quite something. One of my nieces works there. Helps in the kitchen, she does. Not cheap though, is it? You need a few bob to stay there,' she said, giving Charlotte an appraising look.

'Yes, well, it's worth it. And the food is outstanding, so do please pass on my thanks to your niece.' Charlotte flashed the woman a quick smile, aware she was being judged by her clothes and probably her accent. She knew she looked what she was: a successful, elegant businesswoman. But inside she held a knot of tension, desperate to uncoil and feel at ease. The reason she was here.

The woman nodded before releasing her seatbelt and standing up. Within minutes the passengers were filing into the terminal and those collecting their luggage encircled the carousel. Charlotte lifted off her case and wheeled it through to arrivals.

'Charlotte! At last!' cried Louisa, waving frantically before engulfing her in a hug.

As the two women drew apart, faces wreathed in smiles, Charlotte felt a release of some of the tension.

'Come on, we can chat in the car,' Louisa said, linking arms as they walked towards the exit. Louisa steered her to a snazzy blue convertible with the roof tucked away in the boot.

'Like the car.' Charlotte grinned as Louisa stored the case.

'Thanks. I love the feel of the wind in my hair, don't you? Okay let's go, La Folie here we come.'

Charlotte had time to study her friend while Louisa was engaged in negotiating the exit from the airport. Physically there was little difference since they had last met in May, but with Louisa's long blond hair tied back in a ponytail, Charlotte saw the slight downturn to her mouth and the lack of sparkle in her eyes. Something was not quite right. And her guess was it was to do with Paul...

'So, how are things? When we've spoken on the phone you've said how much you love your house, but not a lot about Paul and the job.'

Louisa turned her head, sighing.

'Everything's sort of fine between us, we're just finding it difficult to spend a lot of time together. Something Paul promised wouldn't be an issue.'

'Didn't you say the centre was taking on extra therapists to take the pressure off him?'

'Yes, and that's happened. We have another yoga teacher and I share the physio work with the original therapist, Trevor. So in theory all should be fine. But...' She shrugged, focusing back on the road.

'We can chat later. How's Malcolm? Heard from him lately?'

Louisa's look of pain told her the answer.

'Not for a couple of weeks. He did say he might be off grid for a while and not to worry. Easier said than done when it's your father. Particularly after his mini-stroke...'

'Hey! Stop worrying. If there was anything wrong you'd have heard. And he's a pretty tough cookie, so cheer up. I've been looking forward to coming over and spending some time with you.'

Louisa must have heard the slight rebuke in her voice and she flashed a smile.

'Sorry. I'm very happy you're here and I intend to spend as much of my free time with you as I can. Now, how's the book going? You've not said anything about it on the phone.'

'That's because it's not going well. I've done loads of research, to the extent I could enter *Mastermind* with my speciality subject of Emma, Lady Hamilton and wipe the field,' she said, frowning. 'But I can't seem to get to grips with the fictional characters. I'm beginning to wonder if I'm cut out to be a writer after all.' The knot of tension grew tighter as she said out loud what she'd been thinking for weeks.

'Mm. Why don't you get in touch with Jeanne? You two seemed to hit it off that time in Sark and I'm sure she'd be happy to give you some pointers.'

'Good thinking. As a published author of fiction and non-fiction she's perfect.' Charlotte had forgotten about Jeanne and the thought of talking through her problem with her lifted her spirits. Then she remembered something. 'Ah, wasn't she due to have another baby last month?'

'Yep, she had a little girl, Freya. Very cute and adored by her big brother, Harry.'

'Wonderful! But she's going to be up to her eyes in nappies and everything so won't have much time for chatting.' Her heart sank again. The one person she knew who might understand what she was going through with her writing would be too busy to meet. As a publisher

Charlotte knew many authors, but could not bring herself to admit to any of them her sense of failure. She had her reputation, and that of her company, to uphold. Whereas Jeanne was detached and more likely to be sympathetic. Pity.

Louisa pulled up near the front door of La Folie, the gothic style mansion recently transformed into a beautiful, up-market natural health centre. As they got out of the car, she said, 'Paul's gift to Jeanne when Freya was born was some massages and use of the pool. She's already been and will be back soon so you could chat then. Molly, the counsellor you met here last time, is an old friend and babysits for her.'

Charlotte laughed. A deep, throaty laugh as she was struck by an amusing thought. 'I have the distinct impression everyone on this island knows everyone else. There would be no way of keeping secrets here.'

Louisa grinned. 'You'd be surprised! Come on, let's get you settled in and then we can head off for one of Chef's fab juices.'

The receptionist, Nadine, welcomed Charlotte with a broad smile, telling her she would be in *Serenity* this time. On her last visit her room was *Peace*; all the guest rooms had spiritual sounding names and Charlotte knew this room was the best on offer as Louisa had been installed in it when they first met. Special treatment for the owner's daughter.

Louisa suggested they meet in the dining room in half an hour and left her in the capable hands of Nadine. Moments later Doug, the young Canadian gofer, arrived to escort Charlotte to her room. After flashing his bright white smile, Doug carried her bag upstairs while asking how she was. Charlotte was touched he remembered her, thinking again how well trained were the staff. Malcolm Roget's background had been in hotels, the owner of a luxury Canadian chain before selling up and opening La Folie at the beginning of the year. The attention to detail was superb; something wealthy guests like her appreciated.

Once on her own, Charlotte immediately checked the view from the huge bay window. She had visited Louisa in the room on her previous visit so knew what to expect. The vista of immaculate gardens leading to the cliff paths and ultimately the sea, again made her catch her breath. The garden was as colourful as it had been in spring, but the flowers were different. Charlotte recognised, amongst others, abelia, Chinese lanterns, agapanthus, varieties of daylily, rose and hydrangea. Pinks, blues and reds vied with each other against the green of the foliage. With a sigh of appreciation she turned back to inspect the room, once again admiring the golden maple wood of the four-poster and other furniture, the smooth marble-like walls and the silky ivory bedlinen. Only the best would do for the guests of La Folie.

She unpacked her case before changing into the loose fitting clothes more appropriate for her stay. No longer the publisher, she was now on retreat. As she checked her image in the mirror she saw a very different woman to the one who had stayed here only months before. Now, she was not only slimmer, having lost a stone in weight, but her eyes had more of a sparkle. Charlotte had always been considered striking; tall with glossy brown hair, green eyes and a creamy complexion. But being dumped by her erstwhile husband for a younger model had knocked her self-esteem and she had put on weight and lost her spark. She was glad to have found La Folie, telling herself she looked pretty damn good for a woman pushing forty. Louisa had told her how sad she'd looked when they first met and she was right. Charlotte had been lost but *now*...

For a moment she hesitated. Although she looked and felt better, there was still something not right with her life. It had been liberating to make the decision to become a writer and not just a publisher, filling her with anticipation of a new chapter in her life. She had inherited the company from her father, Michael, and never felt quite comfortable with the idea she had not earned her role as editor in chief. Becoming a writer was meant to establish her as successful in her right, but then she had hit a stumbling block with the actual writing and had lost heart. She had started well but then it became harder, finding it difficult to visualise her characters as real people, living real lives. She could only hope it was temporary, having made the mistake, she now realised, of telling everyone she planned to write a novel and did not want to lose face. A thought too horrible to contemplate.

Her mother's illness also hung over her like a dark cloud. Charlotte planned to ring her soon, but their conversations were always strained and she knew, deep down, she was afraid of possible bad news. It was hard, coming so soon after losing her father, who she missed more than ever. He had been the one rock in her life. Thinking of him now, she had to brush away a tear.

Then there was the question of no man in her life. After Richard had walked out, she had forsworn men, her heart – and self-confidence – shattered into pieces. But there were times when she missed the company of a man – and the sex – and as she headed downstairs to meet Louisa could not help but envy her friend. Paul, although not her own type, was lovely. Surely if there were problems between them they could be solved? She hoped so.

Charlotte found Louisa chatting to a waitress in the dining room, set in the light and airy sun room overlooking the gardens.

'I was asking what today's juice special was and it's Chef's "Energiser". Fancy some?'

'One of my favourites. Shall we sit outside?'

They found an empty table on the terrace and Charlotte, after making sure there was no-one else in earshot said, 'OK, what's the problem?'

Louisa shifted in her chair. 'I think it must be me. I love Paul, I know that. But I...I'm struggling to trust in our relationship. As if some part of me knows it won't last. Ever since Mum died I...I expect to lose people I love.'

Charlotte's heart ached for her, knowing what it was like to lose one parent with the other seriously ill. And to lose a husband to someone younger. She stroked Louisa's arm.

'I understand. You've gone through a lot these past months, but surely Paul's not backing off?'

'It's hard to tell as we don't see a great deal of each other except at work and then we can't really talk. With Dad away I think Paul feels burdened by the responsibility of the centre, even though Dad took a back seat. At least when he was on the island Paul could run things past him.' She sipped her juice and appeared to be debating with herself. Looking at Charlotte she went on, 'I'm beginning to think Paul's not as confident in himself as he appears. He's never had to manage such a new enterprise before and I think he's feeling the pressure. Doesn't want it to fail.'

'I see. Has he said anything to you? About the pressure, I mean.'

Louisa shook her head. 'Oh no. And I wouldn't expect him to. Male ego and all that,' she said with a wry smile.

Charlotte took a sip of her own juice.

'So you need to ask him if he's feeling the pressure. Without sounding as if you're judging him. Offer to help in any way you can. He might be relieved to know he's not on his own.'

'I guess. I'll have a chat with him – if I get the chance! It's been made worse lately cos the new yoga teacher, Judy, has been off sick. But she should be back in a day or two and Paul won't need to buzz around like a blue-arsed fly.'

Charlotte laughed. 'At no time could I imagine cool, calm and collected Paul buzzing around like a fly! Is he running the morning yoga sessions? I always adored those.'

'Yep, at the moment.' Louisa glanced at her watch. 'I'll have to love you and leave you as I have a client booked. How about we all eat together here tonight? Normally I'd go home and cook and Paul would either join me or eat in his rooms.'

'Lovely. I'll see you both later. In the meantime I need to arrange my therapies with Nadine.'

Once her friend had left, Charlotte continued to sit in quiet contemplation of the garden. Fellow guests strolled along the paths and for a moment she found herself studying a lone male. Tall, good-looking and in his forties. In spite of her decision to avoid men, she couldn't help but notice him. Solo men of the right age were conspicuous by their absence in this sort of retreat. Just as she was considering going over and introducing herself, a female guest came out of the dining room behind her and headed, laughing, towards him. His face split into a grin and they shared a hug before sauntering towards the cliff path. She might have known he was spoken for and it was probably just as well. It would be better to focus on finding her writing mojo and forget men. They were always trouble, anyway.

chapter three

The dining room buzzed with muted chatter and laughter. Charlotte weaved between the tables to one set back in a corner, waved on by Louisa.

'Paul won't be long, he's just checking all's well in the kitchen. Which reminds me, Chef says hi and he'll catch up with you tomorrow. So, how's his book going?'

'Very well. We should have it out in time for the Christmas trade. I've had great fun trying out all his juice recipes,' Charlotte replied, wishing she was as good at writing as she was at being an editor and publisher. It had been an inspired decision to offer Chef a publishing deal and she was convinced the resulting book, Juice for Life, would be a best-seller. Juicing was becoming the buzz word in health and nutrition and she herself was both a committed convert and a great advert for Chef's recipes. It was thanks to his juices and low-fat diet plan she had lost so much weight. 'We managed to get an endorsement from that film star who stayed here in May, so it's looking good.'

'As long as Chef doesn't let it go to his head and leave,' Louisa said, frowning.

Charlotte nodded her agreement, not wanting to be the cause of such a loss to the centre. Just then she felt a hand on her shoulder and a familiar voice said, 'Hi, Charlotte, great to see you again.' She stood up to share a hug with Paul, who beamed at her with his usual warm smile. Conscious of what Louisa had said earlier, she searched his face for signs of stress, noting the dark circles around his eyes. Her friend was right: Paul was under pressure, something she could relate to. But for different reasons.

'Hi Paul, how are you? Louisa says it's been busy here lately.'

He shrugged, and dropped a kiss on Louisa's upturned face.

'I'm fine. But it has been hectic these past few weeks, which is great as it means La Folie's proving to be a success. Malcolm should be well pleased when he returns.'

'Which is...?'

'Not for a couple more months at least. Last we heard he's enjoying himself too much, staying at the top-notch spas of the world and he doesn't sound keen to return anytime soon. It's supposed to be research, but I think it's more a chance to be pampered and have fun in exotic places.'

'Bully for Malcolm! If he can't enjoy himself at seventy, when can he? Why, he might even come back with a glamorous lady on his arm.' Charlotte replied, with her throaty chuckle. Registering Louisa's white face she immediately regretted her flippant remark.

Patting her friend's hand, she said, 'Hey, I'm sorry. Didn't mean...'

Louisa took a deep breath and smiled. 'It's okay. Really. It's just me being silly. Of course it would be lovely if he found someone after all those years on his own. He deserves to find happiness after...' She fell silent and Charlotte saw her biting her thumb. Forcing down her own worries, she focused on her friend. It was only eight months since Susan, Louisa's mother, had died after a violent burglary, and Charlotte knew the pain was still raw. Although Malcolm and Susan had parted before Louisa was born, thirty-five years ago, they had each been the one true love of their lives.

Paul flung his arm around Louisa and gave her a squeeze.

'Whether he finds romance or not, Charlotte's right, it's about time Malcolm enjoyed himself. If I were rich and successful, I'd do the same.'

'Oh, would you now? And how about me? Would I be allowed to tag along too?' Louisa asked, sounding hurt.

'Don't be silly! Of course I'd want you with me. If only to keep the adoring females from pestering me,' Paul said, with a smile.

Charlotte watched her friend's face slowly break into a smile and heaved a sigh of relief. My! She is touchy. Talk about being insecure. Which makes two of us. She decided to see if she could help.

'Thank you, kind sir, for allowing me that honour, but as things are at the moment your chances of becoming wealthy are slim. Apart from which, you've always said money doesn't interest you,' Louisa said, giving him a kiss.

'True, on both counts. So it leaves me with no alternative but to vicariously enjoy long foreign trips through Malcolm. But a long weekend would be nice,' Paul said, sighing.

'Isn't there anyone who can cover for you? Surely you don't have to wait until Malcolm's back?' Charlotte asked.

'In theory my assistant could take over but she's been off sick so...' He shrugged. As if realising this was no way to welcome her, Paul brightened and grabbed Charlotte's hand. 'Enough of me, I want to know all about what you've been up to in the big smoke. Oh, and I've already ordered for us – Chef's preparing your favourite meal and the champagne's on ice.'

Charlotte was touched and smiled her appreciation before chatting about her work and the latest publishing 'do' she had attended. At least she had some good things to share. The mood lifted, helped even more by the arrival of a bottle of Krug, triggering a laugh from Charlotte and grins from the others. Charlotte had chosen Louisa Krug as her pen name, partly in honour of her friend and a reference to being distantly related to the champagne family. She felt a quick pang at the thought of never using it. They chatted animatedly through the hors d'oeuvres and the seafood main course, which Charlotte declared to be the best yet at La Folie.

By the time they were sipping herbal teas, it was clear to Charlotte from the way they looked at each other, her friends needed to get an early night. And with each other. She pushed down a momentary feeling of envy.

Finishing her tea, she stood up, saying, 'I don't know about you two, but I'm ready for bed. It's been a lovely meal, thanks so much for organising it. I'll thank Chef in the morning. Night, night.' She kissed them both and left, hoping Paul would take the hint and spend the night with Louisa. Charlotte had to settle for a book.

The next morning Charlotte caught up with Chef and they shared an animated discussion about his forthcoming book. A breezy Canadian named Chris, she found him a joy to work with and he seemed equally relaxed with her, already planning his next book about recipes for healthy meals. The talk of books prompted her to ask Nadine to let her know when Jeanne next booked an appointment so they could meet. She so needed to talk to her.

Needing to make a phone call Charlotte returned to her room. She had been putting off ringing her mother, a task she always dreaded.

'Mother, it's me. How are you?'

'How do you think I am? All alone here and expected to carry on as normal despite...despite being on my own. And you never visit. I could be dying for all you care!' her mother snapped.

Charlotte took a deep breath. It was going to be one of those martyr calls.

'Mother, I know it must be hard, but you do have the staff to help and Daddy was hardly ever there anyway. He was too busy running the business in London. I'm sorry I haven't been up for a while but–'

'I know you're avoiding me. You've hardly been here since...since your father died.' There was a sniff down the line. 'I had to organise the village fête entirely singlehandedly this summer. You could have shown me some support but, no, you were too busy as usual. Playing at being a publisher. No wonder Richard left. You only ever think of yourself.'

She dug her fingers into her hand, determined not to let her mother get to her. But it was hard. Her biggest sin in her mother's eyes was being born a girl. Charlotte had known since a small child Lady Annette Townsend, to give her the full title, had wanted a son – an heir to continue the family name. She had even chosen the name Charles, after her own father. Fortunately for Charlotte, her father had not seemed disappointed, spending as much time with her as he could. He even taught her to ride and accompanied her to the Pony Club gymkhanas, her mother having complained she could not spare the time. In spite of knowing how much her father adored her, it had been hard growing up feeling her mother did not love her, gnawing away at her over the years. And now she had lost the loving parent and–

'Are you listening to me, Charlotte?'

'Yes, Mother, of course. I was ringing to see how you were. Have you seen your doctor yet? When we last spoke you said you were feeling off-colour.'

'Humph. Yes and he's arranged for me to see the consultant in a couple of weeks...' Charlotte's heart raced as the words evoked a feeling of dread, she barely heard her mother's next words. 'I'm sure it's not necessary, just a lot of fuss about nothing. You know how these doctors are. Scared of being sued if they miss anything and charge a fortune for a load of tests.' Her voice changed. Less angry – scared, perhaps? Charlotte felt herself grow cold. If her mother *was* scared then something was badly wrong. It wouldn't be surprising after...But she had to focus, must not let her mother hear her own anxiety.

'I'm sure he's just concerned for your welfare, Mother. Do you still have the pain in your side and feel nauseous?'

'Sometimes, but it's probably just a reaction to the drugs I'm taking.'

'Maybe, but I'm glad you're seeing the consultant. Look, afraid I'm away at the moment but I'll give you a ring when you've seen him. When exactly is that?'

Her mother told her then went on to say how well the roses had done that summer, winning First Prize again at the fête. Charlotte made the appropriate responses before her mother announced she could not waste any more time chatting, the housekeeper needed to talk to her, and rang off.

She was left feeling both exasperated and scared. She had been dreading something like this. Had her mother's cancer returned? And if so, how serious was it?

chapter four

Pushing the dreaded thought of her mother's cancer to the back of her mind, she headed off for her first aromatherapy massage with Lin. A session guaranteed to leave her as chilled as her beloved Krug. Sorely needed.

At lunchtime Charlotte floated on a sea of rose geranium and frankincense towards the dining room in the sun lounge. She was meeting Louisa for lunch and was first to arrive. Charlotte was gazing dreamily out of the window admiring the garden when her friend rushed in, apologetic.

'Sorry to be late, but I had a last minute appointment with the father of Paul's friend. He's not a guest but the friend, Andy, was the brilliant architect who designed the pool and this room. So Paul feels we owe him a favour.'

'No problem. I'm not going anywhere. Had the most divine massage with Lin and can barely function at the moment. You'll have to do the talking and I'll listen.'

Louisa laughed. 'You remind me of how I always felt after a session with Lin. Unfortunately, now I'm staff and not a guest I have to wait in line and Lin's always busy. Right, what shall we have?'

They had just given their order when a man came up to the table and spoke to Louisa.

'Sorry to interrupt your lunch, Louisa, but I wanted to thank you for fitting in my father so quickly. He's been in a lot of pain but says it's a bit better now. I've just come to collect him.'

'Hi, Andy, you're welcome. Oh, let me introduce you to my friend, Charlotte. She's a guest here.'

He turned to Charlotte, offering his hand. 'Hello, pleased to meet you. Is this your first visit?'

For a moment she was dumbstruck. What a gorgeous looking man! Tall, slim with dark, wavy hair, soft brown eyes and a firm mouth which curled up at the ends. She fought down the unbidden attraction, reminding herself she was off men.

'Hello, Andy. Nice to meet you, too. And no, this is my second time, I was here earlier in the year which is when I met Louisa. I gather your father needed her magic touch?'

He gave her a brief smile, saying, 'Yes, he did.' Turning back to Louisa he asked, 'Will he need to return for more sessions? Paul and I have an arrangement if he does.'

Louisa nodded. 'He told me. I'd like to see your father again next week, to check if he's keeping up the exercises I gave him. And his back's pretty stiff, probably from arthritis. Not surprising considering his work.'

Andy was about to say something when the food arrived and he muttered a quick goodbye and left.

Charlotte was left feeling annoyed. Annoyed with herself for her initial attraction to Andy and unreasonably annoyed with him for showing not the slightest interest in her.

'This looks wonderful! Chef told me he's been working on new recipes for the centre and we've been discussing a new book containing them. Perhaps a complimentary book for all guests?' she said, gushing in her need to move on.

'Sounds a great idea. Would need to run it past my father, of course, but I think he would go for it. As long as it's not silly expensive!' Louisa grinned as she filled her fork with seared tuna.

'I've thought of that and we could keep the costs down by printing on demand and also offering the book to purchase by non-guests. Could be a great marketing exercise.'

Louisa agreed and they discussed various ideas before she stood up to leave for her next client.

Charlotte asked slyly, 'So, did you two get an early night?' Louisa reddened and admitted they did and Charlotte offered a thumbs up. She went on, 'Would you like to come for dinner tonight at my place? Paul's coming too,' Louisa said, still pink. Charlotte was happy to accept and, once on her own, her thoughts turned again to Andy. Was he single? Probably not, he was too damn attractive. Stop it! She chided herself. Pulling herself together she slipped outside and strode out towards the cliff path. What she needed was a good long walk and fresh air, not reminders of what she used to have.

The early evening sky was a darkening blue and the sun hung low on the horizon as Louisa drove with Charlotte to St Peter Port. The dark nights were edging ever closer and the women bemoaned the end of summer.

'I've really enjoyed being out in the garden in the evenings after work and at weekends we've had friends round for barbecues. I'm glad Dad snapped up the lease as I'm sure the house would have gone quickly to someone else. It has such a pretty garden which I can't wait to show you, and luckily it's warm enough to eat outside tonight.'

'Lovely. I'm pleased you've settled in, but what are your long-term plans? Will you sell your London house?'

Louisa sighed. 'Depends on what happens with Paul. If we can get over this bad patch the idea is for him to move in with me and then eventually buy our own home. I'm not sure what I'd do if we were to split...' she looked so unhappy Charlotte gripped her shoulder.

'Hey! Don't be so defeatist, I'm sure you two are meant for each other and you'll come through this even more in love. Paul adores you, but you need to tell him you're there by his side. Big Sis says so, remember.'

Louisa turned to face her and grinned. 'Thanks, Big Sis. Always wanted a sister or brother you know. I'd happily settle for you as a surrogate.'

'Good. That's agreed. From now on we're sisters in all but name. Oh! Is this your house?'

Louisa steered the convertible into the drive of the semi-detached house and switched off the engine. 'Yes, lovely isn't it? And it's so quiet in the close that I forget I'm virtually in the centre of Town. Come on, I'll show you around before I start cooking.'

Charlotte admired the 1930s house which appeared recently modernised. Louisa proudly showed her the garden, with a small lawn and patio surrounded by shrubs, offering privacy from the neighbours. It was delightful and Charlotte could see why her 'sister' was so happy there.

'So, what time's Paul arriving?'

Louisa was removing vegetables and chicken breasts from the fridge and said, 'In about an hour. Which is fine as I can prepare the food and cook it as soon as he arrives. We're having an easy stir-fry. Now, how about a glass of wine? White or red? Sorry, we're all out of Krug!' She laughed.

'White would be lovely, thanks. And even I can have too much champagne, you know.' She sat on a bar stool while Louisa poured two glasses of wine before chopping the vegetables. Charlotte felt uncomfortable with the domesticity of it. The preparation of the meal, waiting for the man to arrive – it took her back to the time of her marriage. Not that she ever prepared the food; they had a housekeeper, Mrs Thomas, who moved with them to her father's house in London after his death. But Charlotte had helped to choose the meals and would always make sure there was a glass of something ready for Richard on his return in the evening. Until the excuses about working late began...And now her friend Louisa was worried about her own relationship, albeit for different reasons. She knocked back her wine.

When everything was ready they took their drinks outside to enjoy the last rays of the sun.

Paul arrived, more or less on time, and he set the table outside while Charlotte lit the candles in the lanterns. Within minutes the stir-fry was ready and everyone tucked in. Once they had finished, the plates were cleared and glasses refilled.

'This is heaven. I can understand why you love it here, Louisa. I should eat outside at home, too, but it seems such a fag asking Mrs Thomas to take everything into the garden for me. I usually eat in the breakfast room as the dining room's far too grand unless I'm entertaining. But I don't do much these days, since...since Richard left.' Charlotte sighed.

'Perhaps you will again soon. We'll just have to find you a man! Oh, that reminds me, Paul, Andy brought his father in for a session with me today and I said Jim should come back next week. Is it okay?'

'Sure. I told Andy we'd cover a couple of sessions and he'll pay us a reasonable fee for more if needed. He wants Jim to think we're not charging at all as he's too proud to accept what he'd call charity.' Paul sipped his wine. 'Did you know he wants to uncover what really happened to his grandfather during the occupation? Apparently Jeanne offered to help as she was researching that period for her next book, but she's rather up to her eyes in nappies these days,' he said, laughing. 'A pity, as he seems really keen to help his dad.'

'Sounds intriguing. What's the mystery?' Charlotte asked, leaning forward.

'I don't know the whole story, but it boils down to the fact Jim's father, Edmund, was killed a month before the end of the war, not long after having being labelled an informer by his younger brother Harold. The police never found who did it, although they suspected a POW looking for food. Anyway, Edmund's widow, Madeleine, was apparently shunned by the family and left Guernsey soon after the liberation. Harold later inherited the extensive family property which is now worth a mint, but no-one knew Madeleine was pregnant with Jim. He should by rights have inherited, you see.' He topped up their glasses and leant back in his chair.

'That's so unfair! I'm not surprised Andy wants to help. But surely Jim's the one to demand answers?' Louisa said, looking shocked.

'I agree, but for some reason he's not pursued it. He's much more laid-back than his son, as I'm sure you found. Jim's a lovely guy, salt of the earth, and not got a grasping bone in his body, but he's not very worldly.'

'Is Andy an only child? He seemed quite concerned for his father when we saw him,' Charlotte asked.

'Yes he is. They're very close, both love fishing and often go out in Jim's boat together. We occasionally buy some of their catch for La Folie if they have any spare.'

'Don't their wives mind them going out fishing if it takes up so much time?' Charlotte asked, casually.

'Jim's wife Yvette is only too glad of the fish on the table and Andy was divorced years ago.'

Louisa raised her eyebrows at Charlotte, who pretended not to notice. She swirled her wine around the glass, keeping her face neutral, but inwardly she felt her heart pump faster. Her mind began to race.

'Perhaps I could help.' As soon as the words were out, Charlotte wondered why on earth she had said it. Stupid, stupid, woman! But it would give her something to take her mind off her failed attempt at writing...

Paul and Louisa looked at her, surprised.

'I mean with the research. What if I carry on where Jeanne left off, go through the records etc. See if I can find out anything pertinent to what happened. My forte's always been research and as I'm struggling with my writing at the moment I'd be happy to assist.' She sipped her wine, looking across at her friends.

'That's kind of you, but aren't you here to relax and not tie yourself down with researching in dusty books?

Andy's waited years for answers so I'm sure he can wait a bit longer till Jeanne's back in writing mode,' Paul said.

'Yes, Paul's right. I thought you were here to recharge, not get involved in other people's problems?' Louisa gave her a quizzical look.

'I'm sure I can do both. And it might just kick-start my own writing, which quite frankly, needs something to move it along. But ultimately it will be up to Andy and Jeanne to decide whether they want me to come on board. By the way, how did Jeanne get involved in the first place?'

'Nick and Andy have been friends since boyhood as their fathers were great mates, all living in St Sampson. So he and Jeanne were keen to help in any way they could,' said Paul, emptying his glass. 'Anyone for a refill? I can open another bottle.'

The women shook their heads. Charlotte, thinking Louisa and Paul might want time alone, suggested ordering a taxi. Paul insisted on driving her back, saying he needed an early night with new guests arriving on the first flight from the UK. As she hugged Louisa, her friend whispered, 'I think you've an ulterior motive about this research lark. You can't pull the wool over my eyes!'

Charlotte didn't comment, just smiled before following Paul to his car. Once they were heading out of town, she said, 'I am serious about helping Andy, you know. It does sound as if his family's had a raw deal and I'm all for obtaining justice. Would you mind passing on my offer?'

Paul glanced at her. 'If you're sure, but you know it wouldn't be right for you to work on anything within the confines of La Folie. Strictly against the ethos of the centre. We want to encourage guests to leave the rest of the world behind while they recharge.'

'Yes, of course, that's why I left my laptop at home. But I'm sure something could be worked out if Andy and Jeanne accept my offer. I'm only booked in for two weeks and could stay longer somewhere else if needed. There's no urgent need for me to return home so...' Charlotte shrugged, trying not to think about her mother's illness. For the moment it made sense to be fully occupied with something which had a purpose rather than play at writing a novel, which she still hoped to do. But it was much more important to help a family in need, wasn't it?

chapter five

C harlotte woke the following day after a disturbed night's sleep. In spite of their decidedly tricky relationship, she did love her mother. As an only child she also felt responsible for her, and had promised her father she would "keep an eye on the old girl, m'dear, she's not as strong as she likes to pretend". Easier said than done with a mother who offered only criticism, she thought, struggling to wake up. Feeling guilty about being pampered in the spa while her mother was unwell, Charlotte consoled herself with the thought there was little she could do until she had seen the oncologist, and crawled out of bed to grab a quick shower.

Within a few days Charlotte settled into the calm, relaxed atmosphere of La Folie, allowing herself to step back from her worries and live in the moment. As she walked around the garden one morning she realised the combination of yoga and the ministrations of Lin and other therapists had worked the same magic she had experienced in the spring. Stopping by a colourful display of deep red roses, she bent to breathe in their heady scent and was immediately transported back to her parents' garden in Somerset.

Her mother was inordinately proud of her roses, entering them yearly into the village floral competitions and had always won First Prize. Not surprising as her parents were the local nobs, presiding over local functions with genteel bonhomie. Her mother had always been a snob, but after her father was knighted and she became Lady Annette Townsend, she was much worse. Charlotte used to cringe at the way she talked to staff and villagers, so different to her down-to-earth father. He would never have laid claim to being responsible for the efforts of others, unlike her mother. The fact their gardener was responsible for the lushness of the roses did not seem to stop Annette from accepting her due as a woman with the greenest of green fingers. Something Charlotte could never lay claim to, being hopeless with anything so practical, but she did know the names of plants, drummed into her by her mother from childhood.

Continuing her walk, and admiring the last of the sunflowers and delphiniums standing tall in the sunshine, she wondered how her mother was coping in the house on her own, albeit with the servants. Charlotte bit her lip, feeling the familiar pain of her father's death two years ago. Taught never to display emotions in public, it had been difficult to cope with her loss until she received counselling here in the spring. The grief had been exacerbated by her husband's desertion shortly after and she had become depressed. Gazing now at the daylilies bowing their heads gracefully in the gentle breeze, Charlotte knew she had come a long way since then, but was not as strong as she liked to appear. Boarding school had coated her with a veneer of independence and self-confidence, but inside she was a woman who needed to be loved. As she had been by her father, but not, she thought, her mother: always keen to find fault. And loved only briefly by her ex-husband.

Charlotte made a supreme effort to recapture the feeling of calm now being sabotaged by her memories and imagined herself in a bubble of light, as taught by Molly, the counsellor. It worked and she was able to smile serenely at a passing fellow guest. Glancing at her watch, Charlotte realised it was nearly time for her t'ai chi class and made tracks inside.

As she passed the reception desk Nadine called out to say Jeanne would be in the following morning for her massage and would be happy to meet for a chat afterwards. Charlotte smiled, wondering if Paul had passed on her offer of help. Even if he hadn't, she looked forward to talking to Jeanne about the proverbial writer's block, although a part of her was afraid she was simply a lousy writer. Something far too hard to accept – yet.

At eleven the next morning Charlotte experienced mixed emotions as she made her way to the sun lounge to meet Jeanne. Although it would be lovely to catch up with her, she was having second thoughts about becoming involved with Andy's research. It would be a wonderful diversion, but it would mean spending time with Andy and he was *too* attractive to ignore, even by someone bruised by men. Jeanne was watching for her and waved before standing up to share a hug. Charlotte found herself smiling in spite of her unease.

'How are you? And congratulations on your baby girl. Is she well?'

Jeanne, displaying dark circles under her eyes, but otherwise looking good with gleaming hair and glowing skin, smiled broadly.

'We're both fine, thanks. Fortunately I have quick and easy births and we were home again the same day. But I could do with more sleep!'

Charlotte ordered a juice before replying, 'I bet! But you look wonderful and it looks as if you've lost the baby weight already. What does Harry think about his sister?'

'He adores her, although he was a bit unsure initially when we told him he had a sister. He'd wanted a brother to play with, but once he held her he was hooked and smothers her with kisses,' she laughed. 'I now have to stop him trying to pick her up from her crib whenever he can. And yes, I've almost lost the extra weight. I've been following the healthy recipes Chef cooks up and even Nick's hooked on them. So, how are you? How's the book coming on?' Jeanne looked at her quizzically.

Charlotte took a deep breath. 'Not great. I thoroughly enjoyed the research, but I've been finding it difficult to empathise with my main fictional character and how she would behave at that time. Modern characters would be so much easier, but I love the eighteenth century so...' she went on to describe in more detail what seemed to be holding her back.

Jeanne was sympathetic. 'I can understand the problem. You need to fully immerse yourself in the time-period – the sights, sounds and smells. What people wore, how they talked, etc. Not easy, but possible. Have you read any novels set in that time?' She went on to make more suggestions, admitting she had suffered from writer's block a couple of times and Charlotte began to feel less of a failure. She was simply inexperienced and needed to hear how other writers dealt with such issues. Months before she had joined a local writing group for support using her pen name, but unfortunately someone had discovered both her real name and her role as a publisher and she had been bombarded with submissions. She left immediately, but missed the camaraderie.

Jeanne then brought up the subject of Andy and his family.

'Paul said you'd like to help with the research which is fine by me. But surely you won't be here long enough to trawl through old records and interview people?'

'I can stay longer if need be, so it's not an issue. Even if I did have to return home for some reason I could always come back. My deputy takes over when I'm away and he's excellent. Totally trustworthy, thank goodness. I've finally learnt the art of delegation.'

Her friend grinned. 'A pity I can't delegate the night feeds! But Nick doesn't possess the, er, right equipment. But at least he does spend a lot of time with Harry when he's at home. And he's become quite a good cook since my first book came out.' She sipped her juice before adding, 'Would you like me to ask Andy how he feels about your offer? I understand you met briefly a few days ago.'

'Please. Andy might not remember me as he really wanted to talk to Louisa about Jim. But I'd understand if he didn't want a stranger involved. He...seemed a nice guy,' she said, recalling his warm, brown eyes and sexy body. And quickly pushed away the image as once again she questioned the wisdom of offering to help. Apart from anything else it would be so embarrassing if Andy was completely uninterested in her.

'He is, apart from the chip on his shoulder about the division in the family. And the fact his father was denied his inheritance. Definitely some bitterness there, but otherwise he's a decent guy, if a bit of a workaholic.'

They returned to the subject of writing for a while longer until it was time for Jeanne to leave for Freya's next feed, promising to phone after she had spoken to Andy. Charlotte was left wondering if she would be disappointed if Andy said no to her offer. It was too close to call.

chapter six

The following day Charlotte was relieved to be diverted with an excursion with Louisa, who had a free day. Much as she enjoyed being pampered at La Folie, it was good to get out and explore the island while the Indian summer held sway. They had enjoyed many hours sightseeing during her last visit and today planned to explore the south coast around Jerbourg Point. But first she had a yoga class to attend.

'So, have you heard from Malcolm yet?' Charlotte asked as Louisa drove towards St Martins.

'No and I'm starting to worry. I know he said not to, but I can't help it. Thought I'd give Glenn at the agency a ring and see if he's heard anything, as Dad booked the trip through him. At least I can trust Glenn not to blab on me!'

'True. How's the business going since he took over?'

'Very well, apparently. Glenn always sounds upbeat when we talk. Now *Voyages* handles all the travel arrangements for La Folie, our clients are also using them for their other holidays. It's been win-win since he bought the agency from me.'

'Good. Where was Malcolm when you last heard?'

'Bali.' She frowned. 'Not best known for its health and safety arrangements.'

Charlotte had to agree but didn't say so, not wanting to worry her friend further. 'Hey, I'm sure he's fine. Just being a typical man and not staying in touch. And, to be fair, until recently he had no-one who cared about his whereabouts. Being a father is still quite new for him.'

'Uh huh. I guess. Anyway, I'll ring Glenn and see what he says,' Louisa replied before bringing the car to a halt in the Jerbourg car park. 'Right, let's get walking.'

'What a fabulous view! Herm and Sark are so clear and I can even see France. And that must be Jersey to our right. I must get over there sometime. Have you been yet?'

Louisa shook her head. 'No, but Paul wants to take me for a weekend once he gets the time off, which hopefully won't be long now Judy, his deputy's back. One of our friends, Nicole, was born in Jersey and has the use of her parents' flat. We may be able to stay there when we finally arrange it. Would be nice,' she sighed, before turning to face Charlotte. 'I forgot to ask how it went with Jeanne. You said you were meeting her.'

'It was fine.' She didn't want to say too much as although Jeanne had given her hope, she still had to put her ideas into action. 'Jeanne offered me some helpful tips about writer's block and then we talked about Andy. She said she'd talk to him but I've not heard anything yet.' Charlotte had more or less decided it had been a foolish whim to offer her services and Andy wouldn't want her poking her nose in even if it could be to his advantage. She would need to find something else to give her a sense of purpose and stop thinking about her mother.

'Oh, right. Well I'm glad she helped. Are you going to get back to your novel when you leave La Folie?'

'That's the idea!' she said, forcing herself to smile.

They stood on the edge of the car park drinking in the view. Herm, the smaller island, looking tranquil and inviting, hunkered down in the sea, the nearest beach golden in the sun. Sark, on the other hand, rose up majestically atop steep cliffs.

'What a brill day we had in Sark at Easter. Have you been over again since?' Charlotte asked, remembering their fun day cycling on the island.

'Yes, Paul and I had a day trip a couple of months ago and we've also been to Herm. Gorgeous! You must try and get over while you're here.'

Charlotte laughed. 'What I really need is a retreat at La Folie followed by a stay in a hotel as a normal tourist. That way I get the best of both worlds!'

Grinning, Louisa said, 'You know, you could be onto something there. We could offer a double package for anyone to do just that. Good thinking, Batman.'

Laughing, they set off eastwards along the cliff path, leading ultimately to St Peter Port. They were in no hurry, the day stretched ahead and the sun warmed their faces, the peace only disturbed by raucous seagulls wheeling overhead. The tang of the sea mingled with the scent of the flowering broom and heather. As she chewed on a blade of grass, Charlotte remarked, 'So much has happened to us both since the spring. But particularly you. I don't suppose you ever dreamt you'd end up living here, did you?'

'Nope. I thought I'd find my father and then return to London and...well, pick up the pieces.' Louisa took a lungful of air and released it with a deep sigh. 'It's not been easy, as you know, but once that man was jailed for killing Mum, it made it easier to embrace my new life. All I need now is to know Dad's safe and spend more time with Paul. Easy-peasy!' She turned to face Charlotte, adding, 'And what about you? Happy with the changes you've made?'

Charlotte thought for a moment, not willing to be totally honest with her friend. 'On the whole, yes. I'm no longer upset with Richard and, frankly, he did me a favour. I'm more in control of my life now and there's something to be said for only having yourself to please.' Except there was her mother... 'With regard to my writing, once I'm back on track it will be onwards and upwards.' She smiled at her friend.

They linked arms and continued along the path, aiming to have a snack lunch at Fermain Bay before returning to Jerbourg.

~ ~

35

Andy's mobile rang.

'Hello, Jeanne. How are you?'

He was surprised to hear Jeanne was offering a substitute for his research. Some woman called Charlotte who was staying at La Folie. He'd met her according to Jeanne. After thanking her, he said he'd think it over. Once he'd switched off the phone, he leant back in the office chair, tapping his fingers on the desk. Although keen to find out the truth of what really happened to divide the family, Andy was wary of involving a stranger. Jeanne was fine, married to one of his best friends and a local, he could trust her implicitly. But this Charlotte – who was she? He remembered now he had met the woman, lunching with Louisa the other day. Apart from registering vaguely how attractive she was, he hadn't paid her much attention. Just a guest of the centre. Jeanne had said she was a writer and a publisher from London who loved research. Hmm. Swinging the chair from side to side, Andy stretched out his legs in an effort to ease the stiffness from his morning run. So, Charlotte was well qualified to help with digging up facts, but was she discreet? He stood up and paced around the clinical room constituting his workspace: white walls covered in photos of finished projects and drawing boards bearing his latest plans. He couldn't work in clutter, needing to focus on the job in hand and although there was a window, it overlooked a granite wall, offering not an iota of distraction.

What to do? Should he ask his father if he minded a stranger looking into the family history? As he pushed against a wall while stretching his legs Andy realised that was a no-no. Jim was a private person and hated talking about the family. Whenever Andy asked him why he had not pressed for his inheritance, he had become annoyed, saying he had come to an arrangement with Uncle Harold and not to interfere. Knowing any so-called arrangement had not involved much, if any, money changing hands,

Andy was exasperated as well as puzzled. Something did not add up and although it was all right for his father to act as if he didn't care about money, in reality he needed it now he was retired – meaning Andy had to help out when he could without Jim finding out. At least his mother Yvette was not too proud to accept the few pounds he handed her whenever he was round for dinner. The thing which really stuck in his craw was the knowledge that his good-for-nothing cousin Dave stood to inherit the family fortune and would no doubt blow it away on fast cars and flash holidays, assuming he was not incarcerated at the time. The unwelcome thought prompted Andy to pick up the phone.

chapter seven

As she stepped out of the changing rooms Charlotte was greeted by the sound of arms splashing their way through water. Not a huge fan of swimming, she knew it would be a great way to stay toned, as Louisa's fit body confirmed. Her friend was a passionate swimmer and her trim shape was testament to the value of that passion. Ideally Charlotte would have preferred to swim in a warm sea with mask and flippers while admiring the brilliant colours of underwater creatures and coral reefs. Sighing, she accepted the beautifully designed indoor pool at La Folie would have to do for now and slid reluctantly into the warm water. After a while she was surprised to find it was almost enjoyable and managed twenty lengths before she climbed out, shrugged on her robe and flopped onto a lounger.

Picking a juice from the selection offered by the hovering waitress, she settled back feeling rather smug. Perhaps this exercise lark might not be too bad after all. She was determined to keep her slim figure after all the hard work of watching what she ate, and exercise had to play a part. As she sipped her juice Charlotte allowed her gaze to wander to the kitchen garden visible through the glazed walls. It had been barely established last time she was there but now massed rows of lush vegetables and herbs swayed gently in the warm breeze. Feeling content and soporific in the heated air of the pool, Charlotte's heavy eyelids were drooping when Nadine appeared at her side.

'Sorry to disturb you, Miss Townsend, but Jeanne Mauger has just phoned. She asked if you could call her back when you have a moment.'

'Thanks, Nadine.' Charlotte smiled as the receptionist departed. Wonder if this means she's spoken to Andy? Hope so. She finished the last of her drink and stood up, nodded at a woman lying on a nearby lounger, and returned to the changing room for a shower. Keen to find out what Jeanne had to say, it wasn't long before she was back in her room and reaching for the phone.

'Hi Jeanne. Any news?'

'Yes, Andy's suggested you two meet to discuss things further. I warn you, he's a bit unsure about involving a non-local so it's not a done deal. You'll have to turn on the charm,' Jeanne said, laughing.

'I'll do my best,' Charlotte replied, smiling to herself. Jeanne passed on Andy's phone number and then excused herself as a baby's wail echoed down the line. Charlotte was about to punch in Andy's number when she was hit by her previous doubts. Was it really a good idea to meet Andy? The thought of the research made her tingle with anticipation – something to get stuck into, make her feel she was achieving something useful – but what about the man himself? Did she or didn't she want to see him again? Telling herself it was irrelevant as he had hardly acknowledged her, she made the call and Andy suggested they meet at La Folie the next evening. No longer feeling sleepy, she changed into joggers and trainers and headed outside for a walk. Anything to stop her dwelling on whether or not she had made a mistake.

The next day dragged. Charlotte had booked a couple of therapy sessions in between her t'ai chi and yoga classes and although occupied, did not feel fully engaged with anything. A passive participant at best. But at least, she considered later that afternoon, her mind and body had received due pampering and she was pretty chilled out in preparation for meeting Andy. Glancing at her watch, she saw there was an hour to kill and returned to her room for her swimsuit. Forty-five minutes later she was showered and changed and waiting in the sun lounge. She spotted him hovering in the doorway and waved him over to the tucked away corner table. Wearing a navy T-shirt, a crumpled cream linen jacket and jeans, he attracted admiring glances as he strode towards her with an easy grace. Mm, looks as if he keeps fit. Not bad for a forty-year-old, she thought, reaching out to shake his proffered hand. She felt a frisson of electricity as their hands touched.

'Hi Andy. Thanks for coming. Would you like a drink? They serve a brilliant selection of juices or you can indulge in a glass of something stronger.'

'Juice is fine, thanks. I'll have whatever you recommend,' he said, offering a slight smile.

Charlotte noticed the smile did not reach his eyes and her heart sank. This was going to be tricky. Time for the charm offensive. She summoned up her brightest smile and suggested a Chef's Special juice. The order placed it was time to talk business.

'I understand from Jeanne you're keen to discover what really happened to your grandfather and why the family's been divided since. But I think you're wary of me becoming involved as I'm not a local. Am I right?' She tilted her head and opened her eyes wide.

Andy shifted in the chair.

'Well, sort of. It's a delicate matter, as I'm sure you appreciate. I need to be convinced of your sincerity and absolute discretion and, to be frank, I don't know you.' His eyes locked onto hers and Charlotte had to remind herself this was purely a job interview. Nothing more.

'No, you don't. Not yet. But Paul and Louisa do know me pretty well and am sure would be happy to vouch I'm both loyal and honourable. And as a publisher, I wouldn't survive long if I was ever indiscreet.'

He leant back and smiled. Again it did not reach his eyes.

'Point taken. The thing is my father and I are private people by nature. We don't like the idea of washing our dirty linen in public and, in a small place like Guernsey, it's very hard to avoid. If anything's discovered which could damage our name further, then it must be kept quiet. My father has suffered enough,' Andy said, a look of pain crossing his face.

'Of course, I'd be the soul of discretion. But what puzzles me, Andy, is why you haven't undertaken the research yourself? Keeping it in the family, as it were?'

'Good question. Apart from the fact I've never had much free time to devote to it properly, I couldn't risk my father finding out. It would be bound to get back to him if I was seen to be asking questions and researching archives. But the main stumbling block is the other family members wouldn't talk to me. And, to be honest, Dad's also made it clear he doesn't want the past raked over. God knows why not, as he's the one to have lost the most, what with his inheritance going to that...that reptilian uncle of his, Harold.' His face tightened and Charlotte could see his struggle to stay calm.

'I take it you don't get on with Harold,' she murmured.

Andy grunted. 'It's that obvious, is it? Harold's the key to the whole sorry story. Ideally it would be great to ask him directly what happened but that's never going to happen. We'd have to find a way of uncovering the truth some other way.' He took a sip of his drink, then gave her a searching look. 'How would you achieve that?'

She wasn't encouraged by his manner, he certainly didn't seem attracted to either her or her offer of help. But at least she could answer the question. 'I've thought about it. As Jeanne's novel is set in the occupation, she intended to talk to people with first-hand experience of living here at that time. I thought I could be her researcher, talking to people on her behalf. What do you think? Would it work?'

'Hmm, should do. Old islanders love talking about the war. But it's extremely unlikely Harold would talk to anyone; from what I've heard anything to do with the occupation is a taboo subject. And apparently my grandfather is never mentioned by his side of the family. It's as if he never existed.'

Charlotte saw the tightening of his jaw. This was really a big deal for Andy; it looked as if Jeanne was right about the chip on his shoulder. But at least he was beginning to open up.

'May I ask why it seems more important to find out the truth now? After all, it's been a long time since...' she said, spreading her hands.

Andy twiddled the glass in his hands and seemed to be debating what to answer. At last he said, 'I'm concerned my parents are now struggling financially. Dad had to retire early thanks to his bad back and Mum only earns a pittance as a translator.' Charlotte raised her eyebrows and he went on, 'She's French. Dad was brought up in France, where my grandmother fled after the Liberation. She had family in Normandy, you see, like quite a few locals. My parents were teenage sweethearts and married young. Once I was on the way Dad decided to come to Guernsey so I could be a local and take up my family heritage.' Andy gave a bitter laugh. 'Some heritage! I don't know what happened when my parents arrived here, but Harold has never recognised Dad as part of the family and, more importantly, the rightful heir. And why would he? He'd have lost virtually everything.'

'So your parents received nothing?'

Andy shook his head.

'That doesn't sound right. Can your father prove who he is?'

'You mean he's Edmund's son?'

She nodded.

'I don't know. Don't see why not. Apparently my grandmother didn't know she was pregnant when

Edmund was killed and she left Guernsey shortly after. So I guess it's possible no-one here knew about the pregnancy when she left. But Dad's birth certificate proves he was born less than nine months after his father died, so...' He shrugged.

Now Charlotte was surprised to find herself angry on his behalf. 'This is so unfair. Something doesn't make sense and it sounds as if Jim's been swindled out of his inheritance. I'd really like to help if you'd let me, Andy. We can't let Harold get away with this!'

She felt herself flush as Andy stared at her, eyebrows raised.

'Are you always so passionate about other people's problems? Particularly when you don't even know them?'

Charlotte, embarrassed, laughed. 'Sorry! I did get rather carried away. But I do so hate it when there's an injustice and I meant what I said about helping.'

'In that case it would be churlish of me to refuse,' he replied with a smile. Charlotte relaxed under his warmer gaze. This would be such a worthwhile project to keep her occupied. And not thinking of anything else...

He went on, 'It's not just about seeing my parents enjoy a comfortable retirement, I also want to stop my waste of space cousin inheriting everything when Harold finally shuffles off this mortal coil.'

'Oh, so why's your cousin the heir and not his father? And what's so bad about him?' Charlotte leaned forward, beginning to be fascinated by the unfolding story.

'My uncle Stanley, Harold's only child, died years ago of cancer, leaving a son, Dave. He was a teenager at the time and went even more off the rails than before and has been in trouble with the police more times than I can count. And *he's* the Batiste who will inherit what should be my father's!' Andy virtually spat out the words.

After he had left Charlotte returned to her room to mull over what had been discussed. Grabbing a notebook she jotted down the main points. While a guest at the centre she had no intention of undertaking any research, as she had agreed with Paul, but wanted to be clear about where to start once she left. As she wrote, her thoughts kept straying to Andy. He *was* rather delicious, she decided. But she wasn't ready for a relationship. She simply had to sort herself out first. And although he had thawed a little towards the end, he had not showed any interest in her as a woman. Only as a researcher. Tapping her pen against her lips she gazed out of the window towards the cliffs and the sea beyond. A wind had built up during the day and now white caps topped the waves, adding melodrama to the scene. Mesmerised, Charlotte thought it was a shame she couldn't stay at La Folie until the research was finished. Reminding herself to ask Louisa if she could recommend a hotel, Charlotte glanced at her watch and saw it was time for dinner. After a quick freshen-up she headed downstairs in anticipation of the delights Chef had planned for the guests.

She was crossing the hallway when Louisa appeared from the office, her face ghostlike.

'Louisa, whatever's the matter?' Charlotte cried, rushing toward her.

Her friend's face crumpled as she fell into her outstretched arms.

'It's – it's my father. I've just been on the phone to Glenn who'd been trying to track him down.' Tears soaked onto Charlotte's shoulder as Louisa went on, 'He should have left Bali a week ago and flown to Japan but didn't catch the flight. And – and Glenn's contacted the Bali hotel and Dad checked out as planned but – but hasn't been seen since!'

chapter eight

Charlotte steered Louisa back into the office. Fortunately it was empty and she pushed her friend into a chair before sitting beside her.

'Look, don't get yourself in a state. I'm sure there's a perfectly innocent explanation. Malcolm's free to change his plans if he wants and I'm sure that's what he's done. Found somewhere else to go on the spur of the moment. Which would be so like him, wouldn't it?'

Louisa blew her nose and nodded.

'I guess so. But I don't see why he didn't cancel his flight to Japan. Glenn checked with the airline and they hadn't heard from Dad, which is odd. It's not like him to throw money away.' She sniffed.

Charlotte couldn't help agreeing, but didn't want to worry Louisa further. Holding her hand she asked, 'Has Glenn contacted other airlines which had flights that day?'

'No, he said he can't as they won't divulge passenger lists except to the police and we don't want to involve them – yet. Oh, where on earth is he? He can't just disappear!' Tears tracked down her cheeks, leaving black mascara trails.

'Hey, this is not solving anything. Have you got any clients booked this evening?'

Louisa shook her head.

'Good. Have you spoken to Paul yet?'

'No, I...I was on my way to find him when you saw me. I'm not sure where he is...'

'Right. You stay here and I'll go and find him,' Charlotte said, squeezing Louisa's shoulder. 'How about splashing some water on your face? You can't let the guests see you so upset, now can you?'

Leaving Louisa to freshen up, Charlotte headed to the reception desk to ask where she could find Paul. Told he was due to finish with a client any minute, she hovered outside his therapy room while thinking what could possibly have happened to Malcolm. She could only pray he was all right for Louisa's sake. It would be too awful for her to lose him only months after meeting him for the first time. And so soon after losing her mother...The thought reminded Charlotte of her own mother and the tests she would be undergoing in a few days. Her stomach clenched and she had to take a deep breath. So much for a chill out break. What with her mother and now Malcolm...

'Charlotte, are you looking for me?' Paul appeared at her shoulder and she quickly told him about Malcolm and that Louisa needed him. His eyes widened in shock and he thanked her before dashing off to the office. She thought it better to leave them alone and carried on towards the dining room, even though her appetite was gone.

After another restless night Charlotte dragged herself off to the early morning yoga session, hoping to hear from Paul that Malcolm had phoned. Unfortunately Paul hadn't said anything and was subdued during the class and hurried away afterwards. He told Charlotte that Louisa was calmer but still concerned and was ringing Glenn again that morning. As she returned to her room to change Charlotte prayed there would soon be good news, for everyone's sake. It was always the waiting that was hardest to bear, she thought. Once you knew what had happened, it meant you could deal with it. But when you didn't know *what* you had to face it made it worse. Like not knowing whether or not her mother's cancer had returned...Giving herself a mental shake, Charlotte made tracks for the dining room and a belated breakfast, aware, in spite of everything, she was actually hungry.

Later that morning she caught up with Louisa whose shadowed eyes bore witness to her lack of sleep.

'Any news?' she asked, giving Louisa a hug.

'Not yet, but Glenn's emailing all the major hotels in Bali to see if Dad's staying in one of them. It's going to be a long haul as there's hundreds!' She sighed wearily.

'Oh dear. Look, I'm sure Malcolm is fine and he'd be mortified if he thought you were worrying about him. Until you find out more, isn't it best to carry on as normal as I'm sure you've guests who need you, right?' Louisa nodded. 'How about you try and book a session with Molly, perhaps some of her hypnosis will help you relax? She helped you when you first came here, didn't she? And I found her counselling invaluable,' Charlotte said, forcing herself to sound more positive than she felt.

'You're right, I know. Paul said something similar but it's not going to be easy. I'll see if I can catch Molly, I think she's in today and even a short session might help. Thanks, Charlotte, you always manage to say the right things.' Louisa gave her a weak smile before going to check about Molly.

Charlotte was left feeling pleased she had helped but worried she had been too optimistic. Although Malcolm was a free agent and did not need to report in, she did think it strange he had not been in contact for weeks and was not keeping to his schedule. Now that was worrying.

Time crawled by for Charlotte, concern for her mother and Malcolm gnawing away at what should have been her chance to assuage her grief over her father and re-evaluate her goals. Instead, the possibility something awful may have happened to Malcolm actually reinforced her feelings of loss. And with the uncertainty about her mother's health it was hard to focus on her own possible future. As a writer. With only two days left of her stay at La Folie she was looking forward to diverting herself with the research for Andy. At least her mind would be fully occupied. While Charlotte was having a drink with Louisa in the sun room she asked her about hotels, and her friend immediately suggested she stay with her for as long as needed.

'To be honest I'll be glad of some company while Dad's...missing. I find myself going through all sorts of scenarios and making myself feel worse. You'll be a calming influence and perhaps we could catch a film or something to take my mind off it. Paul's rarely free at the moment and isn't into chick-flicks anyway,' Louisa said, her face pinched with worry.

'As long as you're sure, I'd love to stay with you. But you do know I don't cook? That side of my education has been sadly lacking, I'm afraid.'

'No worries, I don't mind cooking if you'll help prepare. And we might even be able to persuade Chef to provide the occasional takeaway. Being the owner's daughter does offer some benefits.' Louisa sighed.

'Hey come on! No gloomy faces allowed when I move in. I thought you said Molly had helped?'

Louisa nodded. 'Yes, she did. Sorry, I'm being a pain, aren't I? I'm so glad you're here. Paul is so concerned about Dad too; he isn't able to offer me the support I need at the moment. He appears relaxed about it, but I know he isn't. They're so close, more like father and son than employer and employee.' Louisa glanced towards her and grinned. 'I promise to cheer up as I don't want to drive you away. How about we stretch our legs on the cliff path for half an hour? I've hardly been outside for days!'

Charlotte was happy to agree. Although September would soon be morphing into October, the days were still warm and sunny. Linking arms they strode into the garden and headed for the cliff, the tang of salty air soon lifting their spirits.

Before she left La Folie, Charlotte rang Andy to explain she would be staying with Louisa and gave him the phone number.

'Sounds good. Where do you plan to start with the research?' His voice was warm and friendly and she wondered if this was solely because he was keen for her to start or he now liked her. Which might be nice...

'Thought I'd start with the island archives as I understand the German records are kept there. Apparently Jeanne's used them in the past. The downside is my German's a tad rusty so it might take me a while to decipher unless there's a translation. I'm hoping the Germans kept a record of anyone who actively spied for them but it's a bit of a long shot.'

'I see. Well, I wish you luck. Naturally I'm hoping my grandfather's name won't show up but...' She heard his voice catch and fervently agreed with him. It would be too awful. But even if Edmund had been a collaborator, Jim was still the rightful heir and it wouldn't be a total disaster.

'It's possible we might not know one way or the other. I think our main focus has to be on how we can prove Jim is the heir and why he's not acknowledged as such. At the moment I can't see a way to do it without talking to your parents. Any ideas?'

There was silence at the end of the line and Charlotte wondered if it had been too soon to ask. It was obviously a touchy subject.

'Hmm. Let me think about it, will you? See what you come up with from the archives first.'

It was fine by her. They left it she would stay in touch with any progress she made. Or didn't.

Before packing her case Charlotte phoned her mother and as she punched in the number she crossed her fingers.

'Hello, Mother. How are you? What did Dr Rowlands say?' Her heart hammered painfully in her chest as she listened into the silence.

chapter nine

'Oh, he wants me to have a scan and some blood tests. I'm sure it's a waste of time but...' Charlotte heard the doubt in her mother's voice and her heart sank.

'Dr Rowlands was brilliant when you were diagnosed with breast cancer, Mother, so I'm sure he wants to make sure all is well. Did he...say what might be the problem?'

Annette coughed. 'Apparently there's a chance it's secondary cancer. He *says* he's confident it isn't and I'm just run-down after the surgery and chemotherapy last year. The tests will tell us more.'

Charlotte put her hand over the phone while she drew a deep breath. Oh God, no! Not again...Her mother had gone through hell last year but the doctors had been confident the cancer hadn't spread.

'I'm so sorry, Mother. Is there anything I can do? Come up for a while?'

'No, no, there's nothing *you* can do. If only your father were still with us,' her mother said pointedly, '*he* would be a tower of strength.'

Charlotte gritted her teeth. Apart from the fact her father hadn't coped at all well with other people's illnesses, usually disappearing to London if she or her mother were unwell, she *had* supported her mother through her illness last year. Without any thanks. Unsure why she was bothering, she tried again.

'If you're sure. How about my coming with you when you have the tests? So you're not alone.'

'Harumph. That will not be necessary, Charlotte. I'm perfectly capable of attending medical appointments on my own, thank you. Wouldn't dream of taking you away from whatever it is you're doing these days. Didn't you say you were out of the country?' Her voice had regained its usual sharpness.

'Yes. I'm in Guernsey. If you remember I was over earlier this year to stay at a natural health spa. It did me so much good I came back. But I'm about to leave and stay with a friend here while I undertake some research for...for a book. So it's not a problem to come over–'

'I said it's not necessary! Nothing's happening yet anyway. The tests aren't for another week and are perfectly straightforward. It will then be a week or more before the results are back so until then I suggest you continue with this...this research.' Her mother paused. 'Didn't you tell me you were writing a novel set around Lady Hamilton? What has she got to do with Guernsey?'

'Nothing. I've offered to help a friend researching the occupation and–'

'Oh, never mind! You know I'm not interested in anything like that. I must go, I have to chair a meeting of the WI shortly. Goodbye, Charlotte.'

The phone went dead before she could respond. Angry once again she had been given the brush-off, but also feeling sick with guilt at the possibility of the cancer having returned she wondered what to do. There was obviously no point dashing over now as her mother must be coping all right if she could still manage to boss around the members of the WI. And it might appear a tad melodramatic if it turned out her mother was only suffering from a general malaise. Distractedly she began packing her case, the thoughts tumbling through her mind. Deciding her best option was to ring Dr Rowlands after the weekend, she managed to damp down her concern and finish the packing. Louisa was due to take them both to her house when she finished work at six. Charlotte planned to pick up some wine en route. Tonight she desperately needed to switch off.

Louisa was equally keen to blot out her worries about Malcolm and they ended up opening a couple of bottles over dinner. Chef, on hearing Charlotte was staying with Louisa, had presented them with a fully prepared meal which only needed to be finished in the oven. As they tucked into herb-crusted duck and roasted vegetables they raised a glass – or two – to him.

'You know, if I could afford it, I'd steal Chef and install him in my kitchen at home. Everything he produces is superb! Mrs Thomas does her best but...' Charlotte shrugged as she speared a tender piece of duck.

'Come on! I think your housekeeper's a great cook. Not on a par with Chef, I admit, but I think you've been spoiled.' Louisa studied her. 'Have you ever had to cook?'

She shook her head.

'So how on earth did you manage at uni?'

Charlotte had the grace to look sheepish.

'Well, I lived in college at Oxford and all the meals were provided. Most students moved out to house shares in the second or third year but I was too comfortable where I was.' She laughed. 'Basically I'm rather lazy and not at all domesticated as you've noticed, and I've been lucky enough to always have someone to take care of that side of my life.'

Louisa's eyes opened wide.

'Talk about how the other half live! Don't tell me you were brought up with servants at home?'

Shifting in her chair, she could only admit it. 'Yes, I was, but please don't think I'm some sort of aristo. We're pretty ordinary, really. My parents happened to come from good families and my mother inherited the Manor House with...with an estate, but there were no titles. It was my father's charity work which earned the knighthood–'

'I didn't know your father was a Sir! But you're not a Lady, are you?' Louisa asked, open mouthed.

'No, I'm not. Or rather, not one with a title,' she said, feeling as if she should apologise for her background. But she couldn't help being born to wealthy parents, could she? Although the thought did reinforce her own insecurity about inheriting the publishing company...

After more teasing, she was relieved when Louisa changed the subject by asking if she had been in touch with Andy recently.

'Yes, to let him know I'm here. Once I've made a start on the research I'll give him a call. He's so keen to find out the truth about his family but I'm not sure if it will be possible after all this time.'

'So what exactly are you looking for?' asked Louisa, between mouthfuls.

'I'm hoping the Germans kept records of any collaborators or people who actively spied on their behalf. As Edmund, Andy's grandfather, was accused of helping the Germans, I want to see if there's any proof. Of course, they might not have left *written* records but someone must have known who was betraying islanders. Perhaps in return for special favours,' Charlotte said, reaching for her wine.

'Sounds a bit of a longshot. I don't envy you trawling through a load of dusty documents in German. English would be bad enough. What happens if you can't find anything?'

'Haven't a clue! All I can think of is talking to people who were around at the time and see if anyone mentions something useful.' Charlotte sighed at the thought of the potential difficulties in proving anything after more than sixty years. Filling their glasses with more wine, she pushed the thought aside and took a large swallow. Plenty of time to worry about it later.

By Monday morning Charlotte was not only keen to ring Dr Rowlands but also to start her research. The phone call took priority and she waited impatiently while his secretary put her through. She remembered hoping when they last met in Harley Street it would be for the final time...

'Charlotte, good morning. Sorry to keep you waiting. How are you?' Dr Rowland's unctuous tone interrupted her thoughts.

'I'm well, thank you. But I'm concerned about Mother. She told me you're arranging some tests and mentioned the possibility of secondary cancer. Is it likely?'

He cleared his throat. 'Well, as you know I can't say too much, but yes, there is a chance the cancer has spread. But it is only a chance; her symptoms could be the result of a number of issues. I've ordered the tests more as a precautionary measure, so please don't worry unduly.'

'I see. But if it is cancer, Doctor, what's the prognosis?'

'It depends and it's far too soon to speculate. All I will say is we might not be able to operate. But we have a range of treatments available to control any cancerous growth and accompanying symptoms. I do realise you're concerned, but let's wait until we have the test results, shall we? I'd be happy to chat again then. And now I absolutely must go, Charlotte, as I have a patient waiting. Goodbye, my dear.'

Hmm, not particularly encouraging, she thought, hanging up. Typical doctor, hedging his bets. And he was so sure the cancer hadn't spread when the cancer was first diagnosed...Frustrated, Charlotte then rang her housekeeper to check if there were any problems at home before requesting she couriered her laptop and mobile to Guernsey. Another call to her office and she was up to date. Time to visit the archives.

Armed with an A4 pad and pens Charlotte walked across Town towards St Barnabas, the converted church holding the island's archives. Louisa had explained it was at the top of Cornet Street, not far from Victor Hugo's house which they had visited in spring. The climb up the steep hill was as good as a workout and she was relieved to arrive finally at the arched entrance of the Gothic onetime church. Catching her breath, she admired the architecture, so different from Town's church down the hill. A mix of blue and grey granite with featured red brick window arches, a tower and a red tiled roof. Slipping through the inner glass door she was greeted by a woman at the reception desk.

'Good morning, I'm Charlotte Townsend. I phoned last week to arrange to come and see the *Feldkommandtur Verwaltungsgruppe* files.'

'Ah yes, Miss Townsend, we have them ready for you. If you wouldn't mind leaving your bag in a locker, please?'

Once her bag was deposited Charlotte followed the woman to a quiet area possessing tables and chairs with one solitary occupant. She sat at an empty table and waited while the assistant fetched the files from storage.

'These are the records for 1944 to 1945 as you requested. If you need anything else, please ask.'

Nodding her thanks, Charlotte opened the box containing the German Field Command's civil administration papers and hoped her German was up to the task.

By lunchtime her head was spinning and, in need of fresh air and refreshment, Charlotte headed back down Cornet Street to a Thai café she had noticed on the way to the archives. After placing her order she found a free table on the garden terrace with a view over the harbour and out to the islands. Breathing in the salty air tinged with the smells of Thai cooking, she closed her eyes for a moment before opening them to focus on the view. It was blissful after staring at faded typed German documents all morning. The weather was still mild and with only cotton-wool clouds floating in the blue sky, Charlotte sat back in her chair and sipped a chilled glass of wine, wondering how much longer the weather would hold. While she was admiring the varied plants and stone eastern sculptures the ticket number for her food was called and moments later she was tucking into a fragrant Thai soup.

'Hello, Charlotte. Fancy seeing you here.'

Looking up she saw Andy hovering by her table, a glass of lager in his hand.

'Oh! Hi, won't you join me? I'm just taking a break from the archives,' she said, a quiver of surprise – and pleasure – flowing through her.

'Thanks. So, how did you get on?' he asked, pulling out a chair opposite.

'Not great! I'd forgotten how long-winded German officials can be. Talk about dotting the Is and crossing the Ts! I'm still finding my way through the reports and haven't come across anything remotely useful yet.' She grinned ruefully. 'But I've hardly started so...'

He smiled. 'I wasn't expecting a miracle! I'm only grateful you're giving up your valuable time to help me–' Interrupted by the voice over the loudspeaker calling his ticket number he mouthed "excuse me" and went to the counter. Returning with a toasted sandwich he looked preoccupied.

'I've been thinking about how I can repay you for your time–'

'There's no need. It's my pleasure.'

'Maybe, but I think the least I can do is take you out for dinner sometime. If...if you would like to, of course,' Andy said, cutting into the sandwich.

'That's very kind of you and I'd be delighted to accept. Although you don't have to–'

He waved his hand dismissively.

'It would be my pleasure,' he said, his mouth curling upwards.

She returned the smile, enjoying a pleasurable flutter in her stomach.

'I've got several commitments already this week but I'm free on Friday. Would that work for you? I could book something in Town if you like. You may have noticed we're spoilt for choice over here.'

She laughed. 'Yes, you certainly are. Friday would be perfect, thanks. I've not had to eat out yet but Louisa's told me what great restaurants Guernsey has. Her father's taken her to most of them, I think. "A Gastronomic Mystery Tour" she called it.' For a moment the thought of Malcolm still missing caused her to bite her lips. Louisa was so worried...

'Are you all right?' Andy's face was creased with concern.

Charlotte rallied. 'I'm fine, thanks. But I'd better be getting back to the archives. Will you ring when you've booked something?' She stood up and swung her bag over her shoulder.

Andy rose quickly to his feet and, leaning forward, placed a tentative kiss on both cheeks, continental style.

'Yes. I look forward to seeing you on Friday. Don't work too hard, will you?' he joked.

Charlotte smiled and turned towards the entrance, buoyed by the unexpected pleasure of seeing Andy and being asked out to dinner. And she had enjoyed the closeness of his kiss. But during the walk up the hill she began to wonder if she should have politely declined dinner. Even a thank-you meal seemed fraught with danger if a good-looking man was involved. She would have to be on her guard and remain the cool professional. If it was possible. Sighing, and a tad out of breath, she pushed through the door of the converted church, glad to lose herself in dusty documents again.

That evening a tired and listless Louisa cooked supper, assisted by Charlotte who chopped vegetables more willingly than expertly. The strain of not knowing what had happened to Malcolm was taking its toll on Louisa, and Charlotte ached for her friend, the pain at her own loss briefly surfacing again.

'Glenn's emailed the less luxurious resorts as well now. A couple of new ones opened recently and he wonders if Dad might have decided to visit one of them for a comparison. He reckons sometimes the smaller, less glitzy hotels, offer a more personal experience and I think he's right,' Louisa said, pushing her hair back out of her eyes as she checked the chicken under the grill. 'It's worth a try, isn't it?' she turned to Charlotte, who gave her a hug.

'Course it is. Now, here's a glass of wine. Try and relax and let's enjoy our meal.'

Louisa seemed to make an effort and during supper Charlotte mentioned having met Andy at lunch time. And he had invited her out to dinner.

'He hasn't! My, I'm surprised. I understood he was a bit of a recluse where women are concerned. Do you think he's really just re-paying a debt or does he fancy you?' Louisa asked, tilting her head.

Charlotte shook her head. 'No idea. And don't go trying to pair us off as I'm not sure it's what I want right now. To make it harder, so far I haven't found anything in the records about collaborators so my research could take a while.'

'Earning a few more dinners!'

'Hmm, not exactly what I wanted,' she said, wondering what it was she did want.

They were clearing away the plates when the phone rang. Louisa went into the hall to answer it while Charlotte loaded up the dishwasher. She heard an exclamation from Louisa but couldn't hear what she said. A couple of minutes later she came back, with a stunned expression on her face.

'What is it? Is it Malcolm?'

Louisa nodded and slumped into a chair. Charlotte embraced her, praying it wasn't bad news.

'Glenn's found him. He's staying in one of those new hotels I mentioned.'

'What a relief! But that's great news, isn't it?'

Louisa stared at her.

'But he's not alone. He...he's with a woman!'

chapter ten

Louisa bit her thumb, her stomach churning from the news. How could her father behave like this? Like...like a love-struck teenager! She vaguely heard Charlotte saying something.

'He's what? But it's still good news, isn't it? You know he's safe which is the important thing.'

'Well yes, I suppose so. But he could have told me he was all right! I've been so worried...' She grabbed her glass and swallowed deeply.

'I'm sure he didn't mean you to worry. Are you going to phone him? Find out a bit more about this woman he's with?'

'I guess. I'll have to leave it until tomorrow morning as it's the middle of the night there now. Oh, Charlotte, I hadn't really thought of him meeting someone at his age.'

'He's not that old! Seventy's the new fifty or something now, I believe. And he's a very attractive man so why not? Eligible men of his age will have no shortage of interested women.'

She stared at Charlotte. 'You don't think this...this woman could be a gold-digger, do you? After all, Dad's loaded.'

'I didn't say that. And don't jump to conclusions until you've talked to Malcolm. And be happy for him. He's been alone too long,' Charlotte said as she stood up. 'Time for bed. And try and sleep. At least you know nothing bad's happened.'

Louisa nodded and climbed the stairs, convinced she would not sleep a wink. To her surprise, as soon as her head hit the pillow she fell into a deep sleep, and woke the next morning feeling better than she had for weeks.

Once she had arrived at La Folie, Louisa found Paul who had been relieved when she'd phoned the previous night with the news.

'Good morning,' he said before adding, with a chuckle, 'The old devil! Told you a woman was probably involved, didn't I?'

'Hmm. Yes, well, I'm going to ring him now before my first appointment. I'll catch up with you later,' she said, giving him a quick kiss. As she slipped into the office she thought it was typical of men to see another man disappearing to make off with a woman as something to be admired. Instead of thoughtless or selfish. After dialling the number Glenn had given her, she took some deep breaths to steady herself. She simply had to stay calm...

The reception answered and she asked to be put through to Villa 6. The phone rang out for a few moments before her father's voice came on the line.

'Roget speaking.'

'Hello, Dad. How are you?'

'Louisa! How on earth...?'

She told him they'd discovered he'd missed his flight to Japan and were concerned he was okay. And Glenn had contacted the main hotels to try and find him.

'Oh, Louisa, I'm sorry! I never thought you'd be worried about me. I said I might be out of contact–'

'I know. But it scared me when you missed your flight. You're my father, I'm bound to be worried.'

Malcolm was silent for a moment and she heard a female voice in the background.

'Dad, I...I know you're not alone. Have you...met someone?' The catch in her voice annoyed her. She really must not sound hurt. Even though she was.

He cleared his throat. 'Yes, I'd planned to tell you once I was sure it was serious. We met at dinner the first night I arrived. Gillian was on her own at an adjoining table and we got talking and finished up eating together.' His voice grew warmer and Louisa imagined him looking fondly at "Gillian" and stifled a pang of jealousy. 'We spent a lot of time together and then, instead of heading off to Japan, I decided to stay and we moved to this new place as a...couple. I guess I should have let you know I'd moved, darling. I can see now how worrying it must have been for you. Can you forgive me?'

'I suppose. Paul's been concerned too, you know. The centre's been so busy and not knowing if you were...were all right, added to the pressure.'

'Sounds like I've been a pretty selfish bastard, haven't I? I'll make it up to you both when I get home, I promise.'

'And when will that be?' Louisa asked, feeling like the parent instead of the child.

'A couple of weeks, I reckon, although we haven't booked our flights yet. But you'll be the first to know.'

'Good. So, are you going to tell me more about Gillian?'

'Sure. She's a widow and a semi-retired naturopathic doctor and I know you two will get on like the proverbial house on fire. You've a lot in common, Gillian's not only an advocate for natural health but also a passionate swimmer.' He paused. 'Look, would you like to say hello? I've told her all about you and she's dying to meet you when we get back.'

Put on the spot, Louisa could only agree. There was the sound of muffled whispers in the background before a woman's voice cut in.

'Hello, Louisa. I'm Gillian and I want to start by saying how cross I am with your father. He assured me you were not expecting to hear from him until his return and if I'd known the truth I'd have insisted he phone. You must have been so worried, you poor girl! My son insists I ring him every week while I'm away so I can sympathise with you. I do hope you won't hold this against me as I so want us to be friends.' Gillian's warm, melodious voice echoed down the line. Louisa felt her hurt recede.

They chatted for a few more minutes before Malcolm came back on the line to say his goodbye, and offering to ring as soon as the flights were booked. Louisa clicked off the phone feeling a great deal happier than she had before the call. Checking her watch she saw she would need to hurry for her first appointment and left the office with such a bright smile Nadine gave her a quizzical look.

~ ~

Charlotte, meanwhile, was ploughing her way through the occupation files in the archives. Most of the material referred to the day-to-day administration of the island, covering reports of minor offences and requisitioning of food from the island reserves. Pretty tedious stuff, she thought, wondering what had possessed her to undertake the task. Then she thought of Andy and his kiss. Telling herself not to be silly, it was only a friendly kiss, she turned back to the papers in front of her. Somewhere amongst the banal must be a reference to the islanders who informed on their neighbours. It appeared hundreds of people were arrested for breaking German laws and she guessed many were caught after being snitched on by neighbours with a grudge.

Deciding to widen her search, Charlotte asked to see the files of The Controlling Committee of the States of Guernsey and other Guernsey documents covering the occupation and the immediate aftermath. She was shocked to read of the hundreds of prisoners deported to prisoner of war camps or prisons in Germany or occupied France, some of whom never returned, even though they had not committed grave offences. Reading the reports opened her eyes to the full impact on the island of being occupied by enemy soldiers and how embedded it was in the psyche of the locals more than sixty years later. She was about to call it a day when a police report caught her eye and she read on with renewed interest.

That evening Charlotte listened as Louisa described what Malcolm had said during their call and her brief conversation with Gillian.

'So, how are you feeling about the new woman in his life? Any happier?' Charlotte asked as they prepared supper.

Louisa sighed. 'A bit. I'm okay about meeting her, for sure. But I guess I'm scared of being pushed into second place in Dad's affections. After all, we've only known each other for six months,' she said, fiddling with the fillets of plaice.

'I can't see Malcolm pushing you anywhere. You're his only flesh and blood, important to a man like him. And he's only known this woman two minutes! What did Paul have to say?'

Louisa told her, adding Malcolm had since rung Paul to apologise for not being in contact and he would definitely be back in two weeks. 'Which is great, as Paul and I want to get away for a long weekend before the weather turns. Dad apparently said he'd help out if we went away so that's something to look forward to.' She served up the food, asking, 'And how was your day?'

'Not bad. Although I still haven't come across any evidence of named informers, I did find the police report about Edmund's death, which is a result of sorts.'

'Sure. What did it say?'

'Not a huge amount, but it did confirm no-one was ever charged and the only suspect was an escaped POW who was shot later by the Germans. The police must have assumed he was the killer as they stopped looking for anyone else. It's rather inconclusive, but what was more interesting was nothing was said in the report about Edmund being a suspected informer. And surely the police would have known if it was true,' Charlotte said, feeling again the frisson of excitement she had experienced in the archives. 'When I phoned Andy to tell him, he agreed with me, saying he thought it was a significant breakthrough. What do you think, Louisa?'

'I agree, it sounds promising. Well done! I'm not surprised Andy sees it as progress. Talking of which, did he mention your night out?'

'Yes, he said he's booked Le Petit Bistro, in the Pollet for Friday. Do you know it?'

'Yep, Paul and I went a few weeks ago. Has a great buzz, you'll enjoy it. Not long now, eh?' Louisa said, with a cheeky grin.

Charlotte smiled, but inside she still had her doubts about the proposed dinner. If it could be purely business, then fine. Otherwise...But she was pleased by what she had read, or rather, not read in the police file. Perhaps they would yet find the truth about why poor Edmund was killed. And by whom.

~ ~

Andy drew up at Louisa's house on Friday evening wondering what he had got himself into. It had seemed a good idea to invite Charlotte out to dinner as, after all, she was giving up her valuable time to help him. And he desperately wanted to get to the bottom of the family's division and why his father wasn't now living in Harold's house as was his right. But was this solely a means of thanking her or a real date? He sat in the car for a moment, questioning his motives.

Yes, he did want to show his appreciation – particularly after her find in the archives – and, yes he did find her attractive. More than attractive. But someone who, he guessed, was out of his league. Posh voice, posh clothes and able to afford to stay at La Folie. Twice. And there was he, admittedly an up-and-coming architect, but of modest means. On the plus side, on accepting his invite, Charlotte had bestowed on him a warm smile which had lit up her lovely green eyes. Oh, sod it! I'll just see what happens, he thought, getting out of the car.

Charlotte opened the front door and for a moment he was lost for words. She looked stunning in a deep red dress which clung to her curves and emphasised her long, shapely legs.

Swallowing, he managed to say, 'Hi. You look...amazing, that colour really suits you,' before kissing her on both cheeks.

'Why thank you, kind sir! And you don't look too bad yourself. I do love that shade of blue on a man,' she said, nodding at his shirt. The previous day Andy had checked his wardrobe and was so ashamed of the state of his shirts he had rushed out to buy new ones. Now, warmed by Charlotte's dazzling smile, he was glad he'd made the effort.

He opened the car door for her before sliding into the driver's seat and starting the engine.

'Hungry?' he asked, glancing at her profile.

'Yes, I only had a sandwich for lunch. Louisa warned me the servings were generous so I've left plenty of room,' she said, releasing a throaty laugh as she patted her stomach. Her laugh was so sexy!

'Good. Let's go.'

In less than five minutes they were parked in Le Truchot, lucky to find a space on a Friday night and only yards from Le Petit Bistro. Andy steered Charlotte towards the restaurant, its presence advertised by the hum of music and laughter. As he opened the door and ushered her inside, they were embraced by a cheerful wall of sound. A waitress rushed up, menus in hand, and guided them to a small table near the back of the room, took their wine order and left them to peruse the menus.

Charlotte gazed around and remarked, 'It's so French, isn't it? It reminds me of bistros in Paris, a feast for the eye as well as the stomach. Love the stained glass panels and the French signs.' Her eyes twinkled as they swept over the restaurant. 'I take it you've been here before?'

'It's one of my favourites. I've had many a business lunch here.'

Her eyebrows arched.

'Oh, does this count as a business dinner?'

Andy shifted in his chair as the point hit home.

'Not exactly. Sort of half and half–'

'I'm teasing! Which wasn't fair of me. Ah, our wine.' Charlotte smiled at the waitress as she set down a bottle of St Emilion and a carafe of water.

After raising their glasses in salute, they sipped their wine.

'Lovely! A good choice, Andy.' Charlotte picked up her menu. 'Now, what shall I choose? Can you recommend something?'

Andy went through the choices, glad she wanted his input and conscious of her desire to put him at ease. It was years since he'd dated and he'd felt out of the game when he hit forty last year. But this woman re-kindled the desire to become close to someone again, though he knew she was recently divorced and might not be interested in a relationship...

Once they had placed their order Andy asked how the research was going since she had found the police file concerning Edmund's death.

Charlotte frowned. 'I've found references to the existence of collaborators but so far haven't found names mentioned, by either the Germans or the local government. I'll keep looking, but...' she shrugged. After taking a sip of her wine she added, 'It might be time to consider talking to people still alive, preferably anyone who lived in St Martins. Word would have got around if someone was snitching on neighbours, surely?'

Andy was finding it hard to concentrate on what she was saying; she was so attractive. 'Mm, you'd think so,' he replied, bringing his mind back to the conversation and trying to think of the best way forward. 'Parish records would help. You should be able to find the names of those still around who would remember the war. That generation didn't move around much, tending to live in the same parish all their lives. You could contact the rector for potential interviewees for your "research".' Andy paused, struck by an idea. 'How about asking Jeanne what she wants to know for her own book? Then you'll be a genuine researcher!' He grinned broadly.

'What a brilliant idea! I wouldn't be lying to the rector then, thank goodness. Which would have made me very uncomfortable. I can't wait to get started.' Charlotte's eyes gleamed with pleasure and Andy was hooked. She looked radiant and oh so sexy in that dress! He was going to find it hard to separate business from pleasure...

The food arrived, providing a welcome diversion from his erotic thoughts. For a few moments they concentrated on eating before Andy asked about her own family. Tears, quickly wiped away, appeared when she told him about her father's death and then went on to mention her mother had been ill. He gripped her hand in sympathy.

'I'm sorry, you've had a rough time, haven't you? I shouldn't be bothering you with my family's problems.'

Charlotte shook her head. 'Don't be silly. It's proving to be good therapy for me. Saves me thinking too much,' she said with a wry smile. 'I do miss Daddy dreadfully, as we were particularly close, but my relationship with Mother is...strained. I love her because she's my mother but don't really like her much, if that doesn't sound too awful. How about you? Do you and your mother have a good relationship?'

'Yes. French mothers are renowned for being super strict with their kids, but mine was much more laid back. Perhaps it would have been different if I'd been brought up in France. My French grandmother's a bit scary!' he said, laughing.

'My maternal grandmother was too, so we have something in common.' She speared a piece of lamb before asking, 'Do you speak French? I can imagine how useful it would be here with such a strong French influence.'

'I do. As Dad was bought up in France he was bilingual from the word go and he and Mum often chat in French at home so it was natural for me to learn. I can't speak the local patois, though. And you? I know you speak German.'

'I studied French and German at A level, along with English and kept them up at uni but I'm not terribly fluent. But enough to translate documents and menus!' she said, smiling.

'Being bilingual was a plus at school as French, naturally, was one of my strong subjects and I always got top marks. The other boys thought I had an unfair advantage and didn't like me for it,' Andy said, the memory of school causing him to frown.

'You weren't happy at school?' Charlotte asked, head on one side.

'Junior school was fine, but secondary…Not really. Felt like a fish out of water. You see, I was a scholarship boy. After achieving top marks in the eleven-plus, I was awarded a place at Elizabeth College, the private boys school. I'd rather have gone to the grammar with my friends, but my parents thought it was too good an opportunity to turn down. But it wasn't easy coming from a relatively poor family and mixing with the sons of the wealthy.'

'Oh, I can imagine. Did you not have any friends?' She frowned.

'How can you imagine what it was like? You must have gone to a posh school yourself,' he said sharply.

'I did, as you say, go to a posh school. But a few girls were admitted on bursaries, like yourself, and I became friends with one of them. We got on extremely well and she confided in me about how hard it was going back home in the holidays and being ignored by the friends she used to have before she boarded. So I do have some idea of what it must have been like for you,' she said, looking him in the eye.

He felt wrong-footed. 'Sorry, it...it was presumptuous of me. I did have a couple of friends at College, but it wasn't the best of times. I was happy to get away to university.' He grinned. 'What's funny is some of those boys who ignored me back then have become my clients since, so I guess being a poor local lad has paid off!'

After a noticeable coolness in Charlotte's responses, Andy was able to steer the conversation into the safer waters of hobbies and interests. He sensed she had become reluctant to say too much about her background, briefly mentioning the family home was in Somerset and wondered if it was to do with their disparate backgrounds. Apart from that they seemed to share similar interests such as books and films and as the meal progressed Charlotte seemed to thaw a little and he was glad he hadn't bottled it. As he dropped her back at Louisa's he asked what she was doing at the weekend.

'I haven't anything planned. If the weather holds thought I might pop over to Herm as I haven't been over yet.'

'Sounds good. Would you like a lift? I can borrow Dad's boat and show you round if you like.'

'I...I'm not sure. Wouldn't it be taking up a good part of your weekend?' Charlotte's smile looked hesitant and he wondered if he'd been too quick to suggest such a trip. He hadn't planned to ask her out again so soon but now he had, he could hardly back out. Perhaps it would be better if she said no and they could go back to being acquaintances. He *had* messed up earlier...

'No, it's okay, I love any excuse to go over to Herm. It's such a great place to relax,' Andy said trying to sound convincing.

'In that case I would like to accept.' This time Charlotte's smile lit up her face.

He said he'd need to check the times of the tides before making firm arrangements and would phone her. They stood in the doorway while Charlotte fished out the key from her handbag.

'Right, I'll say goodnight. See you tomorrow,' Andy said, before pulling her towards him and kissing her on both cheeks. Pulling back, Charlotte smiled and said, 'Goodnight, Andy, and thanks for a lovely evening.' She opened the door and waved as he returned to his car. Driving off, he told himself he was a fool and wondered what kind of day he had let himself in for.

chapter eleven

Andy phoned Charlotte the next morning to say he would pick her up at ten. This gave her time to call her mother. Their conversation was brief.

'Hello, Mother. Have you had the tests?'

'Oh, it's you, Charlotte. Yes, and for once I wasn't kept waiting. I do so hate it when other people are not punctual–'

'Yes, I know. And when do you get the results? I can fly over and accompany you–'

Her mother gave an exasperated sigh.

'Don't be ridiculous! As I've said before, I'm perfectly capable of attending an appointment on my own. And, as it happens, I've been feeling somewhat better lately and I'm sure it's all a fuss about nothing. My appointment is in ten days' time. I assume you're still on that island – Guernsey, wasn't it?'

'Yes, I am.' Charlotte groaned inwardly. It was like talking to the proverbial brick wall! 'Look, Mother, will you at least promise to call me when you've seen Dr Rowlands? So I know everything is all right.'

'If you wish. Now, unless you've anything else to say, I must be off. Can't hang around on the phone all day, you know.'

'Goodbye, Mother, I'll wait for your call. Take care.' She clicked off the phone and threw it on the bed in frustration. Determined not to let her mother's intransigence spoil her day, she pushed down her annoyance –and concern – and forced herself to smile before joining Louisa for breakfast.

'How did it go last night? Good, er, meal?' Louisa asked, smiling as she set out muesli and juice.

'It was lovely, thanks. Lively and good food, just as you said. And Andy proved to be great company.' She sat down as Louisa placed a mug of coffee in front of her. 'He's taking me over to Herm today in his father's boat and offered to give me the grand tour. Should be fun,' she said, trying to keep her voice neutral.

Inside, she wasn't quite as sure. The thought of a day with such an attractive man was both heady and worrying. Where on earth could it lead? Nowhere was the honest answer. But at least it would stop her thinking about her mother.

Louisa's eyes rounded.

'My, he hasn't wasted any time, has he? Paul had said he was shy where women are concerned. Just goes to show men don't understand each other any more than they do us women.' She pulled out a chair opposite and took a sip of her own coffee before adding, 'I think he must fancy you, after all. And you're keen, too, methinks.'

Charlotte nearly choked on her drink.

'Well, he *is* attractive but we've only just met and hardly know each other, so...' she said, waving her free hand. Where had Louisa got that idea from?

'Would you be interested in a relationship if he was?'

'It's too soon to speculate, but I'm definitely over Richard, thank goodness, and would like to think I'd meet someone again one day. But at the moment men are not top of my agenda.' She found herself growing alternately hot and cold as Louisa stared at her and dropped her eyes, focusing on her muesli.

Louisa appeared to let it go, asking if she would be back for supper. Charlotte assumed so but said she would phone if not. They continued with their breakfast while Louisa chatted about her own plans. Paul was taking Sunday off and they were going out for lunch and a drive.

'You'd be welcome to join us, of course.'

'No, you two need some time on your own. I'll be fine. Might walk into town and have some lunch. It's a pity the shops are shut though–'

'Why don't you borrow my car? We'll use Paul's, then you can go wherever you like. Okay?'

'Thanks, I'd like that. I'm sure there are loads of places I haven't been yet.'

Louisa made a few suggestions before they cleared away the dishes and Charlotte nipped upstairs for a final freshen up. She was waiting downstairs when Andy arrived, dressed in jeans and a patched Guernsey sweater.

'Morning.' He gave her a quick kiss on the cheek before scrutinising her outfit of cotton slacks, long sleeved T-shirt and cotton sweater. 'You'll need something a bit warmer for the crossing, as it's chilly on the sea this time of year. Have you got a jacket or something?'

'Sure. Give me a minute.' Charlotte ran upstairs to fetch a lightweight padded jacket.

'That's better. You can leave it in the cabin when we're ashore.' Once in the car he headed down towards St Julian's Avenue before turning left at the roundabout.

'Oh, where's the boat? I'd assumed it would be in the marina,' Charlotte said, pointing to the QEII marina in front of them.

'Dad keeps it at Bordeaux. It's near his house and cheaper to moor there. It's not far.'

They fell silent and Charlotte gazed out of the window, conscious of his closeness as Andy drove along the coast to The Bridge in St Sampson, circled the harbour and followed the road to Bordeaux. He pulled into the car park and pointed to a white motorboat with a small cabin, dipping gently on the water a few yards from shore.

'There she is. Can you roll up your trousers to wade out? Or will I have to carry you?' he asked, a wicked grin splitting his face.

She laughed. 'Don't worry, I'll cope! Not sure you'd manage the weight!'

He shook his head. 'I could carry you, no problem. But if you can walk, so much the better, as I have to get the fuel on board. Right, let's go.'

Slinging their trainers round their necks they approached the shore with Andy carrying a jerry can. It was high tide and moments later they reached the boat. Andy hopped aboard first and gave Charlotte a hand. Once the tank was re-fuelled he started the outboard and pointed the boat towards Herm, clearly visible straight ahead of them.

Charlotte settled onto a seat opposite Andy and watched as he steered. She fought down a tinge of unease, feeling vulnerable in such a small craft. She had imagined it would be larger, with proper seats and a steering wheel like the smart boats lined up in the marina. This looked like a toy boat in comparison and was a new experience for a landlubber like her. Not wanting Andy to think she was a wimp, she fixed a bright smile on her face and told herself to relax. He was the son of a fisherman, experienced with boats and clearly knew what he was doing. Turning her head she focused on Herm, its golden beaches topped by green fields and trees. She had agreed to come with him and there could be no turning back, in spite of the chill running down her arms.

'It looks beautiful, doesn't it? Will it be packed with people on such a lovely day?'

Andy, keeping one hand on the tiller, pushed his hair back with the other. 'No, the odd thing about Herm is, no matter how many people pile in for the day or even longer, you only ever find a crowd in the pub. After their pit stop, everyone drifts off to different parts of the island and none of the beaches ever get crowded. Mind you, today isn't hot enough to lie on a beach for long, so most will be taking long, leisurely walks.'

She let her gaze travel over the fast diminishing stretch of water. 'Gosh, this is quick. I expected it to take a lot longer.'

'Takes about fifteen minutes. Much quicker than taking the Trident and I'll be able to drop you off by the harbour. So you won't get your feet wet!' he said, with a grin.

Charlotte smiled, twisting her head round to watch the east coast of Guernsey fall behind. Dotted between the two islands were rocky outcrops which Andy skilfully avoided with quick flicks of the tiller. Beyond Herm the outline of Sark reared up; a reminder of the fun day she and Louisa had enjoyed in the spring. Moments later and the harbour wall was upon them and Andy cut the engine as he manoeuvred close to the steps, taking hold of the rope as he jumped out.

'Okay, if you get out now, I'll moor up properly and join you in a minute.'

She climbed to the top and watched as he throttled up and moved a few yards away before dropping anchor and wading the few feet to the beach. As he joined her on the jetty he asked what she wanted to do first.

'I'd really like a coffee, please. I need warming up,' she said, rubbing her arms. Although the day was warm, she still felt the chill from the boat ride.

'Sure. Let's head to the Mermaid and we'll soon have you warm again.'

He strode off to the left, passing shops hidden behind brightly coloured displays of remnants of the holiday season. Bargain-hunters chatted happily as they searched the rails and bins for the must-have buys. Charlotte was entranced as she took in white stone cottages covered with flowers and shrubs rubbing shoulders with the little shops. Perhaps Andy was worried she might join the shoppers as he moved on quickly to the adjoining pub. For a moment she wanted to hold back and look at the shops, annoyed with Andy. But admitting to herself she needed a coffee more than shopping she let him lead her on. She could go shopping later.

'Inside or out?' he asked, as they walked under the stone arch into the courtyard, filled with benches and tables. Some in the sun were empty and Charlotte said she'd prefer outside, and headed for one of them. Andy went inside to order the coffees while she people-watched. The other customers were in a relaxed mood, sharing jokes as they planned their day, and small children ran around tables under the watchful eyes of their parents. Charlotte found herself unbending in the laid-back atmosphere, in spite of the memory of the conversation with her mother forcing its way to the surface. There was nothing she could do except wait for the phone call. Today she had to let go.

Taking a deep breath of the ozone-laden air, she experienced a frisson of anticipation at the day ahead. It had been so long since she had been on a date – or whatever this was – not since she first met Richard, ten years ago. A lifetime. Or so it felt. Pushing to one side the obvious complications of living across a stretch of water and their different backgrounds, she thought she might as well enjoy any time she spent with Andy. As the thought flittered across her mind, the man in question appeared from the pub bearing two mugs of coffee.

'You look lost in thought. Everything okay?' Andy asked as he sat beside her.

'Absolutely. I was thinking what a lovely day it is and how happy everyone looks. It's such a shame summer's officially over. Does the island close down for the winter?' She had no intention of sharing her real worries with him. It would make her more vulnerable.

'Not completely. The White House Hotel near the harbour will close next weekend until spring, but the self-catering cottages are rented out through the year. And the Mermaid and the shops open for shorter hours in the winter. So there's usually someone staying here, along with the inhabitants, naturally.' He sipped his coffee before adding, 'You know Jeanne and Nick were married here?'

'Yes, what a fab place to choose. I expect all you Guerns know the island well.' She stirred the froth on her drink as, not for the first time, she wondered what it would be like to live on a small island.

'For many of us growing up in Guernsey, Herm was where we went for holidays. Getting off the island to go abroad was too expensive but it always felt like being in another country coming over here. My parents hired frame tents in the Seagull campsite above Manor Village and friends would join us and we had a whale of a time. Nick was one of them. It's a children's paradise, as you'll see when we go round.' He rubbed her arm. 'Warmer now?'

She smiled, enjoying the touch of his hands. 'Yes, thanks. This place is a real sun trap and the coffee was just what I needed. Shall we go?'

He stood up and offered his hand as she stepped over the bench. 'We'll head towards the common first and continue round the coast until lunch time. I've booked a table at The White House for one thirty, if that's okay?'

She nodded and they joined the coastal path outside. A minute later Andy unfolded a map and explained their route, first pointing out Fisherman's Beach on their left. 'The island has several great beaches which is why they never get crowded. The best, in my view, is Shell Beach on the east coast.' He went on to tell Charlotte a little more about Herm and she listened avidly as the island gave itself up to her gaze. A small boy, rushing around a bend, bumped into her and she had to hold onto him to steady them both. His parents caught up and mumbled an apology before grabbing his hand. Charlotte smiled. It was lovely to see children running free, even if they did nearly knock you over.

As they continued on the path the number of walkers thinned until they found themselves alone on the sandy track leading to the common – home, according to Andy, to Neolithic burial grounds. Warming to the theme of Herm's history, he became more animated, waving his arms in the way of those of Latin blood, and she smiled inwardly, recalling his French ancestry. He was definitely more passionate than she had guessed and wondered idly if the French blood would out in other ways too. She felt her face grow hot at the thought and when he brushed her hand, she pushed it in her pocket, worried he was going to hold it. Looking puzzled he carried on with the story.

Charlotte enjoyed listening to Andy's tales of Normans, monks, pirates and Prussian princes, all former occupants of Herm. But, for her, the biggest surprise was learning the writer Sir Compton Mackenzie, whose work she admired, had leased the island in the 1920s. At this point in his tale they had reached Shell Beach and the glimmering expanse of sand – actually crushed seashells carried by the Gulf Stream – looked too inviting to resist. Pulling off their trainers they ran along the shore edge, laughing as the sea lapped at their ankles. At one moment they came to a stop to avoid a dog splashing in the shallows and Charlotte lost her balance. Andy grabbed her and she found herself staring into his eyes. He leant down and kissed her. Charlotte closed her eyes and allowed herself to melt into the kiss. Coming up for air, she pulled back slightly and smiled.

'That was some kiss! What brought that on?'

'You looked so carefree and happy and...and beautiful. I couldn't resist. Did you mind?' he asked stroking tangled hair off her face.

'Nooo...Although we do appear to have an audience,' she said, pointing.

He turned round and saw three small faces gaping at him, goggle eyed.

'Are you two married, then? That was so soppy!' declared a freckle-faced lad of about seven, building sandcastles with what appeared to be a younger brother and sister. He pulled a face in disgust.

Andy laughed.

'No, we're not married, just friends. Don't you like seeing people kiss each other?'

The boy shook his head.

'Nah, not in public, anyways. Suppose it's okay if you're on your own. My mum and dad never kiss in front of us kids,' he said, nodding towards a couple sitting fully clothed on a mat about a hundred yards away. Charlotte glanced towards them, noting they appeared to be arguing and felt a pang of sympathy for the boy and his siblings.

'Well, I'm sorry if we offended you, young man. We'll move away and let you build your sandcastle undisturbed,' Andy said solemnly. Charlotte saw his mouth twitching and had to stifle a giggle.

The boy nodded and turned back to his digging while Charlotte and Andy ran a few yards before collapsing into helpless laughter.

'Well, that told us, didn't it? Public displays of affection are a no-no if there are kids about,' Andy spluttered.

Charlotte allowed him to hold her hand as they continued up the beach, away from critical eyes. Coming across a sheltered spot, Andy suggested they sit down and they snuggled up together, feeling the sun's warmth on their faces. Charlotte was content to sit quietly, every fibre of her being tingling. In spite of her reservations about the wisdom of allowing Andy to get under her skin, his kiss had woken something in her and it felt good. Very good. Like coming out of hibernation after a cold, long winter to find the sun and warmth on your body once more. Even if it was likely to be short-lived.

'You look as if you haven't a care in the world. Do you?' Andy asked, stroking her face.

Instantly she was snapped into reality. Her mother. Groaning inwardly at the thought of what might lay ahead, Charlotte replied sharply, 'Of course I have cares! Doesn't everyone? And it's something I'd rather not talk about.'

He leaned back, frowning. 'Sorry, didn't mean to pry. Shall we make a move for the restaurant? All this walking is building up my appetite.'

She let him help her to her feet and they walked side by side, but not holding hands, as they retraced their steps to the harbour village and The White House.

The conversation over lunch in the Conservatory Restaurant was initially stilted and Charlotte, aware she had ruffled Andy's feathers with her sharpness, tried to defuse things by encouraging him to tell her more about his work.

He appeared to regain his earlier humour and they spent the afternoon exploring the rest of the island, or at least a good part of it. Charlotte continued to be enchanted with everything she saw, declaring the tiny Norman chapel of St Tugual to be one of the 'sweetest chapels I've ever seen'.

Andy kept an eye on the time, saying he needed to catch the high tide to float the boat from its temporary mooring. As they made their way from the Manor Village in the centre of Herm he announced there was just time for a quick look round the shops if she wished.

It proved to be an expensive 'quick look' as Charlotte ended up buying a couple of tops to see her through the cooler weather and three paperbacks to replace those she had finished reading. Pleased with her purchases, she allowed Andy to hold her hand as they strolled the few yards to the harbour.

He left her on the jetty while he waded out to the boat and brought it back to the steps. Minutes later Charlotte was safely aboard and gazing wistfully at Herm as they sped away.

'You can always come back, you know,' Andy said, glancing at her. He frowned, adding, 'You're not planning on leaving for a while yet, are you?'

'No, but I can't stay forever. Perhaps another two or three weeks tops, depending on whether or not I can discover the answers you need. I...I might have to go home for a while.' She chewed her lip.

He grunted and appeared lost in thought as he held onto the tiller. Charlotte, reliving the day, could not help wondering where they both stood in terms of a relationship. Were they becoming closer – or not?

chapter twelve

A ndy was in thoughtful mood on Sunday morning as he left his cottage in St Peters. His parents had invited him for Sunday lunch and as he drove up to St Sampson he could not get the thought of Charlotte out of his head.

He was falling for her and he knew he shouldn't. It was hopeless. She was way out of his league and apart from anything else, lived on the mainland. Hardly conducive to a romantic involvement even if there wasn't such a social gulf between them. The thought was depressing but at the same time his heart skipped a beat at the memory of their kiss on the beach. And their goodnight kiss when he dropped her off at Louisa's.

In the heat of the moment Andy had invited Charlotte round for lunch on the following Saturday and now he wondered if it was a mistake. Should he back off before he got in deeper? But he couldn't withdraw the offer without looking like a complete pillock so…The sound of a blaring horn brought him up sharp and he just managed to stop at a junction as another car drove past. Get a grip, man! Andy told himself, shocked at the near miss. Resolving to forget about Charlotte for the moment, he focused on arriving at his parents' house in one piece. Twenty minutes later he pulled into the drive of their tiny cottage.

'Hello, son. Good timing, your mother's just about to serve up. Fancy a lager with your dinner?' his father said as he ushered him into the dining cum sitting room. Andy thought Jim looked tired and hoped he'd not been overdoing things again.

'Thanks. I'll get them, Dad, you sit down.' Andy walked through into the kitchen, barely big enough to hold two people, and gave his mother a hug as she stood dishing out portions of vegetables to accompany the meagre amount of roast pork on the three plates. The memory of the meals he had enjoyed with Charlotte in the last two days made Andy feel guilty. As his mother turned to give him a kiss, he slipped a twenty pound note into her apron pocket. 'Hello, *Maman*, looks delicious. Hope you made your incomparable apple sauce to go with it?' he asked, returning her kiss.

Yvette smiled. 'But of course. Your father would not forgive me if I do not! You take the lagers and wait while I bring in the plates in one little minute.' She patted her pocket and mouthed "thank you" before turning back to the task in hand. Andy collected a couple of cans from the fridge and returned to the dining room.

'How are you, Dad? How's the physio going?'

Jim took the proffered can before replying, 'Not too bad, son. That girl Louisa's been making me do lots of exercises at home and it seems to ease the pain. Not as stiff as I was, for sure.' He took a sip of the lager before adding, 'The only thing is she wants me to cut down on the fishing for a bit. Said it wasn't helping. But you know I love going out in the boat and we enjoy the fish I catch. Bit of a bummer, really,' he said, frowning.

'It's a pity, but if your back improves won't it be worth it in the long run? Did she say you could get back to the fishing one day?' Andy was concerned. Not only did his parents need the fish themselves, but his father earned good pocket money from the extra he sold.

'She didn't say one way or the other. I guess it depends how well the treatments work and I'm not sure how many they'll let me have.' Jim stared at Andy. 'You know I can't abide charity. I prefer to pay my own way, always have–'

'But do not go on at the boy, Jim. You should instead be glad one thinks so well of Andy's work to wish to help you,' Yvette said, coming into the room with a plate in each hand. Andy stood up and fetched the last plate from the kitchen.

His mother flashed him a smile as they sat down to eat. Jim grunted before tucking into his food. While they ate, Yvette asked Andy about his latest projects and the meal passed off pleasantly as he described a barn conversion he was designing. While they were eating the pudding of French apple tart Andy had an idea.

'Dad, you remember Nick's wife is a writer?' Jim nodded. 'Well, she's planning to write a novel set during the occupation and wants to get hold of as many first-hand accounts as she can. As you know, she's not long had a baby so can't get out and about much and asked me to pass the word around,' he said, before taking a final sip of his lager. 'I remembered you saying once that your mother kept a diary during the war and wondered if you still had it. It'd be just the kind of thing Jeanne's looking for.'

Jim pursed his lips. 'I don't rightly know if we have. It was with some bits and pieces we kept after she died, but could have been thrown out long ago.'

Andy turned to his mother, who looked thoughtful. 'We kept all the old family photos and various papers, I am sure. If it is there the diary will be in the attic in the box with those other things. Do you want to have a look while you are here?'

He looked at his father, shifting in his chair.

'Is it all right with you, Dad?'

'I'm not sure. Don't like the thought of other people poking about in our private business–'

'*Mais, c'est bete*, Jim! After so long a time, it cannot do harm for this nice girl Jeanne to read Madeleine's old diary. And if it may help with her book, why not? There is nothing to hide, no?' Yvette laughed.

Andy held his breath. If the diary *was* in the attic why was his father reluctant for anyone to read it?

Jim seemed to do battle with himself, before finally saying, 'No, there's nothing to hide. Suppose you can see if it's still there.' He stood up and, rubbing his back, stretched a bit before stomping off to the sofa.

Yvette raised her eyebrows as she shot a glance at Andy, who shrugged. He helped clear the table before going upstairs to check out the attic. Access was easy thanks to the inbuilt ladder attached to the hatch and the attic was both floored and well lit. As a boy he had played in there with a battered train set passed down by friends of his parents. Nick had joined him on occasion and he smiled now at the memory of happy times pretending to run a railway. Shoved towards the shallow part of the eaves he found the boxes his mother had suggested he search first. Kneeling down, he remembered years ago looking idly through old photos stuck in albums and wondering who everyone was. His curiosity at the time had not been strong enough for him to question his parents, which he now regretted. But this was not the right moment to ask, and he concentrated on looking for the diary.

A couple of boxes later he pulled out a likely contender, a thick, brown hardback book bearing the title *Journal* in faded gold lettering. Andy held his breath as he looked inside. He let out a long sigh. The inscription, *To my darling wife, Madeleine, on the occasion of her birthday*, was written in heavy script across the page. The original book must have consisted of blank lined pages and Madeleine had filled in the dates of her diary entries. Flicking through he noted the diary spanned the years from 1943 – when Madeleine married Edmund – to 1946. The handwriting was not easy for him to decipher and Andy, not wanting to give his father time to change his mind, decided to leave and look at it later.

~ ~

Charlotte phoned the rector of St Martins first thing Monday morning, eager to begin what she hoped would be a more fruitful line of research. She asked if they could meet and he suggested the following morning. Pleased, she slipped out into the garden to test the temperature. With October only days away, the air was cooling and Charlotte was glad of the warm sweaters she had bought in Herm. Idly dead-heading the roses her thoughts turned to Andy and his excited phone call on Sunday evening.

'You'll never guess, but I've found my grandmother's diary from the occupation!' he cried, as she answered the phone.

'What! But how...?'

Andy explained how it had happened and she congratulated him on his brainwave. 'Have you read it? Anything interesting?' she asked.

'Well, to be honest I've flicked through, but apart from the fact the writing's hard to read, I...I feel uncomfortable reading it. She was my grandmother, after all and...and newly married–'

'Oh, that's so sweet! You don't want to be a voyeur. Perfectly understandable, but I doubt if there'd be much, ahem, in the way of bedroom secrets in a young woman's diary during enemy occupation,' she said, wondering if Andy blushed when embarrassed. 'Would you prefer me to read it? At least I'm impartial and would only share what was important or relevant.'

She heard his sigh of relief.

'Would you? If you didn't mind–'

'Of course I don't mind. I absolutely adore reading through old diaries and we do need to know if Madeleine mentions anything about Edmund and collaboration. She, if anyone, would have known, I'm sure. Oh, this is exciting! I think we're beginning to make progress at last. When can I see the diary?'

'I can call in at lunchtime tomorrow if you like, I'll be en route to an appointment.'

They talked for a few minutes more before saying goodbye and Charlotte was left tingling with excitement at the prospect of reading the diary. Surely it *had* to hold something of significance, she told herself.

The last rose now devoid of dead flowers, Charlotte could only wait impatiently for Andy to arrive; he wasn't due for another two hours. What to do in the meantime? For a moment she was tempted to call her mother to persuade her to let her accompany her to the doctor's the following Tuesday. But the thought of another brush-off stopped her. Instead she walked down to Candie Gardens to check out the latest display in the museum before having a coffee in the café and admiring the view over the harbour. Sitting quietly gave the chance to try and make sense of her confused feelings about Andy.

Their goodnight kiss had been as intense as the one on the beach and she had not wanted it to end. Her body was saying yes while her head was saying no, this is not what you want right now. It had caused her a couple of restless nights and she was no clearer as to what to do. And now she was even more entangled, with the chance to read the diary and receive help from the rector! She relieved her frustration by kicking out at the leaves in the gardens before making her way home.

Andy arrived in a rush. 'Sorry I can't stop, but I'm running late as usual. Here's the diary and I hope you can fathom the writing better than I could. I think Madeleine was trying to cram as many words as possible onto the pages!' he said.

Charlotte glanced through. The writing *was* tiny, but legible, she thought.

'I'll start reading it now and will keep you posted. Oh, and I'm seeing the rector of St Martins tomorrow morning so that's another potentially useful line of enquiry.'

'Great. Look, I'd better shoot. Call you later,' he said, hesitating before kissing her quickly on the cheek.

Charlotte waved him off, not allowing herself to dwell on his hesitation, and carried the diary, a notepad and pen outside. The garden was a suntrap and she was determined to sit out as long as it stayed warm. It took a while to adjust to Madeleine's handwriting, so it was a slow start.

Most of the earlier entries referred to the increasing lack of food and the distress caused to islanders by harsher and harsher restrictions imposed on them by the Germans. Charlotte began to understand Madeleine was using the diary more as a way of relieving her feelings than as a factual recording of events, although these cropped up occasionally. She described her husband in glowing terms:

"My Edmund's working so hard to finish the cottage. Not easy with materials being scarce. Particularly paint. But today he went round asking if anyone has any spare and everyone was so kind and he came back with a few tins. They would not be my first choice but I must not complain. It's good to see how well-liked he is, for sure. Mind, I always knew that – everyone likes Edmund. Everyone except his horrible brother, Harold. But of course, he's just jealous..."

Charlotte sat up straight. If Edmund was such a nice guy he wasn't likely to have betrayed his neighbours, was he? She knew it wasn't proof of his innocence, but it did support Andy's belief in him. Of course, Madeleine was biased, but...Charlotte carried on reading, skimming through the long passages bemoaning the lack of proper tea and soap until she came to an entry which caused her to feel shocked. Surely he hadn't dared...She had to tell Andy – now.

chapter thirteen

It's about Harold! Madeleine wrote early in the diary he wanted her for himself but she preferred Edmund and he couldn't bear being rejected. He was only seventeen and, according to your grandmother, good looking but with an aggressive nature. She fell in love with Edmund for his gentleness and sense of humour.' She paused, gripping the phone as she chose the right words.

Andy chipped in. 'Go on. I take it there's more?' His voice was eager.

'Yes, there is. Well, Madeleine doesn't say much more about Harold until about a year after her marriage, in '44. Apparently tensions were rising as Neville, your great-grandfather and Harold were buying on the black market but Edmund never went along with it, saying he and his wife would prefer to starve rather than take food from the mouths of others. I have to say, Andy, your grandfather sounds like a really decent man,' she said, clearing her throat. She found herself feeling emotional at the thought of the suffering of the islanders, so graphically described in the diary.

'I'm sure he was; which is why I want to clear his name. Does the diary say anything about that?'

'Not so far, but there's quite a bit I haven't read yet. Anyway, going back to Harold. She recalled the words from the diary.

"Oh, what a day it has been! I still feel sick to my stomach at what happened. While Edmund was busy – helping a neighbour – broken fencing, Harold turned up at our cottage, knowing I would be alone. I was in the kitchen. He tried to force himself on me. It was hard to fight him off. He is so big. I managed to grab a heavy saucepan – hit him on the head. It knocked him out for a few minutes. How

afraid I was! I thought I had killed him but I could see his chest move. I was scared what he would do, so I ran out and hid behind a bush. I could see the front door – prayed Edmund would not return and find his brother on the kitchen floor. Thank God he did not! Harold staggered out – bleeding head – towards the family farmhouse. I went back and cleaned up the blood. I had just finished when Edmund returned. I must have looked bad, he asked me what was the matter – but I said was tired from cleaning, had an empty stomach."

As she finished Andy let out a horrified gasp.

'My God! How awful. So my grandmother says Harold tried to rape her and she didn't tell her husband?'

'No, she couldn't. She didn't want Edmund getting into a fight with Harold as he was bigger and stronger and was worried Edmund would be killed. I can understand that, can't you? Remember everything was topsy-turvy in the occupation, tempers and nerves were stretched, and fights would break out easily. Or that's what I've read in the police reports. And, as it happens, Madeleine was right not to say anything as next time she found herself alone with Harold, he threatened to hurt her if she told anyone. Poor girl. What a horrible thing to happen. Her own brother-in-law!'

'I've always thought Harold was an unpleasant piece of work, but I had no idea he was capable of something like this. Makes you think, doesn't it? It sounds to me as if he's the one more likely to be an informer and not Edmund. It would fit his character, wouldn't it?'

'I hadn't thought about it, but you're right. Perhaps there'll be more answers later in the diary. So far Madeleine hasn't said much about collaboration or informers but I get the impression she led a sheltered life down in St Martins. I don't think she and Edmund socialised much as the neighbours were pretty scattered across the open fields.'

'Hmm. Well, thanks for telling me, Charlotte. This does give me cause to hope we'll find something concrete.' He was quiet for a moment before continuing, his voice bitter, 'If I were to meet Harold now, I'd be tempted to punch his face in, if he wasn't such an old man. And to think he had the nerve to not acknowledge my father. He's a far better man than bloody Harold ever was.'

Charlotte felt so sorry for him, determined now not to give up until Jim regained what was due to him – and to his son.

The next morning Charlotte drove Louisa's car out to St Martins' vicarage. She had dropped Louisa off at La Folie earlier and had the use of the car for the day and planned to drive around the parish which had been home to the Batistes for generations. Except for one particular branch. There had been little time to read any more of Madeleine's diary as Louisa had returned home early from work and had cooked supper for them both. Louisa had been intrigued by the diary's revelations and they spent the evening debating what really happened to cause the family split. As Charlotte parked the car at the vicarage she crossed her fingers, hoping the rector, Martin Kite, would be willing to help.

She need not have worried. On explaining she was acting as a research assistant to Guernsey writer Jeanne Le Page, the rector gave her his blessing.

'Jeanne's books are wonderful and her research is immaculate. I particularly enjoyed the first *Recipes for Love*,' he said, smiling. 'There's been one or two non-local writers who have twisted the facts in their books and it's upset some locals, I'm afraid. However, as it's Jeanne's novel, then I'm sure my elderly parishioners will be happy to talk to you. Not that there's many left, now. And some of them are, shall we say, not as nimble mentally as they were,' the rector said, with a sigh. 'I'll ask around and pass on the contact details of anyone willing to chat. Would that suit?'

'Oh, marvellous, Vicar. Thanks so much, I do appreciate you taking the trouble. As a thank you, I'd like to make a contribution to parish funds. I know how much churches rely on donations to keep a roof over their heads these days,' she said, pulling out her purse and extracting fifty pounds.

'You're very generous, my dear. Thank you. And do please call me Martin. How about a cup of tea before you go?'

Charlotte accepted his offer, happy to talk further to someone who knew the parish well. She had to hold back from asking if he knew Harold Batiste. Be patient, she told herself, someone's bound to know him from the war...

After saying goodbye to the rector, she drove off down Grande Rue before turning into one of the lanes on the right, leading towards the cliffs. Louisa had left her a copy of a Perry's guide containing maps of the island so she would not get lost. The winding lanes meant Charlotte had to concentrate on any oncoming traffic and only managed to catch glimpses of her surroundings. Deciding it would be better to walk, she spotted La Belle Luce Hotel and pulled into the car park. Pleased to find a venue for lunch later, Charlotte set off for her walk. Having passed a cemetery along the road she headed there first, wondering if it was where the Batistes were buried. Seemed likely. Charlotte had always liked cemeteries and churchyards, finding them peaceful and soothing. Not morbid unless you had recently suffered a bereavement.

She bit her lip as the memory of her father's funeral flashed into her mind. A grand affair it had been too, as her mother had asked most of the county, or so it seemed. But Sir Michael had been much liked and the church was full to the point of bursting, with a number of people crowding outside to pay their respects. Charlotte would have preferred a quiet, family service so she could express her grief instead of needing to hide behind a frozen mask for the day. Her mother had played the part of brave, grieving widow to perfection, dabbing at her eyes occasionally, but never allowing tears to fall. Charlotte had never been sure whether or not it had been a true love match. Her parents did seem to care for each other, but spent much of the time apart. 'Oh Daddy, I do miss you!' she cried softly, trying to hold back the threatening tears.

Taking a couple of deep breaths, she began weaving her way around the serried ranks of graves, larger ones containing generations of families. The names were predominantly local, with the occasional foreign and English name confirming the ingress of immigrants. Some tugged at her heart: the loss of a young child or an adult dying well before they reached their prime. Just as Edmund had done. Moving further into the cemetery she found his grave. The inscription on the plain granite headstone was brief:

Edmund Batiste

1924–1945

Dearly loved husband

God Bless

Charlotte was shocked Edmund's family had not acknowledged him, leaving his widow to bury him and provide the headstone. Nearby stood the grave of his parents, Neville, who died in 1947, and Enid in 1925. Andy had mentioned she had died giving birth to Harold. The headstone was large polished granite.

A chill took hold of her, like the proverbial walking over the grave and she shivered, turning back to Edmund's grave. For the first time she noticed the shrivelled up flowers sticking out of the inset vase. Someone still cared, she thought, and assumed it was either Jim or Andy. Glancing further along, Charlotte saw an impressive, polished headstone belonging to another

Batiste. This time it was Harold's son, Gregory, who had died in 1985, and apparently merited a much more elaborate headstone than his uncle.

She gritted her teeth in anger at the snub accorded to Edmund and, with a shock realised she was taking it all personally. As if she was a part of the family and not an impartial researcher. She needed to stand back, not let it get to her. After all, she might be leaving the island soon and had her own pressing problems...

A few minutes later Charlotte returned to the hotel for lunch, which left her calmer. She followed it with a brisk walk down the lanes towards the clifftops. The views and sea air worked their magic and she found herself humming a tune as she gazed over hedges into fields of grazing cows. It was all so peaceful now, but what had it been like during the occupation? With a shortage of manpower it must have been hard work looking after livestock and any surviving crops.

Charlotte felt guilty as she considered her own pampered life. Hardly her fault. Fate – or karma as Buddhists believed – played a part in which family and generation you were born into. She had listened with rapt attention to Paul's lectures on Buddhism at La Folie and had loved the idea of karma, similar to the Christian idea of "As ye sow, so shall ye reap". As she stood on the cliffs overlooking Moulin Huet Bay, the heartland of the Batiste family, she was convinced if there had been any skulduggery in the past, then it was high time it was revealed. An unwelcome thought floated into her mind. Was she being entirely altruistic with her offer of help? Or was she beginning to enjoy spending time with Andy and wanted to continue? With a toss of her head, she turned round and strode away.

Later that afternoon Charlotte settled down in the dining room with Madeleine's diary, using the table as a desk. Following on from Harold's attack, Madeleine made sure she was rarely alone until one day she heard he had a girlfriend, Maud. She described her relief Harold would no longer need to *"bother her"*, adding, *"I wonder what this girl is like? Harold's such a brute and is so full of himself. What girl would be attracted to him?"* Charlotte recalled Andy saying Harold's wife was called Maud and she was still alive but frail and virtually bed-ridden. So, the attraction must have been mutual. She read on.

It was now late in 1944 and Madeleine wrote in detail about the lack of food and other essential supplies since the D-Day landings in the August. The Germans – and hence the islanders – had relied on France for supplies but the usual routes were now cut off with the Allied advance.

On a personal note Madeleine confided their plans to start a family had been postponed as both she and Edmund were concerned about the impact of pregnancy on her starved body. The family was better off than most as they grew their own food and had a few cows, but they had to share any so-called excess and the quotas per head were reduced from August onwards. Charlotte was intrigued to learn Madeleine prepared her own spermicidal sponge as a contraceptive device and her supplies of spermicide and soap were dwindling.

Charlotte stood up and made herself a cup of tea, her head full of pictures of thin, weary islanders becoming more and more desperate as the war dragged on. Young women like Madeleine, barely twenty, dreading becoming pregnant at a time of shortage of both food and basic medicines. That last winter was particularly harsh, colder than ever and with no fuel for heating or cooking after the loss of both gas and electricity by December. As she stirred her tea, Charlotte could not begin to imagine how awful it must have been and hoped to get the chance to talk to those who had lived through the nightmare.

Sighing, she returned to the diary and Madeleine's tale. In spite of the deprivations, she appeared to be more upbeat as the year drew to a close. Life-saving supplies from the British Red Cross arrived aboard the *SS Vega* in December and the ship returned another four times before the end of the war. Madeleine wrote how the word was going around the Germans were losing the war and it could not be long before the islands would be relieved. She described how hidden, forbidden wireless sets kept the islanders updated with the latest defeats in Europe and how happy she was it would soon be over. Charlotte's heart ached for the girl, wishing she didn't know the unhappy ending. Forcing herself to read on, she came to the entry dated 5th April, four days before Edmund died. Would there now be some clues about what happened?

chapter fourteen

As she read Charlotte became excited, convinced it was significant. *"I was in the kitchen and looking out of the window – saw Edmund and Harold arguing – was bad as Edmund's face was red – shook his fists at Harold who laughed at him. Edmund looked even angrier – thought he'd explode, wondered if I should go – calm things down. But Harold walked away – my husband stood there, his head in his hands. I felt sick to see him so. That bastard, Harold! He has to spoil things. Edmund – usually so calm – looked up and must have seen my face – gave me a quick smile before walking off in opposite direction. When he came back later I asked – what was he arguing about – said it was a difference of opinion. But he – strange mood the rest of day and the days following – struggling with something weighty. Not like to pry..."*

Could it be relevant to Edmund's death only four days later? For the first time she pondered the idea Harold might have had something to do with what happened to his brother. But what? She continued reading, dreading Madeleine's reaction to her husband's death. A couple of days after the argument, she told of her puzzlement when her normally friendly neighbours don't return her greeting and turn their backs on her. When she told Edmund, he admits the same thing happened to him. Neither of them could explain it and she wrote how worried they both were and Edmund's mood grew darker. The neat, tiny writing changes for the entry on the 10th became more of a scrawl, blotted with splashes of ink and what could only have been tears.

"Dead! He's dead. I know – I saw his body. It's horrible, I feel sick. Can't stop crying. Me – a widow! At twenty! It makes no sense. Only yesterday he was in my arms. And they say he was an informer! I cannot believe that. I know

for sure my wonderful husband is dead, but he was no traitor! He did not come home last night after going to his father's. I did not know until this morning. While I slept he...Oh, God. Oh, God! What am I to do? I feel so ill. Edmund never arrived at his father's. I went to see. The local constable started a search. With the neighbours. Said something about an escaped POW. We all live not far from the cliffs at Jerbourg. They headed there first. I had to stop to be sick. Rushed to catch them up. Someone was pointing down at Van Bêtes bay. The rocks! The constable tried to stop me. But I ran past and looked down. Sprawled on the rocks was his twisted body. I can't stop seeing it. Oh, Edmund! My dear, dear Edmund! How will I live without you."

Charlotte found herself wiping away a tear as she read and grabbed a tissue to blow her nose. The poor, poor girl! Even though she had already known what happened, somehow reading Madeleine's account made it more personal, more real. Getting up, she made herself another cup of tea, deciding she had read enough for the day. As she stood by the sink nursing her mug, visualising the horror of finding Edmund's body, Louisa burst in, cheeks flushed with excitement.

'Dad's home! Or at least he's arrived in London and will be flying over tomorrow. Oh, I can't wait to see him,' she said, flinging her bag onto the worktop.

Charlotte slowly took in her words. 'How...brilliant. I thought he wasn't due back until the end of the week.'

'That was the plan, but apparently he decided he couldn't stay away any longer and Glenn found him a couple of last minute tickets. First class, of course.' She grinned at Charlotte, who gave her a hug, trying to shake off the horror of what she had read to share Louisa's joy.

'So, you'll be meeting the mysterious Gillian. I assume she's coming too?'

'Yes, so I'll not have him to myself, which is a shame. But she's only staying for a few days before returning to

England to see her son. Guess she needs to tell him about my father.' Louisa looked thoughtful as she made herself a cup of tea. 'I remember, on the odd occasion Mum brought home a man, how chippy I was with them. Poor Mum. I turned from a well-behaved, pleasant girl into a rude whirling dervish. She must have been so embarrassed!'

'Do you plan on resurrecting the dervish when you meet Gillian?' Charlotte asked, smiling.

'I don't think it would go down too well, would it?' Louisa chewed her lip. 'I admit I do have mixed feelings about meeting her. But, as you and Paul said, it's natural Dad wants to have a partner of his own. God knows, he deserves some happiness after working so hard all his life. And as nothing will bring Mum back...' She sipped her tea and Charlotte noticed the moistened eyes.

'Hey, it's okay to be maudlin. Whatever Malcolm feels for Gillian, it won't take away what he felt for your mother,' Charlotte said, stroking her arm. She could identify with what Louisa felt. If her mother were to start seeing someone, what would *she* feel? Refusing to dwell on it and aware it wasn't likely to happen while her mother was sick, she changed the subject. 'I've been reading more of Madeleine's diary and it's so sad...' She described the events of the last few days of Edmund's life and Louisa was all ears.

'I see what you mean about Harold. He sounds fishy to me. And he had more than one motive for killing Edmund. Not only would he become the heir, but there'd be no repercussions from trying to force himself on Madeleine. But it's a bit extreme, isn't it? As well as risky. He would have hanged if caught,' Louisa said, with a shiver.

'Yes, but from what Madeleine writes and Andy's told me, Harold was greedy and ambitious as well as hot-tempered and may have seized the chance when he could. People do strange things when there's a war on and Madeleine writes how on edge everyone was that winter.

Perhaps cold and hunger turned their brains.' She paused as another thought struck her. 'And there's the bit about Edmund being an informer. Where did that come from? He doesn't sound the type, yet he and his wife were being shunned so someone must have thought he was. I wonder if Harold had a part in it, too.'

'Possibly. It may have suited him to blacken his brother's name and it's a bit suspicious coming so close to his death. But without proper evidence I can't see how anything could be proved.'

'That's the problem. Which reminds me, I saw the rector of St Martins yesterday and he's agreed to pass the word around among his elderly parishioners I'd like to talk to them about the occupation. You never know, someone might know something.'

'Sounds promising. And Madeleine's diary might give you more clues,' Louisa replied, pulling food out of the fridge for supper. 'Right, can you give me a hand with the veg? You're beginning to make a half decent sous chef under my expert guidance,' she said, chuckling.

Charlotte aimed a mock blow at her before picking up the paring knife to start work on the beans and carrots Louisa piled in front of her. Secretly, she was pleased to be involved in the preparation, knowing how useless she was on the domestic front. If, heaven forbid, she no longer had a housekeeper to take care of such things, she would be hard pushed to make much more than a slice of toast. She really did need to be more self-sufficient, she admonished herself, recalling what the islanders had endured. Particularly poor Madeleine.

~ ~

The next morning Louisa was like the proverbial cat on a hot tin roof. Malcolm's flight was due in at eleven and she had swapped her appointments with Trevor, the other physio, so she could meet him at the airport. After saying goodbye to a client at ten o'clock, she nipped along to

Paul's office. When she opened the door he looked up from a pile of paperwork and smiled.

'Morning, darling. How are you feeling? Excited or nervous?' He came round the desk to kiss her and she relaxed into his arms. No matter how things went with Malcolm, more than anything she wanted to make it work with this lovely man. All they needed was to have more time together... 'A bit of both. If things work out between Dad and Gillian, she could end up as my step-mother! It's a weird thought considering until a few months ago I didn't even have a father,' she said, frowning.

Paul wrapped his arms around her. 'Must be, but if she's as nice as he says then that could be a bonus, so there's no point worrying about it, is there? And the good news is he's agreed to keep an eye on La Folie this weekend so we can have a couple of nights in Jersey. Assuming you still want to go away with me,' he said, pulling back, his head on one side.

Her heart leapt at the thought of a whole weekend away. Just the two of them...she imagined long walks on a beach, strolling around shops and bars and the nights in each other's arms...

'You bet I do! Are you asking Nicole if we can stay in her family's flat?'

He grinned. 'It's all arranged and she says you can pick up the key any time.'

Her eyes widened. 'Huh! You assumed I'd say yes and still asked me.' She couldn't be cross and stayed locked in his arms a moment longer. 'I saw Nicole the other day and she looked exhausted. Young Eve's teething and no-one's getting much sleep. I'll pop round tomorrow.' She glanced at her watch. 'Better go, the flight's due in a few minutes. Can I have the car keys please?'

Paul handed them over and after another quick kiss she left, a broad smile plastered over her face. Things were looking up. The centre's courtesy car – actually an upmarket people carrier – was parked by the front door and in minutes Louisa was heading towards the airport. Excitement at the thought of the weekend vied with her nervousness about meeting Gillian. And it was hard not to be jealous of this 'other woman' who had stolen her father's heart. As she pulled into the airport she told herself to behave like a grown up and be welcoming.

'Dad!' she called out as Malcolm appeared through the arrival doors pushing a laden trolley, closely followed by the woman she assumed was Gillian. Her father strode forward, blue eyes shining in his tanned face and looking ten years younger, and threw his arms around her.

'Louisa, darling, it's so good to see you. And thanks for picking us up.' He turned to motion Gillian forward. 'And here's the lady I want you to meet. Gillian, my daughter, Louisa.'

For a moment the two women eyed each other up and then, as if choreographed, they smiled in unison. Louisa liked what she saw. A slim, fair-haired woman whose eyes sparkled with humour and intelligence in her suntanned face. And oh, so like her mother! Feeling a tug at her heart, she offered a tentative hug and received a resounding kiss on both cheeks.

'Louisa, I'm so pleased to meet you at last. Your father hasn't stopped talking about you since we arrived back in England,' Gillian said, nudging a beaming Malcolm.

'And I'm happy to meet you, too. I'm sure we'll have lots to talk about!' She turned towards her father. 'Do you want to go to La Folie or your apartment, Dad?' she asked, aware they were attracting some attention from onlookers.

'The apartment, please. Are you free to join us for lunch later?'

She shook her head. 'No, sorry, I've got a full schedule so I'll have to love you and leave you. But I'm free tonight.'

Malcolm continued pushing the trolley, a lady on each arm looking, Louisa thought, the epitome of the proud family man. Experiencing a pang that by rights this happy group should have encompassed her mother and not Gillian, Louisa had to fight hard to continue smiling. Had her father been attracted to Gillian because she reminded him of her mother?

'Tonight will do fine. I'll book a table at Le Fregate and do ask Paul to join us,' Malcolm said, as they arrived outside. Louisa agreed and went over to unlock the car, relieved the initial encounter had gone well.

~ ~

While Louisa was busy meeting Malcolm, Charlotte sat at home absorbed in Madeleine's diary. The aftermath of Edmund's death was worsened for the girl by the family's apparent acceptance that Edmund had been an informer, responsible for at least one neighbour's arrest.

Madeleine's grief permeated her writing: *"I cannot believe no-one seems to mourn Edmund as they should. His father and brother say he is no longer part of the family and I must organise, and pay for, the funeral. Harold even seems happy my husband is dead! He strides around as if he owns the farm and cottages. Which he will, one day. Oh, I can hardly bear it! Edmund! Please come back to me! Don't let you be dead! It must be a horrible dream. Yet I know it's not. It's real. The police say they are looking for the killer, interviewing our neighbours. But no-one saw or heard anything. He had been beaten before being pushed over the cliff, the constable said, his eyes avoiding mine when he told me. Even he must believe those terrible rumours! My neighbours avoid me as if I have the plague! This hurts the most. Edmund was a good man and a good friend to everyone. How can they now turn their back on him when he can no longer speak for himself? And I feel so ill! I'm sick to my stomach and can keep little down, not that there's much to eat. At least the vicar is kind, helping me organise a decent burial for my beloved..."*

Charlotte felt waves of anger flow through her, anger at Madeleine's betrayal by family and friends. It was painful to read the pages describing the funeral, with

Madeleine the sole mourner apart from the paid coffin bearers. Having seen the grave, Charlotte found it all too easy to imagine the scene: the lonely widow swathed in black standing almost alone at the graveside as she threw soil onto her husband's makeshift coffin, followed by a small bunch of bluebells.

In need of air, Charlotte rushed into the garden, taking several gulps before she was able to shake off the heart-breaking picture. Pacing up and down the garden, her mind sifted through what Madeleine had said and she became convinced Harold had been behind Edmund's death. Everything pointed to him, but at the time it seemed no-one suspected him of fratricide. The escaped Polish POW was captured and questioned and protested his innocence, but, according to the diary, he was shot regardless by the Germans. Madeleine noted the investigation was quietly dropped. Within four weeks the war was over and everyone had more pressing things to consider. The Liberating forces arrived on 9th May aboard the *HMS Bulldog* and the Germans surrendered before the Union Jack was raised on the Royal Court. Madeleine describes how she hitched a lift into St Peter Port to join in the celebrations, although *"heartsick my beloved Edmund wasn't there to celebrate with me"*.

Charlotte had realised Madeleine must have been pregnant by this time, although it seemed she had yet to find out. She returned, almost reluctantly, to read what happened over the following months. The pages of sprawling, blotched writing described Madeleine's decision to leave Guernsey where she felt betrayed and unwelcome, and go to live in France with her late mother's family in Normandy. The move was arranged via a series of telegrams in the weeks following the Liberation. Once she had ordered a memorial for Edmund's grave, using her meagre savings, she left. By the end of June Madeleine was reunited with her French cousins. It was not until then she realised she was pregnant, but this at least was good news.

chapter fifteen

Andy was pottering in the kitchen on Wednesday evening when the phone rang. Hoping it wasn't another call from the extremely fussy client he'd been on the phone to earlier, he picked it up gingerly.

'Andy, it's me. I've read more of the diary and there's a lot to tell you...' He listened with increasing feelings of anger towards Harold, Neville and all those who had deserted Madeleine when she needed them most. By the time Charlotte had finished he was ashamed of being a Batiste.

'What happened to my grandmother was inexcusable, no wonder she never talked about it much to Dad. I always wished I'd met her but she died when I was a baby. She sounds very brave.' He remembered a photo of Madeleine, taken by his father when she was in her forties, and now kept on show in his parents' sitting room. What struck Andy, apart from her beauty, was the air of sadness around her. Madeleine's soft brown eyes gazed into the distance and a barely formed smile hovered around her mouth, as if she was afraid or unwilling to smile properly. Andy had often wondered what had been going through her mind. Perhaps now he knew...

'She *was* brave. To be forced to leave her home when she'd lost her husband...what reading the diary has done, Andy, is to make me even more determined to find out what really happened to Edmund,' Charlotte said, finding it hard to let go of the imagined picture of Edmund's body lying shattered on the rocks. She cleared her throat. 'By the way, I visited the cemetery yesterday and noticed someone still leaves flowers on his grave.'

'I take some every once in a while. For some reason, Dad says he doesn't like going, and it's the least I can do.'

'That's kind of you. Not everyone can cope with cemeteries.'

Andy was silent, unsure whether to mention the proposed lunch on Saturday, when Charlotte said, 'Still on for Saturday, are we? I'm looking forward to seeing your home as I don't think I've seen inside an architect's house before. I always imagine they're terribly up to date and full of gizmos. Very avant-garde.'

He laughed. 'Well, you'll be disappointed with mine! It's an old cottage which I've renovated but kept the original features. And Guernsey doesn't really do avant-garde, the planners prefer the cosy cottage look. Of course it's still on for lunch. I thought about one o'clock, if that's okay?'

'Perfect. I'll see you then, but will phone if I learn anything I simply have to share. Goodnight, Andy.'

'Night.' He poured himself a glass of wine while mulling over what Charlotte had told him. He'd dearly love to grab hold of Harold and shake him until he admitted what had really happened in '45. But he began to feel a glimmer of hope they were getting closer to the truth and he thanked heaven for sending Charlotte to him. Until she started searching the archives he'd completely forgotten about his grandmother's diary. And as well as her gift for research, she was one hot lady and he wanted to take her to bed. If she'd let him – although he was dubious about becoming involved with an upper class lady like Charlotte. And he did not see her as someone happy to enjoy one-night stands. Groaning, he finished his wine.

~ ~

When Charlotte walked into the kitchen on Thursday morning she found Louisa had already prepared breakfast for them both and was dancing around to Guernsey FM on the radio.

'Morning. You look happy. How did the meal go last night?' Charlotte said, smiling at Louisa's impromptu dance. She sat down at the table and Louisa sashayed towards her with the coffee pot.

'Fine. I like Gillian, she's fun and I can see why Dad fell for her as she's so warm and friendly. As well as pretty attractive for a woman in her sixties. They're both coming to La Folie today and Dad will no doubt be giving her the grand tour. He's out to impress her, all right.' Louisa sat down, looking pensive. 'I think he wants Gillian to fall in love with Guernsey and consider moving here. He was in full sales pitch mode last night.'

'How would you feel about that?'

'Oh, okay. I'd rather she came here instead of Dad going to England. But her son Matthew's there and she's bound to have friends and family so...' Louisa shrugged.

'Well, I look forward to meeting the lovely Gillian. Are you inviting her round here before she leaves?'

'Hadn't thought about it but sounds a good idea. I'd like you to meet her, see what you think as you're more impartial.' Louisa buttered her toast before continuing, 'I finish early this afternoon so could invite them round for supper tonight if you're free.'

'Perfect. And I'll give you a hand with the preparation.'

'Thanks. I'll give Dad a call in a minute. What are your plans for today?'

Charlotte leaned back in the chair. 'Nothing much. I'll read the rest of Madeleine's diary but as she's now settled in France I'm not sure I'll learn much of importance. Still,' she yawned, 'could be interesting. She'll have given birth to Jim before the diary finishes and I'd like to know how she coped. Must be terrible to have a baby after losing your husband.' She took a bite of toast before going on, 'Which reminds me, how's the therapy going with Jim? Andy's said how much his dad misses his fishing.'

Louisa frowned. 'I can imagine, but he has to watch it or he'll continue to have pain. My aim is to wean him off the prescribed painkillers, which aren't good for him anyway, and I will ask Paul about a herbal alternative. He's a whizz with his concoctions and helped Dad when they met in India. If he wasn't so busy, I'd suggest he set aside more time for his herbal treatments.'

'Can his herbs help with life-threatening illnesses like...cancer?' Charlotte asked, thinking of her mother. If the test results weren't good then perhaps...

'He hasn't said so, but maybe. Why? Do you know someone with cancer?' Louisa gave her a searching look.

'My mother was diagnosed with...with breast cancer and had chemo and radiation more than a year ago. It was horrible and if she were to, to get sick again I wondered–' she dug her nails into her hand.

Louisa gasped. 'Oh, I'm so sorry! You told me she'd been ill, but not what it was. You poor thing. And your mother! You should have told me before.' Louisa gripped her hand. 'If the cancer came back I'm sure Paul would help in any way he could. Does your mother agree with alternative therapy?'

She frowned. 'That's the problem, I doubt it. She's one of those people who think doctors are omnipotent. Still, if the cancer has spread and the doctors can only offer limited treatment, Mother might be persuaded to try an alternative.' Charlotte hoped it wouldn't come to it, but her stomach still knotted up every time she thought about it. The first time it was diagnosed she was sure her mother would die, from the treatment if not the cancer. She had been so ill...but it felt good to know there might be another option. La Folie's team of therapists had given her such care and support, she felt sure her mother would also benefit from a stay.

'Are you okay?' She heard the concern in Louisa's voice.

Lifting her head, she smiled at her friend. 'I'm fine, thanks,' she said, knowing she was anything but. The spectre was ever present. 'The problem is, as I mentioned that day in Sark, Mother and I have a tricky relationship. She never listens to me and can't abide being told what she should do, so...' She spread out her hands. Not wanting to say more, she added briskly, 'Now, weren't you going to phone Malcolm about tonight? If they're coming round I'll tidy up.'

Louisa, looking as if she wanted to say something but changing her mind, reached for the phone while Charlotte cleared away the breakfast things. She loaded the dishwasher in silence while Louisa chatted to Malcolm. Coming off the phone, Louisa said, 'It's all arranged. They'll be here at seven and as I know Dad loves fish, I think I'll cook some wild salmon and steamed veg. Gillian's into healthy eating so I can't go wrong with that.' She glanced at the clock. 'Right, I'd better get a move on. See you later.'

Charlotte called goodbye as Louisa shot out of the kitchen and headed for the front door. Satisfied the room was clean and tidy she walked through to the dining room and picked up the diary. Her mind was full of all the things unsaid to Louisa but hoped the diary would prove a distraction. The last entry she had read was when Madeleine had discovered her pregnancy and was experiencing a mix of hormonally-charged emotions.

*"I came back from the doctor's and hid myself in my room. Such a shock! We had so wanted to have children but dare not. Now Edmund's baby is growing inside me but **he** has gone. Oh, my darling, I'm so happy to have your child but so sad you can't be here. I know you would be so proud to be a father! And a wonderful father. Oh, how am I going to manage without you, my love? Our child will be fatherless..."*

The entry was blotched with what Charlotte assumed were tears. Madeleine continued to pour her heart out onto the page, writing as if she were talking directly to Edmund. Charlotte began to find it too painful to read and skimmed through to see if there was any mention of

Guernsey or the Batiste family. But on that subject Madeleine was silent. Once she had shared the news of her pregnancy to her aunt and cousins, Madeleine was swept up in a wave of congratulations and excited plans. Her family were farmers and provided her with a small cottage on their land which had lain derelict for years. In return for her help on the farm, for which she was amply qualified, her family asked for no rent and paid her a small wage. Her gratitude shone through her words: *"My own little home! For myself and my child – I could not be more content except if Edmund were to walk through the door! Such generosity I had never met until now. And Aunt Therese has promised to help when baby arrives, reckoned to be in late November. In the meantime there's much to do to make the cottage habitable..."*

Charlotte was about to continue reading when the phone rang. It was the rector of St Martins.

'Morning, Charlotte. I've been chatting to some of my parishioners and one dear old lady, a Mrs Vaudin, said she'd be happy to talk to you about the occupation. Here's her number...'

'Thanks, Martin. I'll give her a ring. Do you think there might be others willing to see me?'

'I'm sure there will. Give me a few more days and I'll have made some house calls. It's usually the ones who can't get out who are the most willing to talk to anyone,' he said, chuckling. 'Good luck.'

She wasted no time and was soon talking to Mrs Vaudin and they agreed for Charlotte to call round on Friday morning. She checked the address in the Perry's guide and saw it was located near the shops in St Martins and easy to find. Pleased someone was willing to talk, Charlotte settled down with the diary. She flipped through the pages and found no reference to Madeleine's past life, all was centred on the upcoming birth. James Batiste arrived on 19th November 1945 and according to his mother was *"the most beautiful baby boy, with a thatch of dark hair"*. From this point on it appeared James was the centre of Madeleine's life and her diary recorded his progress over the next few months, with the occasional reference to his sorely missed, dead father. The diary finished later in 1946, the last page of the book now filled.

As she closed the diary, Charlotte pondered on the life of the woman she had come to know so intimately. If she walked into the room now, as a young woman, she felt she would have recognised her. The essence of Madeleine, more than the physical body. Although her life in France looked to be peaceful and without drama, she had suffered much so young and Charlotte shed a tear for her. And, unbidden, came the unwelcome thought of how was she going to find out the rest of the Batiste story.

Early that evening Charlotte and Louisa were busy in the kitchen preparing the evening meal.

'It's a pity Paul can't come, too, but he's so busy making sure all is up to date before we fly to Jersey tomorrow evening. He and Dad had a long discussion about staffing today so I'm hoping he'll agree to take on more therapists,' Louisa said, preparing the fresh salmon steaks for the oven.

'That's good. Then you'll be able to take more breaks together. What did Gillian think of the centre?'

'Oh, she loved it. Said she wouldn't mind a stay some time so, of course, Dad offered her a room whenever she wanted. But with him living so near it would be a waste for her to stay there. I think it'd make more sense if she popped in for a few treatments next time she's over.' Louisa turned to Charlotte, laughing. 'They're like kids, they can barely keep their hands off each other. You'd think they'd be past it at their age.'

'Oh, I don't know. Falling in love at any age can be quite heady, so I'm told.' Immediately an image of Andy's face popped into her mind and her pulse quickened. But it wasn't as if *she* was falling in love, was it? Clearing her throat she went on, 'And Malcolm is young for his age and from what you've said, so is Gillian. Do you think they'll want to leave early tonight?' she asked, eyebrows raised.

'Possibly. They've only got two more nights together before Gillian returns to England on Saturday. I don't know when they'll next meet.' Louisa slid the fish into the oven and Charlotte popped the vegetables into the steamer. 'Right, that's done. They should be here soon, time to open some wine.' Louisa retrieved a bottle of wine from the fridge and poured out two glasses and they made themselves comfortable in the sitting room. Ten minutes later the doorbell rang and Louisa jumped up to let them in.

'Hi, Dad. Gillian. Please come in and meet my friend Charlotte.'

'Charlotte my dear, it's great to see you again. How are you? Had a good stay at La Folie?' Malcolm beamed at her, before giving her a warm hug. Charlotte agreed with Louisa, he looked both younger and happier. Jubilant even.

'I'm very well, thank you, Malcolm. And yes, I enjoyed my stay at your wonderful centre.' She turned to Gillian, hovering beside him. 'Hello, Gillian. Pleased to meet you.' She surveyed the fair-haired lady whose eyes sparkled with fun and intelligence and shook hands.

'And I'm pleased to meet you, too. I've heard so much about you from both Malcolm and Louisa I feel I know you already.' Gillian smiled warmly, her blue eyes surveying her.

'Now I'm worried.'

'You needn't be, it was all good, I assure you. And I was fascinated to hear you own a publishing company. I'd love to know more,' Gillian said, as Louisa ushered everyone into the dining room.

'And I'd love to hear more about your work as a naturopathic doctor. I'm becoming more and more fascinated by alternative medicine.'

Charlotte and Gillian were soon lost in deep conversation and the evening sped by. It was approaching eleven when Malcolm suggested they leave and a taxi was ordered.

'What a wonderful evening, my dear. I think it's fair to say Gillian and Charlotte hit it off, don't you agree?' Malcolm said, giving Louisa a hug as they said their goodbyes.

She grinned at Charlotte who could only nod her agreement. She and Gillian exchanged a quick hug, promising to keep in touch.

Once the guests had left the two women retreated to the kitchen to clear away.

'Well, that went well and I'm pleased you liked Gillian, though I thought you would. As she lives in Richmond you're not too far from each other. Assuming she stays there and doesn't move here.' Louisa, loading the dishwasher, turned to face her. 'Do you think they make a great couple? As in permanent?'

Charlotte, washing the glasses in the sink, looked up and smiled. 'Absolutely. You can see how much in love they are. Even when they were talking to someone else, their eyes kept glancing towards each other. I think it's very sweet and I'm pleased for them both. Gillian's a lovely woman and too young to stay a widow forever. Has Malcolm said anything to you re his plans?'

Louisa shook her head. 'Not exactly. But the fact he's keen for my approval speaks volumes, doesn't it? But it's early days, so...' she shrugged, yawning. 'I must get to bed or I'll be fit for nothing tomorrow night. I think Paul's planning to take me out to a nightclub he's heard of so it could be a late one.'

Once Charlotte was in bed her thoughts turned to the loved-up couple and their obvious happiness. Genuinely pleased for them, she could not help feeling a twinge of envy. They had been given a second chance at love and she hoped it could be true for herself. Her face warming, she recalled the passionate kisses she had shared with Andy. There was definitely a spark between them. But was it lust – or love? And what about the big divide socially? She didn't give a fig for class, she told herself, but deep down she knew it would be hard to relinquish the trappings of wealth. And it was clear Andy wasn't comfortable about her background – and his. So, where did that leave them?

chapter sixteen

There was an autumnal edge to Friday, not surprising as October had crept in a couple of days earlier, almost unnoticed under the guise of warm sunshine. But now it was grey and clouds scudded across the sky, chased by a north-easterly bringing a Scandinavian chill to the island. Charlotte shrugged into her warmest sweater and topped it with a lightweight jacket labelled "Windproof and Stormproof". She hoped it was true as she dashed out to Louisa's car parked on the drive. Her friend had said she could use it while she was in Jersey and Charlotte had dropped her off earlier at La Folie. The couple planned to take a taxi to the airport straight from work later that afternoon and Charlotte had wished her a good weekend. Accompanied by a wink, which made Louisa blush.

Now Charlotte was on the way to visit Mrs Vaudin in St Martins and, in spite of the cool wind, felt a tremor of excitement. Reading Madeleine's diary and the files in the archives, had brought the occupation to life for her and it would be fascinating to talk to someone who had lived through it. It was a matter of minutes before Charlotte pulled up outside the cottage off La Route des Camps.

The door was opened by a stooped old lady, leaning on a stick and trussed up in layers of old cardigans. She peered at her with bespectacled eyes.

'You must be Charlotte Townsend. Come in, girl, out of the wind.'

She followed the old lady down a tiny hall and into a cramped sitting room where chairs and sofas jostled for space. Charlotte glanced around at shelves stacked with photographs and painted ceramic figurines.

'Would you like a cup of tea, my dear? And some Gâche? I can't carry a tray these days so if you could give me a hand–'

'Of course! Lead the way.'

Mrs Vaudin shuffled through to the adjacent kitchen and switched on the kettle. On the side lay a tray already set with cups, saucers and a plate of buttered Gâche, a local fruit bread. Charlotte was glad she had accepted the offer as it must have taken the old lady some effort to prepare. Once the kettle was boiled she filled the teapot and carried the tray into the sitting room while Mrs Vaudin followed.

'This looks lovely, thank you. Shall I pour? Sugar?'

'Two sugars please. I still have my sweet tooth even though I've lost most of my teeth!' The old lady cackled, displaying a gummy mouth. She stared at her. 'You're not local are you? And that accent of yours means you must be posh. Why are you talking to the likes of me?'

Charlotte wriggled on the chair. 'No, I'm not local, but I am a friend of Jeanne, the writer of the book I'm...researching. She wants me to talk to anyone who lived here through the war, so you're absolutely the right kind of person for me to meet.' She flashed her warmest smile and the old lady nodded. 'I understand you've lived all your life in St Martins and remained here during the occupation.' Charlotte sat back, equipped with tea and Gâche.

Mrs Vaudin grunted, her eyes appearing even cloudier. She described her earlier years in the Parish and during the war, saying it was very different at that time.

'I'm sure it was. Could you tell me a little bit about what it was like back then? My friend Jeanne wants to make sure she gets her facts right in her next book.' Charlotte fished in her bag for a pen and notepad.

Mrs Vaudin talked and Charlotte wrote, asking the occasional question. Her account of what happened while under German rule tallied with what Charlotte had read, both in the archives and in Madeleine's diary.

'Did you hear anything about informers, Mrs Vaudin? I understand there were those who reported their neighbours for having forbidden radios and things like that.'

'I did hear my parents talking about such things when they didn't know I was listening, but no names were mentioned, like. People were angry about it, for sure. By the time we were liberated, everyone was looking over their shoulder. Bit paranoid we were. A bad business, all told,' she said, with a shake of her head.

'Yes, I absolutely agree.' Charlotte coughed. 'I understand a certain Edmund Batiste, who lived near St Martins Point, was accused of being an informer before dying in mysterious circumstances. Did you hear anything about that?'

The old lady sniffed. 'Well, I know the Batistes, for sure. Everyone round here does. Old Harold's the local bigwig, thinks himself some sort of lord of the manor! Not a real one, mind. Not like Mr Peter de Saumarez, who's a proper gentleman and lives at Saumarez Manor down the road,' she said, waving her arm yet again. 'But I never heard of no Edmund Batiste.' She frowned. 'Died in suspicious circumstances, you say? What happened exactly?'

'He...he was beaten up and pushed over the cliff at St Martins Point. He was Harold's older brother.'

Mrs Vaudin's mouth opened wide.

'You don't say! Well, I never! I didn't know there was a brother. All I know is Harold took over the farm and everything else when old man Batiste died. My pa did some work for him once, said he was a right stingy bugger with a vicious temper. Mmm,' she said, looking deep in thought.

Charlotte, anxious not to cause rumours which might get back to the rector, went on to say it was only a story she'd heard, and it may have been far from the truth.

'Oh, I know how easy it is for rumours to spread here! People's words get twisted, like those Chinese whispers thingy. I had a friend once who said she thought her little girl might have an ear infection, and before you knew it, the word went round the little mite had gone deaf!' Mrs Vaudin chuckled. 'Wasn't funny at the time, but it goes to show you have to be careful what you say, doesn't it?' She tapped her nose. 'Don't worry, my dear, I won't repeat what you said. Wouldn't want you getting into no trouble when you're only trying to help your friend.'

She breathed a sigh of relief. That had been close! 'Thank you, I appreciate your discretion. Now, I'd better leave you in peace. Let me clear everything away first. And is there anything else you'd like me to do while I'm here?'

Mrs Vaudin brushed aside any offer of further help, other than the taking of the tray to the kitchen. As she left, Charlotte opened her bag and pulled out a box of chocolates – soft centres fortunately – and handed them to the old lady.

'Thank you so much for your time, you've been a great help. And for the lovely tea and Gâche. Goodbye.'

The old lady grinned and waved her off before shuffling back into the cottage.

Charlotte was left feeling somewhat wrung out, but pleased someone from outside the family had a poor opinion of Harold. A picture was building up of an unlikeable, greedy man which fitted Madeleine's description perfectly. As she started the car she thought of the close call when mentioning the Batistes. She would need to be more careful another time.

~ ~

Andy checked the casserole slow-cooking in the oven. Yes, it should be cooked in time but perhaps he should add a drop more wine? He was on a mission to impress and the boeuf bourguignon was part of the plan. That and his natural charm and good looks, he teased himself. Although he had spoken to Charlotte on the phone a few times during the week, he had only seen her briefly when dropping round the diary. The memory of their day in Herm was still up there as one of the best days he'd experienced in a long time. Years, if he was honest.

Watching the potatoes simmering on the hob reminded him he had not invited anyone, let alone a beautiful woman, around for a meal for ages. Since splitting with Julie, he had thrown himself into the practice, working hard to build up his client list and achieve a measure of success against fierce competition. In this Andy thought he had succeeded. Word was spreading and he was now so busy he wondered if it was time to take on a young graduate. He shook his head – time to think about the business later.

For the moment the priority was impressing Charlotte. She was working hard on his behalf with the research and he wanted to show his appreciation. And he would like to think she was interested in him as well as the family schism. And proving what a dab hand he was in the kitchen might help, he thought, straining the cooked potatoes prior to creating a buttery mash.

The food was keeping warm in the oven when Charlotte arrived on time. Checking he hadn't spilt anything on his clothes – no, all was well – Andy ran a hand through his hair before opening the door.

'Charlotte, great to see you again. And looking so...well,' he said, wanting to say gorgeous but thought it might be too much. Even though it was true. She was wearing a brown suede skirt and red sweater which emphasised her green eyes. He felt self-conscious in his jeans and open-neck shirt, standard weekend wear.

She smiled, her eyes sparkling as she thrust a bottle of wine into his hands.

'You're not looking too bad yourself,' she replied as they moved forward into an embrace. He kissed her lightly on the mouth and felt his body respond. Quickly moving back he ushered her inside.

'Umm, something smells delicious! Is cooking another of your talents?' she asked, as he led her into the kitchen diner.

'Well, I wouldn't go so far as to call it a talent, but I'm not bad. Having a French mother does have advantages where cooking's concerned. You know how important food is to them,' he said, encouraged by her compliment. 'Please, take a seat and I'll pour some wine. Lunch will be ready in five minutes.' Once Charlotte's glass was filled he checked the vegetables before joining her at the round table set with his best china and cutlery. She gazed around at the handmade wooden kitchen units, topped with a gleaming granite worktop set against soft green painted walls, and smiled.

'What a lovely room. I like the way you've kept a cottage feel but included some modern touches. Feels cosy. And welcoming,' she said, her eyes locking onto his.

He licked his lips, his mouth inexplicably dry. 'Thanks, I'm pleased with the way it turned out. And...and the rest of the cottage, which I'd be happy to show you after lunch, if you like.'

'Love to. In the meantime I'm starving! My gastric juices have gone into overdrive thanks to that wonderful aroma. Would I be right in guessing you've added wine to whatever it is you're cooking?' she said, her head tilted.

Andy laughed. 'You'd be right! A good old-fashioned boeuf bourguignon positively swimming in Burgundy. And accompanied by mashed potato and steamed beans. Would Madam like to eat now? Or we could wait a little longer–' he teased.

'Now, please! Do you need a hand?'

He was already lifting the casserole out of the oven to put on the worktop before taking out the dish of mashed potato and the warmed plates.

'No, it's all done. I only need to strain and butter the beans. You stay put while I prove to you I'm not only a great cook but also a rather mean waiter.'

He set the dishes on the table with a flourish and gave a slight bow.

Charlotte chuckled. 'Not bad so far. And it all looks divine. Your mother taught you well.'

He sat down, beginning to feel his tense shoulder muscles relax under her smiling gaze.

'I guess. She was determined I would make someone a good husband one day and saw my being a reasonable cook as a step in the right direction. I did share the cooking with my ex, and she seemed to enjoy what I made. My father, on the other hand, has no interest in anything which happens in the kitchen except when the meals are served in front of him. He's a relic of the chauvinist era, I'm afraid.'

Charlotte helped herself to the food and waited while Andy filled his plate.

'Well, I have a confession to make.' He looked up, shocked. 'Oh, don't worry, it's nothing terribly awful, but I've never learnt to cook. Never needed to, you see. But I'm making an effort now and Louisa is helping me. I've progressed from being completely useless to knowing how to prepare vegetables and, at a push, how to cook them.' She beamed at him and he couldn't resist laughing.

'I see. My mother would be horrified but...' he waved his arms, 'I'm not. Surprised, yes. Presumably there's always been someone to cook for you?'

She told him a little about her background, enough for him to realise her upbringing was even more privileged than he'd imagined. While he chewed on this distracting thought, Charlotte took a mouthful of the casserole.

'Andy, this is wonderful! My congrats to the cook and whoever taught him,' she said, her eyes dancing.

'Thanks. I'm glad you like it. I've made a French apple tart for pud and before you ask, yes, it's another of Mum's recipes.' He released an inward sigh. Knowing Charlotte must have dined at the very best restaurants had been a huge concern. Andy acknowledged he was no Raymond Blanc.

'Lovely. I look forward to it. Now, I simply must tell you what I've found out...' Andy was all attention while she gave him the gist of what Madeleine had written in the remainder of her diary. Although there were no revelations, he was content to listen as Charlotte, in a husky voice, which he found incredibly sexy, described his grandmother's experiences. It made it so much more real to him and he wondered how much his father knew. Sometime soon he'd have to raise the subject with him but Andy wanted to wait until he had something concrete to impart. Something that would change his father's life.

'...and I went to see this sparky old lady yesterday and although she couldn't tell me much, what she said did corroborate Madeleine's view of Harold.' Charlotte filled him in further as they ate their food, which, he had to admit, was cooked to perfection. He sent a mental 'thanks, Mum' to his mother as he listened.

'So, there we are. What do you think?' Charlotte asked, before scooping up a final mouthful.

'I think the finger's pointing at Harold, for sure. We just can't prove it, yet. And nothing you've learnt incriminates Edmund in any way. I'm more and more convinced he never snitched on anyone. Sounds totally out of character. Whereas Harold...well, it's something I could imagine him doing. We know he and his father were happy to buy on the black market and hide some of their extra food, making both of them unscrupulous. And Harold tried to rape Madeleine which puts him beyond the pale.' He stood up and paced around, anger at Harold taking hold. 'It would give me enormous pleasure to bring the bastard to justice, and it can't come soon enough. But how can we prove it?' His heart raced and blood pounded in his ears as he pictured his uncle's smug face.

'Andy? Are you all right? Do please calm down. There's no point giving yourself a heart attack. I'm sure we'll find a way to prove what actually happened. Someone has to know and I'm sure it can't be long before the truth will out.' He felt Charlotte's hand on his arm and raised his eyes to her face, her forehead creased in concern.

'I'm sorry, for a moment I...I lost it.' He grinned ruefully. 'It's become a bit of an obsession, I'm afraid, and I mustn't let it control me. But that bastard Harold!' He added, his fists clenched.

'I know and I sympathise, I really do. I'm not even part of the family and my blood boils too! Now, I don't know about you, but I was really looking forward to a slice of apple tart as promised. If it's as scrumptious as the casserole–'

Andy took a sharp breath. He was meant to be impressing this gorgeous woman with his culinary skills and instead had acted like a crazed idiot. Hardly the way to a woman's heart!

'Sorry. I shouldn't let Harold get to me like this, but because of...of what my father's lost, he does. Promise I'll calm down,' he said, smiling. 'I'll serve the tart. Would you like some fresh Guernsey cream with it?' He cleared the plates and various dishes before taking the foil off the apple tart. Using a pastry brush he swirled apricot glaze over the circles of apple slices.

'Cream would be lovely, thanks. To hell with the diet,' she said, laughing and Andy's shoulders dropped in relief. Perhaps all was not lost.

Once he had served up slices of tart and cream they each took a bite. He looked at her enquiringly.

'Delicious! You really can cook, Andy. What's your signature dish?'

'You've just eaten it. Boeuf bourguignon has always been my favourite and rarely lets me down. Although my coq au vin has won me some praise over the years,' he replied, trying hard not to imagine what it would be like to take Charlotte to bed. Watching a woman licking a spoon was *so* sexy. Swallowing, he reached for his wine.

'What a coincidence. It's another of my favourites. It's hard to beat those classic French favourites, isn't it? I do get so tired of the modern food trends like sushi, or a miniscule piece of meat or fish perched on a jus that wouldn't feed a mouse. Do you agree?' She tilted her head and gazed at him, a spoonful of French apple tart poised in mid-air.

Andy forced himself to concentrate and for a while the conversation turned to tastes in food and the atmosphere seemed to lift. He sensed Charlotte was determined to jolly him out of the earlier mood as she recounted tales of underwhelming meals at overpriced posh restaurants as well as some of the more memorable ones. He made a pot of fresh coffee and once they had finished he offered to show her around.

'This was originally two small cottages and I had them knocked into one to make a decent family home as well as providing me with an office,' he said, leading the way into the hall.

'Was this where you lived with your wife?'

He turned to face her. 'No, we rented a flat in Town as we didn't earn enough to buy. We were very young. I only bought this place five years ago so I chose everything. It might be a bit too masculine for your taste,' he said, leading her by the elbow into the sitting room.

He watched as Charlotte looked around and he tried to see it through her eyes. The room was large, two rooms knocked into one, and he had kept it simple. Pale cream walls contrasted with the oak beams of the ceiling and the original fireplace, now housing an enormous fire basket filled with logs, ready for when the weather turned chilly.

A large modern rug, swirls of blues and greens, sat on the reclaimed oak floor in front of a dark grey low-line sofa long enough for him to stretch out on and watch the huge television opposite. A window at the front gave a view onto the drive and the French window at the rear led onto the neat garden composed of a patio, a small lawn and flower beds.

Charlotte turned and smiled. 'It's definitely a man's room but beautifully done. I'd guess you don't spend a great deal of time in here.'

Andy nodded. 'You're right, I don't. I'm either in the kitchen knocking up something to eat or in my office when I've brought work home. Which is probably most nights. I need to get a life,' he said, realising he sounded a bit of a saddo.

'You're not the only one! Although I've stopped bringing work home, I don't get out much since my divorce. Coming over to Guernsey is my attempt at being normal; spending time with people and making friends,' she said, her face clouding. 'It's not easy to start again, is it? How did you cope?'

'Oh, to be honest, it wasn't that bad for me. Julie and I drifted apart, realising we weren't right for each other quite early on. So it was all very amicable and we stayed friends. She's remarried and had kids and we bump into each other occasionally. Hard not to on a small island! I carried on as usual, working hard and seeing mates when they dragged me out of my cave,' he said, his hands thrust into his pockets.

'And haven't there been any women to drag you out of your cave? Bearing the proverbial club in an act of role reversal?' she asked, hands on hips.

Andy swallowed. If she only knew! 'Nooo, but I sense it's time to come out of hibernation and join the real world a bit more. Now the cottage is finished and the business is going well, I have no more excuses.' He jingled the loose change in his pocket, watching her reaction.

Charlotte stared at him for a moment and then lowered her eyes so he couldn't see her expression.

'No, you don't have any excuses.' Looking up she smiled, saying, 'Are you going to show me the rest of your home? I'd love to see the garden as well.'

'Of course, let's go outside first.' A pulse beat in his neck as an image filled his head of Charlotte, bearing a club and wearing a skimpy animal skin yanking him into a cave for nefarious purposes. He hoped the air outside would cool his erotic thoughts. Opening the door, he stood back to let her go past and her arm brushed against his. His body's response did little to temper the thoughts and Andy took a couple of paces away from Charlotte as she studied the garden.

'How charming! Small but perfectly formed, with enough space to eat outside and catch some sun. And low maintenance. Perfect!' she cried, turning around.

'Thank you. The original gardens were tiny but added together they are, as you say, perfect. I'm not much of a gardener so Jeanne helped me with the beds. Their cottage has a fab garden, enormous compared to mine. The gang often end up there for a BBQ.' He walked to the edge of the lawn, surveying the plants and shrubs displaying the last of the autumn colours of red and orange.

Charlotte shivered. 'It's too cold to stand outside, let's go in and you can show me the rest of the cottage.'

Once inside Andy led her to his office, across the hall from the sitting room.

'My main office is in Town, but it's handy to have a designated space here too,' he said, waving his arm around the room, a miniature version of his professional office. White walls, white desk and shelving full of books. A small window gave a restricted view of the back garden.

Charlotte nodded and he then showed her the downstairs cloakroom before offering to continue the tour upstairs. At this point Andy wondered if showing her the bedroom – tidied and immaculate just in case – was appropriate. Would it look like he was coming on to her? She had come for lunch as a *friend*. Not on a date, exactly.

'I'd love to see upstairs, Andy. How many bedrooms have you got?' she asked, her eyes large and soft.

'Uh, three. I turned a fourth into an en suite–' he was interrupted by the shrill ring of the phone. Muttering 'excuse me', he lifted the receiver to find it was his mother.

'Hi, *Maman*, everything all right?'

'Oh, Andy, *mon chèr*, you are there! Your father has been so stupid! He was lifting a heavy box, which he has been told not to do, and his back, it gave way and he fell on the floor and cannot move. Can you come, please, and help get him to bed? He is too heavy for me.'

Andy was jilted out of his good mood. 'Of course, don't worry, I'll come right away. Are you sure he doesn't need a doctor or go to A & E?'

'No, once he is lying down, all will be well. Thank you, *mon chèr*. I will tell him you are coming *toute de suite!*'

He cursed under his breath. Great timing, Dad! Turning to Charlotte, he explained what had happened and he had to leave.

'Of course, absolutely. I do hope your father's better soon. And thank you for a wonderful lunch, Andy. Will you phone me later?' she said, picking up her bag and jacket. He thought he saw a flicker of disappointment in her eyes. Or was he fooling himself?

'Yes, for sure. Perhaps we can go out for dinner again soon.' He helped her with the jacket and kissed her gently on the mouth. The thought of his father bent in agony distracted him. He had to go.

'Sorry,' he mumbled.

'It's okay, another time. You must hurry...' she kissed his cheek briefly before opening the front door and striding to the car. Starting the engine, she gave a quick wave and left. Andy grabbed his keys and banged the front door shut, hoping his father hadn't caused himself too much damage this time.

chapter seventeen

Charlotte drove away from Andy's house holding on to the look in his eyes as he kissed her, the wanting mixed with disappointment. It echoed her own feelings and if it had not been for the phone call who knew what would have happened. Gripping the steering wheel, she also acknowledged an element of relief. They hardly knew each other and she wasn't up for a brief fling. Which maybe was all Andy wanted. He admitted to not having dated for some time so was he ready for a relationship? The arousal in her body was still strong in spite of the lack of resolution and she shifted in the seat.

Forcing herself to concentrate on the road, Charlotte pushed down the thoughts of bodies entwined in bed and took some deep breaths. What she needed was a brisk walk on a beach and she headed to the west coast instead of home. Parking at Vazon, she joined the dog walkers recently allowed back on the sands and strode along the firm sand. A cool breeze whipped through her hair and reddened her nose. The tide was coming in and the sound of waves crashing on the shore grew louder, mixing with the shrill cry of gulls searching in vain for easy food. It was too cold for picnics and the gulls were forced to dive for the small fish in the shallows.

As Charlotte watched their antics she thought about Andy's father, hoping he would make a quick recovery. At least it wasn't as serious as cancer, she told herself, frowning as her thoughts shifted inevitably to her mother. In a few days they would have the test results and then...She shivered, whether from cold or fear, Charlotte wasn't sure. Turning around she made her way back to the car and headed home.

Andy phoned later that evening.

'Hi, sorry about this afternoon. I managed to get Dad into bed, not easy as he was bent almost double, and after taking some strong pain killers he fell asleep. I stayed to make sure everything was all right and got home a few minutes ago.' He sounded tired and Charlotte wanted to rush round and take care of him.

'I'm glad he's okay. How's your mother?'

'She's fine, but annoyed with Dad as he brings these things onto himself. He'll be stuck in bed for a few days until his back sorts itself out, which it will, but it means she has to look after him as well as work. Fortunately she works from home, but it's not great.' He let out an exasperated sigh. 'Anyway, enough of my family, what have you been doing?'

Charlotte told him of her walk and said again how much she had enjoyed the lunch. Feeling self- conscious at how close they had been to going to bed together, she dried up. Andy, perhaps thinking along similar lines, also seemed a bit hesitant. He did say he would have to go round to his parents on Sunday but would have loved to see her.

She was disappointed but tried to sound casual, saying, 'Another time. Didn't you say something about dinner?'

'Yes, let me take you out, to make up for having to leave so suddenly. Are you free on Wednesday? I'm sorry, but I've got meetings booked for Monday and Tuesday otherwise–'

'Wednesday would be perfect, thanks. I look forward to it,' she murmured.

After saying goodbye, Charlotte sat staring into space, lost in a daydream involving Andy leading her upstairs to his bedroom and...Giving herself a shake she switched on the television, searching for an escapist film. Anything to stop her thoughts taking over.

Sunday morning dragged. The house was so quiet with Louisa away and for the first time since she'd been in

Guernsey, Charlotte felt alone and at a loss. There was nothing she could do with regard to Andy's quest, the only reason for staying on here. Her thoughts turned to England – and her mother. In a couple of days the test results would be back, meaning either the end of the anxiety or the beginning of even more. Charlotte's stomach clenched as she recalled Dr Rowland's comment "we might not be able to operate".

Not particularly reassuring, she thought, making herself a third cup of tea. Knowing she would go mad if she sat around all day, she hit on the idea of inviting Malcolm to join her for lunch. He was delighted to accept and suggested The Old Government Hotel, within walking distance for both of them. After making a reservation Charlotte changed into something more suitable than jeans and sweater and immediately perked up. Malcolm was good company and would provide a great diversion to her problems.

Charlotte woke with more enthusiasm on Monday than on the previous day. Not only had she enjoyed her lunch with Malcolm, but Louisa had returned from Jersey in a bubbly mood. She and Paul had loved their trip and, according to Louisa, had talked through their issues.

'I did as you suggested and told him about my insecurity and we also discussed the pressure he'd been under at work,' Louisa said, giving Charlotte a hug. 'It felt so good to bring it all out into the open, for both of us, and we've promised not to let things build up like it again. We both want our relationship to work and agreed if things are going well in three months' time, we'll move in together.'

'Wonderful! I'm so pleased. I've always thought you two made a great team. Will you say anything to Malcolm?'

She shook her head. 'No, not yet. Paul wants Dad to agree to more staff so he's not as tied to La Folie. We'll take it a step at a time,' Louisa said, filling the kettle. 'How about your weekend? How was lunch with Andy?'

'It was lovely, thanks. Andy surprised me by being a great cook, the food was delicious and I liked what I saw of his cottage,' Charlotte said, chewing her lip.

Louisa gave her a searching look.

'I sense a 'but'. What happened?'

She told her about Jim and his back and Louisa nodded her head in sympathy, saying she would ring him on Monday to check how he was. Charlotte went on to say she had lunch with Malcolm, Andy being needed at his parents' house, and Louisa wanted to know how it went. By the time they'd caught up with each other it was late.

Lying in bed on Monday Charlotte recalled what Louisa had said about her and Paul living together. It brought home to her how much *she* wanted a committed relationship. It was now more than a year since her divorce and, pushing forty, was running out of time for a family. If she wanted one.

Sitting up, the duvet tucked under her chin, she examined the idea of having children. Richard had been unable to father children so it had not been an option. She would never have considered a sperm donor, having few maternal instincts. Or so she had assumed. Maybe that was because of Richard, she now asked herself; he was stridently anti-children, always insisting they booked adult only holidays. The thought of nappies, sleepless nights and leaky boobs was not appealing but...she sighed. That wouldn't last forever and friends like Jeanne seemed to find motherhood rewarding. Perhaps it could be fun to have a little person or two to care for and call her own. If it ever happened she would definitely not be like her mother, who showed a distinct lack of maternal instinct. Telling herself it was all academic, as unless she found a partner there could be no children, her mind veered to the one potential candidate in her life. Andy.

She was attracted to him and might have ended up in bed if it hadn't been for his father but...would they be able to overcome their differences, including the stretch of water? Not allowing herself to go down that route, she swung her legs out of bed and stood up. Time to get a move on, she told herself. In more ways than one.

Later the same morning, Charlotte received two phone calls. The first was from Martin Kite, the rector of St Martins.

'Good morning, Charlotte. How did you get on with Mrs Vaudin? She told me you'd been round.'

'Morning. Yes, it went well, she gave me a clear picture of events from her perspective. I'm beginning to agree with you about older people like nothing better than to talk about the past, particularly if it was later viewed as important. Do you have any more candidates for me?'

'Yes, which is why I called. It's a housebound lady who doesn't get the chance to meet people much now and I think gets lonely, even though her husband is still alive. He's a...difficult man and is very controlling so the lady has asked me to arrange any visit for when he's out. Apparently, he plays euchre several times a week so it shouldn't be difficult to find a mutually convenient time.'

'Euchre? What's that?'

'Oh, a card game, extremely popular here, particularly with the older locals, and her husband plays on Monday, Wednesday and Friday afternoons. I wondered if this Wednesday would suit? Mrs Batiste has a chiropodist appointment this afternoon.'

Charlotte's heart skipped a beat. Surely it couldn't be?

'Wednesday's fine by me, Martin. And...and where does Mrs Batiste live?

'In a big old farmhouse off La Route de Jerbourg. You can't miss it, it's called La Vielle Manoire. I'll give you directions, but if you get lost just ask anyone where Harold and Maud Batiste live...'

Charlotte felt lightheaded as she made a note of the address and how to find it. Not that she needed to write it down as no doubt Andy knew it off by heart. She was being handed the chance to enter the lion's den itself. And all thanks to his unsuspecting wife.

She stood for a moment after disconnecting the call as first doubt and then fear crept in. Could she be stirring up the proverbial hornets' nest? If Harold found her there, how would he react? Charlotte paced around the kitchen, her thoughts flying around, scattergun fashion. The ringing of the phone brought her to a halt.

'Hi, Charlotte. It's me. I just wondered how you are,' Andy's welcome voice echoed down the line.

'I'm fine, but you'll never guess what's happened...' she told him about the rector's call.

'Wow! What a turn up for the book. If you'll excuse the pun,' he said, sounding excited. 'Fancy Aunt Maud offering to talk about the war. I didn't realise she was compos mentis, to be honest. I did know she was pretty much housebound and her sight's going. Haven't seen her since I was a kid and that was only by accident when Dad and I were walking at Jerbourg one time. We were never invited round to their house, of course.'

'I know it's an absolutely brilliant opportunity, but do you think it's safe? I don't want to raise the alarm in Harold's mind.'

'Why should you? He's not going to be there and even if he did meet you, he doesn't know you're connected to me in any way. As long as you mention Jeanne's name it should be all right. In fact, I'd better call and bring her up to speed in case the rector or anyone else gets in touch.'

Charlotte thought it over. 'You could be right. I've built up this big bogeyman image of Harold in my mind and the thought of entering his personal space and talking to his wife seemed a bit unnerving. Silly, really, I suppose.'

'Well, whatever Harold has or hasn't done in the past, he's not likely to present much of a threat now at 84. Come on, Charlotte, don't be a wimp!'

For a moment she saw red. 'Hey, it's not you who has to walk into the proverbial lion's den! He may be 84 but apparently he's still a big man. Remember I don't have to do this. I'm not part of your...your family,' she said sharply.

His voice softened. 'I'm sorry, Charlotte. That was crass of me. I wouldn't dream of letting you put yourself at risk. From anyone or anything. But I genuinely think you'll be quite safe. And there's bound to be someone else there if Maud's housebound. A carer or something. Please, Charlotte, this is such a great opportunity.'

She let the anger melt away. Perhaps she had overreacted. And he was right, it was too good a chance to miss. 'Oh, all right I'll do it. I am intrigued by Maud and it will be fascinating to talk to someone who's been married to a man everyone seems to dislike. But I'd still rather not meet him,' she said, calm again. 'I forgot to ask about your father. How is he?'

'Better, thanks, though still in bed. He phoned to say Louisa is calling round later to do some manipulation on his spine, which is good of her. Look, once you've seen old Maud, you will phone me, won't you? I'll be on tenterhooks until you do. Can't wait to hear what she's got to say! Sorry, must go, a client's arriving in a minute, will speak later. Bye.'

Charlotte was left wondering if Andy's interest in her might be more because of the valuable information she had fed him than her attraction as a woman. The unhappy thought deflated her earlier excitement and, too hyped up to settle, she threw on a jacket and walked to nearby Cambridge Park.

The grass was barely visible under a thick carpet of golden brown leaves turning crisp in the autumn air. She kicked through them as she had loved doing as a child.

Slowly her head cleared and she decided, whatever was going on in Andy's head – and heart – it was great luck Maud, of all people, had offered to talk to her. And she would not miss it for the world.

By Tuesday Charlotte was on edge again. Not because of Maud, but because of her mother. Annette was due to hear the test results that morning and it had been agreed between them Charlotte would ring her at lunchtime. It was all very well her mother saying there was nothing to worry about, but she would not be much of a daughter if she didn't. Settling down with a paperback, Charlotte managed to lose herself in the story for a couple of hours. She made a cup of coffee before phoning her mother, heart pounding a rapid tattoo in her chest.

'Hello, Mother, how did it go with Dr Rowlands?'

'Oh, hello, Charlotte. He didn't say a great deal, except I'll need to take some new medication and I should feel better soon. Nothing much to worry about, as I said.' Her mother sounded flat, deflated. Charlotte wasn't satisfied.

'Did he say what the drugs were for? What's the problem?' She kept her voice light, neutral.

'Well, you know what doctors are like, they come out with their long words and you don't want to look as if you don't understand. Something about my liver, but not serious,' her mother replied in the same flat voice. Then she added briskly, 'It was good of you to phone, Charlotte, but I simply must go now. Goodbye.'

She stared at the phone long after her mother had clicked off. Something wasn't right and she meant to find out what. When her mother had first been diagnosed with breast cancer she had researched the possibilities of it spreading. The liver was mentioned and it hadn't been good. Worried now, she phoned Dr Rowland's clinic. Eventually, after the usual hanging on, he answered.

'Charlotte, my dear. I take it you've spoken to your mother? I'm sorry it was such bad news–'

'Bad news? But she said it wasn't serious! What exactly is wrong with her, Doctor?' She felt her palms become clammy as she gripped the phone.

He coughed. 'I did explain it quite clearly to Lady Townsend and hoped she would tell you herself. But the truth is your mother has developed a particularly aggressive form of secondary liver cancer and the prognosis is not...good. We can treat the symptoms to an extent, but there's no cure, I'm afraid.'

Charlotte found herself losing her balance and sat down quickly.

'Do you mean it's...it's terminal?'

'Yes, it is. I think your mother has about a year to live. With luck.'

chapter eighteen

Charlotte's immediate instinct was to phone her mother and she started punching in the number. Before pressing the call button, she hesitated. Would it be better to simply turn up unannounced? Her mother would have to be honest with her face to face. Slumped in the chair, she felt the energy drain out of her body, leaving her frozen in inaction. She had asked Dr Rowlands if there was any chance of error in the diagnosis and he had said, in a kinder voice than usual, there was not. It appeared the cancer had been eating away for months, unnoticed. Or at least unreported by her mother. Making a big effort, Charlotte roused herself enough to make the necessary phone calls. After booking a flight to London, she rang Andy and explained about her mother.

He sounded genuinely upset for her. 'I'm so sorry, Charlotte. What a dreadful thing to happen. I had no idea your mother had been treated for cancer. Why didn't you tell me?'

'I'd hoped it was cured so there was no point mentioning it. You've enough on your plate as it is. But you do realise I need to go and see her? I've booked my flight for tomorrow morning. There's not much I can actually do when I'm over there but I'd like to try and persuade Mother to consider alternative treatments. By the sound of it she has nothing to lose,' her voice caught on a sob and she grabbed a tissue.

'Of course you must see her and alternative treatments might be worth considering. Do you know someone in particular?'

'I was wondering about Gillian, Malcolm's girlfriend. She's a qualified doctor but specialised in naturopathic and herbal medicine and Mother might be prepared to listen to her. There's also Paul and his concoctions. If I can persuade her...' she trailed off, painfully aware of how difficult it might prove.

'Look, I know you'll have a lot to do today, so can I take you to the airport tomorrow? It's the least I can do.'

'Thanks, I'd appreciate it. If you could pick me up at ten, please.'

After saying goodbye Charlotte rang the rector to say she couldn't meet Mrs Batiste because she had to fly to England urgently for family reasons. He agreed to let the old lady know and would re-arrange a time on her return. Charlotte hoped this would be by the end of the week but...She then rang La Folie, asking to speak to either Louisa or Paul. Louisa was busy and she was put through to Paul. She told him what had happened and asked if he thought he could help.

'To be honest, Charlotte, I've not worked specifically with cancer patients, but I know people who have. I don't think anyone would make any promises but it could be worth a try. Let me look into it and I'll get back to you. Are you going to suggest your mother comes to La Folie? If so I can check if we have a spare room.'

'Ideally I'd like her to come, yes. If you could check, please.'

The line went quiet for a minute.

'We could fit her in either next week or the following. Or both, of course. I'll hold them for you if you could confirm one way or another within 48 hours.'

'Brilliant. Thanks, Paul. I'll get back to you.' She then rang Malcolm, explaining about her mother and asking if he thought Gillian might be willing to help. After expressing his shock about her mother's illness, he said he would talk to Gillian and get back to her.

The phone calls left her feeling a little less helpless. She was doing what she could and everyone was so kind and willing to help, surely it was a good omen. And now it was time to pack.

It was a relief to Charlotte to finally board the plane on Wednesday morning. The process of talking to different people and repeating the same story had prompted an emotional breakdown and Charlotte had cried herself to sleep the previous night. It occurred to her she had been initially too shocked to grasp the full implications of what Dr Rowlands had said but it sank in over the repeated tellings. Her mother was going to die, probably in less than a year, unless there was a miracle.

Gillian had called during the evening and had been both supportive and helpful. She was willing to help in any way, but offered no guarantees.

'There are some brilliant natural treatments we can use and I've known patients go into long-term remission. A lot depends on your mother's general state of health and how much she's prepared to help herself, including a change of diet. But it might be we can only offer palliative care and prolong her life for a year or two,' Gillian said gently. 'I'm sorry I can't be more definite until I've examined her.'

Charlotte had thanked her, her heart feeling like a lump of lead filling her chest.

Now, with the plane taxiing along the tarmac towards the runway, she acknowledged the fear she might, in a matter of months, be truly alone. An orphan, without a partner for emotional support. Closing her eyes, she allowed herself the one tiny ray of hope – Gillian's treatments. And Andy's goodbye kiss had been so passionate at the time, everything else had fled from her mind and all that mattered was being in his arms. The image was firmly imprinted like a photograph in her mind's eye and she hugged it to herself during the flight. To her surprise and delight he had offered to fly over to join her if needed, but Charlotte knew it was better if she handled her mother alone.

After arriving in Gatwick she headed to her home in Bloomsbury, keen to catch up with the housekeeper, Mrs Thomas, and to collect some clothes. She had phoned ahead to explain why she would be in London and Mrs Thomas proved to be a brick, fussing over Charlotte and insisting she take a long, soothing bath while lunch was prepared. Happy to agree she felt renewed by the time she was dressed and downstairs again.

Mrs Thomas had set out a mixed salad and plate of crusty bread in the breakfast room and brought in a fresh pot of tea.

'Lady Townsend arrived on Sunday, without any warning as usual, Madam, not mentioning why she was in London. I did think she looked a bit peaky and made sure she had a good breakfast before she left, although she only picked at it. Your mother did ask when you were expected home and I said I didn't know.'

Charlotte sighed. 'Thank you for looking after her, Mrs Thomas. I know Mother still thinks of this house as her own London residence, which of course it was when Daddy was alive. I don't think she's likely to change now. This looks lovely, by the way. While I'm eating I'd be grateful if you'd pack the clothes I've left out on my bed as I plan to drive up after lunch.'

'Certainly, Madam. Do you know when you might be returning?'

Charlotte shook her head. 'It depends on Mother. I'll ring you.'

Mrs Thomas left and Charlotte ate her lunch, enjoying the stillness of the sunny room which had always been her favourite. Designed to catch the morning sun, it was more intimate than the formal dining room on the next floor, now rarely used. Sitting at the round mahogany table she could see out to the garden, the autumn sunshine creating shades of light and dark. A man came in regularly to keep it in shape and she noted, with approval, how neat the lawn and shrubs were. The garden was generous for London but small by comparison with the family's country home and Lady Townsend had insisted it be maintained to her own high standards, taking a particular interest in the rose bushes, always her favourites. Charlotte guessed her mother would have been on a tour of inspection while here, passing on to Mrs Thomas any instructions for the gardener. It was bittersweet to think her mother might not be laying claim to the house for much longer. With this thought she finished eating and checked on Mrs Thomas.

Her case was packed as neatly and efficiently as ever and Mrs Thomas had called the garage to bring the car around. In this part of town, the houses did not have their own garages and Charlotte's car was kept in commercial garaging when she was away. An arrangement set up by her father. Once the boot of the Jaguar was loaded she headed out of London to pick up the M3 to Frome, feeling anything but keen to arrive.

'Charlotte! What on earth are you doing here?'

Her mother's tone was not encouraging. Charlotte had parked at the front of the house and been welcomed by the butler, Phillips, with a smile and raised eyebrows. After unloading her case he walked ahead to the sitting room to announce her arrival to her ladyship.

'I came to see you, Mother. What else?' Charlotte replied, giving her a kiss on the cheek. Her mother responded with a glare fierce enough to stop most people in their tracks.

'There was no need to come haring down, as I said quite plainly yesterday. But as you are here, I expect you would like some tea. If you could bring us some, please, Phillips.'

'Very good, Madam.'

Once the butler had left, softly closing the old oak door behind him, the two women faced each other.

'I know the truth, Mother. I phoned Dr Rowlands and he explained about the cancer and...and it's not good news. Why didn't you tell me?'

Charlotte sat opposite her mother, noting the dark circles under her eyes and a pinched look that wasn't there last time they met. And she had most certainly lost weight. Normally a generous size sixteen, she looked more like a size twelve. At her words, her mother's face seemed to collapse; changing from the initial angry, defiant glare to the sagging softness of defeat.

'He had no right to tell you!' For a moment there was a spark of anger before she continued, more quietly, 'It was a shock, as you can imagine. I was convinced as was apparently Dr Rowlands, it was nothing serious and when he told me...I didn't want to acknowledge the truth. The last thing I needed after leaving the clinic was to explain everything to you. I neither want nor need your pity, Charlotte,' she said, her mouth tight.

Charlotte knew she should offer a hug, but the words stopped her. She sensed the brick wall her mother had built around herself was now further fortified and was at a loss as to how to breach it. It had been so different when her father was taken ill. Not one to make a fuss, nevertheless, he had explained the seriousness of his illness and his days might be numbered and he intended to make the most of the time left. They had gone on trips, seen plays and films and generally had a great time full of laughter till the end. Annette had not always joined them and it seemed to Charlotte she was burying her head in the sand. As she appeared to be doing now.

'Mother, I–' before she could continue, Phillips knocked on the door and entered with a tray bearing the accoutrements for tea.

'Leave it on the table, Phillips, my daughter will do the honours.'

The butler bowed and left.

Charlotte poured tea for them both and offered her mother the plate of dainty sandwiches, which she refused, saying she wasn't hungry. Helping herself to a couple, she sat down again.

'You started to say something?' her mother said, her face having regained a shuttered look.

'I was only going to ask if you would consider spending a week or so at the natural health centre in Guernsey. They offer fantastic treatments and might be able to offer an alternative therapy for – your illness.' She couldn't quite bring herself to say cancer.

Annette pursed her lips. 'I can't see any reason for me to do anything other than take the medication Dr Rowlands has prescribed. Surely if drugs are not sufficient to prolong my life then nothing else will help?'

'It might and you could continue with the chemo as well. I've spoken to Paul, the manager at La Folie, who's experienced in Eastern medicine which might be worth considering. Also, I know a medical doctor who specialises in natural approaches and she is willing to talk to you. As Gillian lives in Richmond it would be easy to meet up. She's a close friend of the owner of the health centre in Guernsey.' Charlotte held her breath. Would her mother be prepared to try unconventional treatment?

Her mother's face remained closed but she noticed a slight twitch under the left eye. She must be so frightened. Her heart went out to her.

'Harumph. I'll think about it. I don't see any point in prolonging the inevitable and if it's my time to go, then so be it,' she said, bleakly.

Charlotte was relieved. 'Thank you. It might be possible to...to gain you more time, Mother, as well as make you more comfortable,' she said, reaching over to touch Annette's arm. Her mother recoiled as if burnt and Charlotte drew back, biting her lips. The woman was impossible!

'If it's all right with you, Mother, I thought I'd stay a night or two.'

Her mother simply nodded and Charlotte stood up and made towards the door. As she opened it, she turned around and saw tears trickle down her mother's averted face. She left quickly before Annette became aware. Once in the hall Charlotte gripped her hands into fists, tension making its way across her shoulders and down into her arms. What could she do? Her mother pushed her away even now and she could hardly force her to accept help. Any normal mother would be glad of a daughter's concern but not *her* mother. Lady Annette Townsend was a law unto herself and Charlotte was strongly tempted to leave – now. But it would put her in the wrong and she couldn't do it. She owed it to her father to at least try to help. As she stood in the vast panelled hall, surrounded by his lovingly collected paintings, Charlotte ached to be in his arms again. 'Oh, Daddy, what shall I do?' she whispered, looking around as if he might suddenly appear. She jumped as a door opened, but it was only Phillips.

'I've taken the case up to your room, Miss Charlotte, and cook has been advised there will be two for dinner. Lady Townsend eats in the breakfast room at seven these days. Is there anything else you need?'

'No, that's fine, thank you.'

He gave a slight bow and she ran up the ornately carved staircase, keen to reach her room and desperate for someone to talk to. She remembered Andy had offered to come over with her so perhaps he'd make a good listener.

chapter nineteen

Andy answered immediately and Charlotte found herself hesitant, realising she was about to expose her inner frustration and worry to someone she hardly knew. His sympathetic and consoling manner, telling her to let it out, broke through her reserve and she poured out her feelings, becoming tearful in the process.

'Please don't cry, I'm sure your mother will realise you're only trying to help and be more grateful. She sounds like the proverbial tough old boot who doesn't want to admit to any weakness. How did she react when she first had cancer?'

'Oh, she was worse! It was shortly after Daddy died and she buried herself away, not wanting to see me or anyone else. I only discovered she had cancer when I found a letter from her oncologist she had accidentally left in my house,' Charlotte said, pacing up and down her room. The sound of Andy's voice helped her to calm down a little and she was glad she had phoned him, in spite of not having any right to involve him in her problems.

'Mothers can't be seen to be weak; my own was the same when she was seriously ill a few years back. Just be patient and be there for her. That's all you can do.' His voice softened. 'I miss you, Charlotte. Are you sure you don't want me to come over?'

She felt her insides melt. It was so tempting.

'No, much as it would be lovely to see you, it's better if I handle this alone. I'll be back as soon as I can, I promise. I...I miss you too.' Saying the words made her realise they were true.

She asked him how his latest project was going and they talked for about twenty minutes before she reluctantly ended the call, promising to ring him the next day. Sitting still, she recognised their relationship had become closer. Anxiety about her mother had precipitated emotions to the surface, including her growing attraction to Andy. And he had made plain his willingness to help her through this awful time.

After unpacking her case she had time for a quick freshen up before going down to dinner. Assailed by the aroma of chicken cooked in wine, Charlotte anticipated an enjoyable meal until Phillips said her mother was too tired to eat downstairs and a tray had been taken to her room, where she was not to be disturbed.

For a moment Charlotte felt a flash of anger, sensing her mother was deliberately avoiding her. Then common sense prevailed; her mother had looked ill and it was natural if she preferred to stay in her room. Sighing, she sat down and allowed the butler to serve the food which, as usual, was delicious and accompanied by one of her favourite wines. Smiling at Phillips for his thoughtfulness, she raised her glass in a salute to her mother. Hopefully she would be willing to talk in the morning and they could agree on possible alternative treatments. If they didn't then the future for her mother looked bleak.

The next morning when Charlotte walked into the breakfast room she was relieved to see her mother already sitting at the table, albeit pushing food around her plate.

'Good morning, Mother. Do you feel better today?' she asked, taking a seat next to her.

'A little, thank you.' Her mother had dark rings around her eyes and her usually immaculate hair looked unwashed.

Charlotte helped herself to the hot buffet laid out on a side table and Phillips arrived with a fresh pot of tea. Lapsang – her favourite.

Once seated she concentrated on her food, unsure how to approach the subject uppermost in her mind. Annette continued playing with her food, taking the occasional mouthful.

'You don't seem to have much of an appetite, Mother. Is it because of your illness?'

'Yes, I find it hard to swallow and don't enjoy my food,' her mother replied, sucking in her gaunt cheeks.

'I see. Will the chemo help?'

'Apparently. I've been booked into the clinic on Monday and will stay until Wednesday while I undergo treatment.'

'In which case I'll stay in London until you leave, Mother.'

'There's no need–' her mother waved her hand.

'There's every need. I want to be near so I can visit and bring anything you require. Just as I did last time you had treatment.' Her mind raced. It was so soon…

'Have you given any thought to my suggestion about talking to Gillian, the doctor I mentioned? Perhaps you could see her before entering the clinic?'

Her mother shrugged.

'Not particularly. I'm not sure there's any point.'

'I can't see any harm in talking to her and she might be able to suggest something to make the chemo more bearable. Remember how ill it made you last time? She did also say she's helped patients go into remission, Mother, and at the very least it should be possible to provide a tolerable treatment which might prolong your–'

'What, my life?' Annette snorted. 'And what makes you think I want to live longer? In pain and not able to do the things I enjoy. What would be the point?' She glared at Charlotte, eyes blazing and lips stretched tight.

She reeled back, shocked at her mother's words.

'But…but you're a fighter, not a quitter! You always taught me only cowards gave up. And you're no coward, Mother! Surely, if we could find an approach which gave you a chance to beat this disease, or at least become pain-free and able to enjoy life again, it would be worth taking?' Charlotte said, leaning forward.

Annette's eyes opened wide.

'I'm surprised you care. We hardly have a close relationship after all. It's my life we're discussing here and I can make my own choices, thank you.'

Charlotte re-filled her cup of tea, her hands shaking. Her mother was so pig-headed! Taking a deep breath, she tried again, her voice calm. 'Of course it's your choice, Mother. But what have you got to lose by talking to someone who's willing to help? At the very least we might be able to make your last months, possibly years, more comfortable and fulfilling. And for the record, I *do* care, you just make it clear you...you've never loved me.' Tears threatened to spill down her cheeks and she brushed them away.

Annette gasped, and her jaw dropped.

'What nonsense! I do love you, Charlotte, I'm just not one of those huggy people who fuss over their children. Your father was more like that and when you two were together I couldn't get a look in.' She sniffed, reaching for a handkerchief in her cardigan pocket. 'I do miss him, you know. I've been quite lost without him and now...' She blew her nose, turning her head away.

Charlotte felt her stomach tighten and she risked touching her mother's hand. This time she did not recoil, but left it on the table. Charlotte gripped it, feeling the cold thinness of the fingers. Leaning forward, she put her arms around her mother's shoulders and they remained locked in an alien, but somewhat comforting embrace. They quickly drew apart when Phillips knocked on the door, asking if they needed anything else. On being told they did not, he left.

An awkward silence followed. Charlotte sensed the shift in their relationship and did not want to push her mother too far. She could almost hear the eggshells crackling under her feet.

Her mother coughed.

'Well, it would seem we both have learnt something this morning.' She smiled faintly, her eyes glistening with unshed tears. 'I do appreciate your concern, Charlotte, and you're right to say I have nothing to lose. My life already hangs in the balance, so what harm can it do to seek help?' She dabbed at her eyes, and straightened her shoulders. 'If you would be so kind as to give me Gillian's number, I will phone to arrange an appointment, if possible before I enter the clinic.'

Charlotte felt a rush of relief.

'I'll fetch it now. I'm sure she will be able to see you soon as she's semi-retired and I'm happy to take you to London once you've arranged a time. You need to be there before Monday, anyway.'

Annette nodded and Charlotte ran upstairs for her phone, praying Gillian would be free at such short notice. Once she had passed on the number she left her mother to make the call and went off to the kitchen to chat to the cook. Mrs Combe, a rotund, cheerful woman who had been the family cook for as long as Charlotte remembered, gave her a big hug, saying she looked thin and needed fattening up.

She laughed. 'No, I don't, Mrs C. I lost weight deliberately and feel so much better for it. But I did enjoy my dinner last night, thank you. You haven't lost your touch,' she said.

Mrs Combe grunted. 'I wish Lady Townsend agreed with you. She hardly touches anything I make these days and it's worried me, it has.' She gave Charlotte a keen look. 'Is there anything wrong, Miss Charlotte? Your mother always loved her food, she did.'

Charlotte was torn. She did not want to discuss her mother's illness, knowing she would be mortified, but...

'She's not been well, Mrs C, but the doctor's sorting her out and I'm sure her appetite will return soon. Please don't say anything to her. You know what a private person my mother is.'

Mrs Combe tapped her nose.

'I won't be saying anything, Miss Charlotte. I'm just glad to hear whatever was wrong is getting put right. Now, how are things with you? I heard you were spending a lot of time in Guernsey lately and wondered what the attraction was?' she said, her head tilted to one side.

Charlotte felt herself flush. 'Oh, I've been staying at a fabulous health centre and made friends with some of the locals. It's been good to get away from London,' she said, flicking her hair.

'Good. I can't imagine why anyone would want to actually *live* in London, myself. So busy and noisy and everyone in such a hurry! Give me the countryside, anytime, I say,' Mrs Combe said, hands resting on her stomach. For a moment Charlotte found the image of the cook hurrying about the streets of the city quite incongruous and suppressed a smile.

Saying she must get back to her mother, Charlotte left the kitchen and returned to the breakfast room where she found her mother looking out of the French windows at the rose garden, her pride and joy. She felt a lump in her throat as she tried to imagine her mother's thoughts. Annette turned round and Charlotte caught a hint of sadness around her mouth, quickly replaced with a tight smile.

'I had a long conversation with Gillian Henderson and she's kindly agreed to see me tomorrow afternoon in Richmond,' Annette said in her usual brisk tone.

'That's good news, Mother. We could travel up to London tomorrow morning and I can drive you to Richmond later.'

'Thank you, Charlotte. Now, if you'll excuse me I need to talk to Phillips.'

The Family Divided

Charlotte was left feeling as if she had been dismissed and gritted her teeth. It would seem her mother's earlier softening was not yet permanent.

They arrived at the house in Bloomsbury at eleven the next morning and Mrs Thomas, forewarned this time, had prepared a room for Lady Townsend. After taking their cases upstairs she served them coffee and biscuits in the morning room.

Charlotte observed her mother as they sipped their coffee. She was concerned with what she saw. Her mother's skin had a yellow tinge and the dark circles under her eyes were more pronounced. Her stomach clenched. Perhaps it was too late...She had been on the internet to learn more about metastasis of the liver and the prognosis was not good. But for her mother's sake she had to be seen to be optimistic. The previous evening she had spoken to Andy and just knowing he was there for her helped. Once the chemo was over, she hoped to persuade Annette to return with her to Guernsey to spend some time at La Folie. Gillian was due to fly over on Sunday to stay with Malcolm so it would work out perfectly, as long as her mother agreed.

The drive to Richmond was slow, thanks to a build-up of traffic leaving London for the weekend, but they arrived in good time and Charlotte waited in an airy sitting room while Gillian took Annette off for the consultation. An hour later the women returned and Charlotte was relieved to see her mother smiling.

'Thank you for bringing your mother, Charlotte. We've had a long chat and I've made up some remedies which will help mitigate the effect of the chemo next week as well as kick-start the healing process,' Gillian said, turning to Annette and giving her a hug. Charlotte saw the flash of warmth between them and smiled.

'That's wonderful. Thanks again for seeing my mother so soon.'

As they walked towards the front door, Annette turned to say goodbye, adding, 'I look forward to seeing you next week.' Charlotte was puzzled but followed her mother outside.

'I understood Gillian was off to Guernsey, so how can you see her next week?'

Annette smiled. 'She told me how wonderful La Folie is and I've agreed to fly over after I leave the clinic. Gillian has offered to be on hand to begin a treatment programme. Wasn't it kind of her?'

'Yes it was. And I'm so pleased you've decided to stay at the centre. We can fly back together.' Charlotte sent up a silent prayer of thanks as she started the engine. As long as the chemo went smoothly, she would be back in Guernsey on Thursday and free to see Andy again. Something which made her feel a great deal more cheerful.

chapter twenty

The weekend was spent quietly with Annette resting most of the time and Charlotte nipping out to Frome to buy Napoleonic era novels as recommended by Jeanne. She wanted to fully immerse herself in the period before starting the actual writing. Her work for Andy and the talk with Jeanne had rekindled the desire to crack on with the novel. Still a bit tentative, she began plotting a more thorough outline of her story. All being well, it would be something to look forward to after she completed the Batiste family history. Assuming there was more to learn, she told herself. The thought of not having a reason to stay in Guernsey for much longer was not a happy one. Even her mother being there for treatment was not entirely positive unless it worked better than hoped. She pushed it to the back of her mind.

By Monday both she and her mother were feeling nervous about the chemo and although Annette looked pale, she told Charlotte she was feeling better. At least her skin was not as yellow and the dark circles were diminished. Annette credited the improvement to Gillian's remedies and Charlotte was happy to agree. So far so good.

Once Annette was settled in her room at the clinic Charlotte returned home. She would visit her mother in the evening and in the meantime arranged to meet her deputy, Tony, at the office to discuss, among other things, the new cook book from La Folie. The hours sped by and she left for the clinic uplifted by Tony's enthusiasm for the project. Bearing a bouquet of heavily scented roses, she was ushered into her mother's room to find her mother attached to a drip and barely awake. After a brief chat she left, promising to call in the following day.

The treatment continued to take its toll over the next couple of days, but on Wednesday afternoon Charlotte was told her mother could leave that evening. It was a relief to see her colour had returned and Annette insisted she felt well enough to travel to Guernsey the next day.

'I haven't had the debilitating nausea I experienced last time and I'm sure it's down to the pills Gillian gave me. Dr Rowlands is pleased with my liver function tests and said I will not need further chemo for four weeks,' Annette said, sitting upright in the chair, her packed bag on the bed.

'Brilliant! The flight's booked and Paul's expecting you at La Folie. Now, let me carry your bag.'

Annette walked unaided to the lift and minutes later they were in the car heading back to Bloomsbury.

As the plane approached Guernsey airport Charlotte's stomach fluttered with excitement. The week in England had brought home how much she loved the island and missed Andy. They were to have dinner together that night and she could barely wait. They might become even closer…

'Well, it looks much smaller than I imagined,' commented her mother, occupying the window seat. 'And why are there so many empty glasshouses? I thought growing was a main industry here.'

Charlotte explained how far fewer flowers were grown since cheaper imports from Holland and further afield had created strong competition. 'La Folie was bought by growers after the war and before the house was turned into a spa, I understand old greenhouses were still visible. Tourism's now a big source of income for the island, together with the financial industry, of course. I'm sure you'll love it here, Mother. It's a bit like Somerset, but completely surrounded by sea, with lovely cliffs and loads of beaches.'

Her mother smiled faintly. 'I'm not sure how much time there will be for me to explore. I imagine most of my day will be spent at the centre.'

Charlotte felt a pang of remorse. For a moment she had forgotten her mother's illness and how weak she was. She touched her arm. 'If you like, I'll take you out in a car. We can circumnavigate the island in about an hour. And if you're up to it, the cliff walks from La Folie are stunning and quite gentle.'

Annette pursed her lips and Charlotte sat back, bracing herself for the landing.

They were met by Doug from La Folie, who welcomed them with a bright smile before steering them outside to the courtesy car. October had now put its stamp on the weather and there was a distinct coolness in the air even though the sun happily played catch with the soft white clouds. Charlotte relaxed into her seat while Annette looked out of the window, appearing keen to take everything in.

As they turned the last corner in the lane leading to La Folie, Annette let out a gasp. 'What an odd building! It looks like a Gothic castle and not at all what I expected.'

'Don't worry, Mother, it's beautiful inside and the back is more Victorian country house. I think it was aptly named, don't you?'

Charlotte led the way while Doug brought in their cases. She was going home with Louisa later and planned to stay for the afternoon, wanting to make sure her mother was well settled. She noted with amusement how Annette's gaze swept over the old mahogany staircase and panelled walls, not unlike those of the Manor House. Catching her mother's eye, she smiled. 'See what I mean?' she said. Annette nodded, looking more at ease and Charlotte continued towards the reception desk where Nadine, her hair spiralled around her head, was ready to greet them.

'Lady Townsend, on behalf of La Folie, I'd like to welcome you as our guest and wish you a pleasant and healthy stay. Doug will take you up to your room shortly.' She turned to Charlotte and grinned. 'It's good to see you again, Miss Townsend. Your mother will be in *Serenity*, which I'm sure you'll agree is very comfortable.'

'It is. Has an appointment been set up with Paul yet?'

Nadine nodded, her curls bouncing in unison. 'Yes, for two o'clock, so you have time for lunch. Oh, and Dr Henderson will call in about four.'

'Thanks, Nadine.' Charlotte turned to her mother. 'While you're settling in I'll catch up with my friend Louisa. Nadine will show you the dining room and we can meet there for lunch.'

Doug led Annette upstairs while Charlotte nipped along to the dining room to see Louisa. Time for a quick catch up.

Before Charlotte left with Louisa later that afternoon, she visited her mother in her room.

'How did you get on with Paul? Has he come up with a treatment plan?' she asked, joining her mother on the small sofa near the window.

Annette, looking tired she thought, managed a small smile. 'He seems very knowledgeable and was extremely thorough in his questions. Felt a bit like the third degree! But he has suggested various treatments and a combination of Ayurvedic herbs which, apparently, have been approved by Gillian. I think they must have put their heads together before I arrived, but I mustn't complain as they are both being very kind and...and professional.' She sighed and looked down at her hands, twisted together in her lap.

Charlotte, aware of what her mother faced, laid her own hand on top of hers.

'It's a lot to take in, isn't it?' she said gently.

Her mother nodded and said she wanted to rest. Charlotte gave her a quick kiss and left, heavy with the thought that even though the alternative treatments would help, her mother's illness was still likely to be terminal.

Back at Louisa's house, Charlotte quickly unpacked and changed for the meal with Andy. She forced herself to focus on the evening ahead and not what was happening with her mother. It was out of her control.

Andy arrived, enveloping her in his arms and kissing her until she had to pull back laughing, needing to breathe. It felt so right to be in his arms, being kissed – and perhaps loved?

He grinned. 'I had to make up for not seeing you for more than a week. And now, Madam, I'm taking you to one of my favourite restaurants, Da Nello's. Ready?' he asked, his eyes twinkling.

'I certainly am. Lead on.'

While they drove down towards North Esplanade by the marina, Charlotte briefed him on what had been proposed for her mother's treatment and he squeezed her hand in support.

'All you can do is stay positive and be there for her. I'm pleased you suggested she stay at La Folie, which alone will do her good. Am I going to meet her?'

'Of course. Although I haven't told her about you yet as we've not really been going out. And it wouldn't seem right under the...circumstances. But I will, in a few days when she's feeling stronger,' Charlotte replied, flashing a smile.

'Good. I look forward to it. Now, for this evening at least, I hope you can relax and enjoy yourself. The food's delicious and I think you'll love the surroundings.'

Andy parked on the Crown Pier and they crossed over and walked towards the Lower Pollet, a matter of yards up from Le Petit Bistro. He reached out for her hand and she allowed him to take it, enjoying the touch of his fingers on hers.

'I've passed this several times and thought how intriguing it looked, with the engraved writing on the windows. And I love Italian food.'

He gave a small bow. 'If the *Signora* will follow me?' He opened the door. She grinned in delight, and entered the small bar at the front of the restaurant. Once they had ordered their drinks they were presented with menus and Charlotte's eyes widened.

'What a choice. It's going to be hard to choose as I like virtually everything,' she said, lifting her eyes to gaze at Andy. He smiled in return, saying she couldn't go wrong with fish, a house speciality. Their Proseccos arrived and they clinked glasses in salute. The wine bubbled through her veins, and she let out a small sigh of pleasure. Delicious! For a while they were lost in contemplation of the menu, only marginally aware of other guests arriving and taking seats nearby. Once their order was placed, Charlotte studied her surroundings, taking in the exposed granite walls, white painted beams and limestone floor with a centred mosaic pattern.

'This is fab. And it looks so old, but new if you know what I mean.'

'The building's about 500 years old and it's been a restaurant for more than thirty. Cosy, isn't it? And not too noisy so we'll be able to hear each other speak. It's... good to be with you again, Charlotte. So much better than talking on the phone,' Andy said, lightly touching her arm.

She smiled. 'I agree. I think we're both visual people and need to see rather than hear, yes?'

The maître d' arrived. He coughed. 'Your table's ready, *Signor*,' he murmured, waving his arm.

He escorted them through the main restaurant and up a short flight of stairs then down again into a room resembling a courtyard, with a pitched glazed roof. Their table was in a far corner and as they followed the maître d' Charlotte spotted a plaque bearing the words *Il Cortile*.

Once they were alone she exclaimed, 'This is perfect! And I can see the moon. It's like being outside, isn't it? Thank you for bringing me here, Andy. Just being in this lovely space is food for my soul.'

'You're welcome. And I think you'll find the food for your body is as good,' he said, smiling.

He was right. The food – and the company – matched the ambience perfectly and she found herself melting inside as the evening progressed. Andy made her laugh with his stories of mishaps during his career as an architect and the combination of fine wine and succulent food was increasingly seductive. She wanted to go to bed with him and was sure he felt the same, judging by the intensity of his gaze and the flirtatious playing with her fingers. He had even put a forkful of his food in her mouth to taste. Naturally she reciprocated and the sheer sensuality of sharing had made her heart race. By the time they finished dessert she was aching to feel his arms around her.

'How about coming back to mine for coffee? I know it's not exactly on the way but–'

She didn't hesitate. 'I'd love to, thanks. I can always get a taxi home later.'

They stared at each other, desire mirrored in their eyes.

'Right, I'll get the bill,' Andy said, clearing his throat. Once the bill was paid, he steered her by the arm back to the bar where she was presented with a single red rose by the maître d'.

'I trust you have had a pleasant meal with us, *Signora*,' he said, bowing slightly.

'Oh, I have. Very much, thank you,' she said, with a lingering look at Andy.

'Then I hope we will have the honour of seeing you again, *Signora* and *Signor*,' he replied, opening the door.

Once out in the street, and uncaring of whether or not they were observed, they flew into each other's arms and kissed. Andy was the first to let go. 'I'd better get you home, young lady, before we disgrace ourselves in public,' he said softly. She laughed and hooked her arm through his as he walked her back to the car.

chapter twenty-one

Charlotte did not need a taxi that evening. Instead she spent the night curled up with Andy in his bed, arms and legs determinedly entwined. When she woke the next morning the memory of their lovemaking flooded into her mind, and she smiled. If she had been a cat she would have purred. Her body felt replete, loose-limbed and at ease with itself. She could have shouted for joy at being wanted by the man whose arm now pinned her to the bed. The intensity of their lovemaking had washed away the incipient feeling of being undesirable which had lingered after Richard's defection to a younger model. Sex – and what sex! – had restored to Charlotte her sense of worth as a woman in her prime.

'Morning, gorgeous. Did you sleep well?' Andy's voice was husky with sleep. He moved his arm and she turned to face him. She stroked the hair out of his eyes.

'Like a baby. Must be the bed!' she said, with a teasing smile.

He reached out and pulled her underneath him. 'I think it was more than my, admittedly comfortable, bed. Let me show you.'

Fifteen minutes later they both laid back on the pillows, sweat cooling on their exhausted bodies.

Andy traced his fingers down Charlotte's stomach before kissing each breast.

'I hate to say this but I should be at work. A new client is due at the office in half an hour. Would you mind very much if we postponed this meeting and re-convened later? This evening perhaps?' The words formal but the tone anything but. Desire still clouded his eyes.

She giggled. 'This evening would be perfect, Mr Batiste. You'd better shower first unless we can double up,' she said, stroking the stubble on his cheeks.

Andy swung his legs out of bed, laughing. 'It is a double shower but I think it would be safer if I showered alone. Could you make a pot of coffee while I get ready?' He padded across the floor to the adjoining bathroom, giving Charlotte ample time to admire his athletic physique. The jogging certainly paid off, she thought, as she got up and threw on the robe hanging on the back of the door. In the kitchen she was relieved to see a cafetière on the worktop. That she could manage. The coffee was in a tin in the cupboard above and while the kettle heated up she hunted down mugs and milk.

When Andy came down, freshly shaved with his hair still damp from the shower, her stomach flipped over. Wafting the subtle scent of lime and sandalwood she found him incredibly sexy dressed in a cream open-necked shirt tucked into reddish-brown chinos. He smiled as he spotted the brewed coffee.

'You made it, thanks. Wasn't sure if you knew how, you said you couldn't cook.'

'Well, making coffee is hardly cooking, is it? I'm not completely without talent, you know,' she said, pouring out two mugs, not wanting to admit she had been shown how to make coffee by Louisa. 'I even managed to warm the milk in case you preferred it.' Charlotte pushed the jug of milk towards him.

'Oh I know you're not without talent, Miss Townsend. Far from it if last night was anything to go by,' he said, slipping an arm around her waist.

She dropped her eyes, suddenly overcome with unwarranted shyness. In the cold light of day...

'Don't go all shy on me. I loved what we did in bed. You're not having any regrets are you?'

Charlotte raised her eyes. His forehead was creased in concern.

'No, of course not. It's just...well, it's been a long time since I...I slept with someone other than my husband and it feels...strange.'

His face relaxed and he pushed her hair back behind her ear. 'I understand. It was the same for me after I split with my ex.' Glancing at the clock, he gulped down his coffee, before adding, 'Sorry, I really must go. I'll ring you later about this evening. Just drop the latch on the way out and here's the taxi number.' He scrawled it on a pad next to the phone. A quick kiss and he was gone.

Charlotte sipped her coffee, hugging to herself the thought of seeing him again that evening. In the meantime she had to shower, dress and return home to Louisa's. And make some phone calls.

Louisa had left for work by the time Charlotte arrived home, relieved to put off the inevitable cross-examination. Once she was changed into clean clothes she sat down to phone the rector and advise him of her return. Martin said he was due to visit Maud over the weekend and would ask if a new meeting could be arranged, preferably on Monday. Charlotte did not want any further delays. She then rang La Folie to speak to her mother.

'Good morning, Mother. How are you today?'

'Not too bad, thank you. I had a massage earlier...' She went on to describe what was planned in the way of treatments, adding she had already started taking Paul's "concoctions", as she called them. Charlotte was happy to listen, glad her mother had accepted the treatments without question. She thought Annette was probably reassured by Gillian being a qualified doctor, adding credibility to the alternative treatment. To the best of her knowledge her mother had never even experienced a massage before, let alone the Reiki and chakra balancing Paul proposed. Charlotte had thought to visit her mother that day but it seemed she was too busy with appointments so they agreed she would call in on Saturday afternoon. As she switched off the phone, Charlotte could not help smiling at the thought she might be spending Saturday morning in Andy's bed. But she was fairly sure they would be up and about by the afternoon.

The first thing Louisa said when she arrived home at teatime was, 'I assume you spent the night at Andy's. So...?' She was grinning from ear to ear.

Charlotte gave her an edited version of events and then let drop she was seeing him again that evening and might not be back until Saturday sometime.

'I'm really pleased for you, my friend. You deserve to have some fun and Andy's a nice guy who needed to get out more. I think you'll be good for one another,' Louisa said, giving her a hug. 'Have you told your mother about him?'

'No, it's too soon and, well, while she's so ill it doesn't seem appropriate to talk about my love life, does it?' she said, experiencing a slight twinge of guilt. 'Mind you,' she continued, 'Mother hasn't once asked me if I'm seeing anyone since Richard left. So I don't imagine she's likely to start asking now. She's never been one to show much interest in what I'm doing and it's one of the reasons we're not close. Although since being diagnosed with cancer again, she's thawed a bit towards me. Which is something,' Charlotte said, with a sigh.

'Well, I do hope you two become closer as you don't know how long you have left together. I still miss Mum so much...' Louisa said, wistfully.

Charlotte threw her arms around her and they stood entwined, sending out to each other invisible waves of support. Finally Louisa pulled back, brushing a tear from her eye. 'I'll put the kettle on. Fancy a cuppa?'

'Thanks. Now, tell me about your day before I go and change. And how things are between you and Paul these days.'

They sat in the kitchen as Louisa told her about the new members of staff being recruited which would allow Paul to reduce his hours. In the meantime Malcolm was taking over some of Paul's admin until an office manager was appointed. Consequently Paul was, according to Louisa, more relaxed and they were enjoying spending more time together.

'If we go on like this, then it looks as if we'll be living together sooner than planned. I can hardly wait,' Louisa said, a dreamy look in her eyes.

Charlotte laughed. 'I'm beginning to think there's something either in the water or the air in Guernsey! So many people seem to be coupling up after arriving on the island.'

'Ahh! Do you think it's serious between you and Andy? As in long-term?' Louisa asked, her eyebrows raised.

She shrugged. 'I don't know. It would be so complicated with my living in London so I'm not thinking that far ahead. I have to live in the moment and enjoy it while it lasts,' she said, mentally crossing her fingers.

Andy surprised Charlotte by taking her to The Doghouse, a gastropub famous for live music, on the outskirts of Town. He had been lucky to book a table in the restaurant as the night's entertainment was a popular Stones tribute act over from England.

'I took a gamble on you loving the Stones' music as much as I do. Was I right?' Andy asked, driving down the Rohais.

She smiled. 'You were. I've loved their music for as long as I can remember. Should be fun.'

The familiar sounds of 'Honky Tonk Women' blasted from the speakers as they entered the pub. Glancing quickly at the band, which looked as energetic as the original, Charlotte allowed herself to be steered towards the dining area where the sound was only minimally reduced. A waitress showed them their table and took an order for drinks.

'What a contrast to last night,' she shouted above the music, tapping her feet and hands to the music.

Andy grinned and put his arm around her. There was a small dance area in front of the band and couples took to the floor, waving arms and joining in with the words. The atmosphere was infectious and when Andy grabbed her hand she didn't hesitate, keen to join in the fun. By the end of the evening Charlotte was both exhausted and happy. She couldn't remember the last time she had danced to such lively music and Andy proved to be an enthusiastic dancer. No just waving the arms about for him. She collapsed, laughing, into his car and when he asked where to, her reply was to pull him towards her and kiss him firmly on the mouth.

'I take it that's my place, then,' he said, when he finally eased away and started the engine. She leant back in the seat and smiled. She had brought her toothbrush. Just in case.

~ ~

Andy woke the next morning wondering if he'd died and gone to heaven. The most wonderful woman he'd ever met had spent the past two nights with him and not only shared his taste in music but laughed at his jokes. And enjoyed being in his bed. Carefully turning his head he sneaked a glance at the still sleeping Charlotte. With her flushed creamy complexion and lustrous hair spread out over the pillow, she reminded him of the subject of a Pre-Raphaelite painting. He knew he was falling in love and could only hope she felt the same about him. But even if she did, would it all end in tears? Their backgrounds couldn't be more different, for one thing. And her life was centred in London and he couldn't imagine leaving Guernsey. He'd worked so hard to build up the practice...Charlotte stirred and, opening her eyes, she saw him and smiled. His body tightened with desire as she stroked his face and kissed him.

'Good morning. Thank you again for the most wonderful evening and...night,' she said, her voice husky.

'It was my pleasure. I had no idea you could...dance like that,' he said, folding his arms around her.

She laughed and pushed her naked breasts against his chest. 'Oh, I've always known how to move my body. And you're quite a good mover yourself,' she added, her eyes cloudy with desire.

He was happy to show her a few more moves.

They made it downstairs about eleven and Andy offered to make scrambled eggs with smoked salmon, to be washed down with a pot of coffee prepared by Charlotte. He enjoyed the intimacy of preparing breakfast together and chatting about inconsequential things like the weather.

As they sat down with their heaped plates and steaming mugs, he asked what her plans were for the day.

'I've offered to visit Mother this afternoon, other than that nothing. What about you?'

'I've got some work to catch up on but it won't take long. How about if we go out for a late lunch before you see your mum? I can drop you off and pick you up later. Looks like it might remain fine for a walk,' he said, wanting to spend every waking minute with this wonderful woman.

She smiled dreamily. 'Sounds good to me. After all these wonderful meals I'll need to walk around the island at least twice.'

'I think we'll make do with a quick walk on the cliffs before it gets dark. But we could go for a longer walk tomorrow if you like.' His brow furrowed. 'Assuming you're free?'

'Yes, I'd like that. But don't you go to your parents' for Sunday lunch?'

'Normally, yes, but they're going to friends tomorrow, so I have a clear day.'

Charlotte nodded. 'Good. Let me take you out to lunch somewhere nice. You haven't let me pay for anything yet which is totally sexist and inappropriate in these days of equality,' she said, straight-faced but with eyes dancing.

He laughed. 'It's a deal! Now, is there any more of your delicious coffee, please? For some reason, I feel a little tired this morning.'

~ ~

Charlotte almost floated into La Folie that afternoon. Only the thought of her mother's illness kept her from beaming at everyone she saw. It didn't seem fair when she had finally found something – or rather, someone – to make her laugh and feel good about herself, her mother faced a tough battle in order to live. *C'est la vie* didn't quite sum up her thoughts on the matter and she made a conscious effort to not seem as happy when she found her mother in the sun room.

Annette was sitting at a table by the window, gazing longingly at the garden leading to the cliffs. A keen walker, it was clear from her expression she wanted to be outside. But Charlotte knew for the moment her mother was not strong enough. Feeling guilty over her own rude health, she kissed her mother's cheek before sitting opposite to her.

'Charlotte! I didn't see you arrive. I was admiring the garden and wondering how it would look in full bloom,' Annette said, turning round. Charlotte studied her face. The skin was no longer yellow and the eyes looked brighter, but sadness played around the thin lips.

'It is a beautiful garden but not as lovely as yours, Mother. And I don't think anyone's roses can compete with those you grow back home,' she said, with a smile.

Her mother's eyes lit up. 'Yes, my roses are rather special, aren't they? I only hope Jenkins will prune them properly while I'm away. I don't like leaving such important tasks to him, as you know.'

Charlotte was fully aware Jenkins was solely responsible for the care of the roses and her mother barely lifted a pair of secateurs to them. But if it made her happy to think otherwise...

'You're looking better, Mother. What treatments have you had over the past couple of days?'

Her mother described the therapies in a way which made it clear she had forgotten Charlotte had twice been a guest at the retreat. And as she had always loved being the centre of attention, had welcomed the fuss made of her as perfectly natural. Charlotte listened to descriptions of the other guests, only some of whom her mother felt able to socialise with. She couldn't help thinking maybe not everyone wanted to befriend her mother either, but kept quiet. As the waitress served them cups of tea and Chef's low-fat cake, she gave Charlotte a sympathetic smile. Whether because of her mother's illness or for being her mother's daughter, she wasn't sure.

An hour later she left her mother to be taken off for a hydrotherapy session and promised to call again.

'There's no need for you to do that, Charlotte, I'm being perfectly well looked after, as you can see. Please don't put yourself out on my behalf,' Annette said, dismissively.

Gritting her teeth, she gave her mother a brief kiss and walked into the garden. All the warm, fuzzy feelings she had arrived with had evaporated. As she sent a text to Andy saying she was ready to be picked up, she hoped he would be able to re-ignite them.

chapter twenty-two

Charlotte was pacing up and down in front of La Folie, telling herself to calm down, her mother was unlikely to change, when her mobile rang. It was the rector, saying he had seen Mrs Batiste and she would be happy to see Charlotte on Monday afternoon around three. She was so excited that all the hurtful feelings her mother's attitude had evoked dissipated into the air, like a burst balloon. When Andy pulled into the drive minutes later she was all smiles.

'Well, you look pleased to see me! Missed me that much, did you?' he teased, before giving her a kiss.

She chuckled. 'I've just arranged something which will please *you*. I'm seeing Maud Batiste on Monday afternoon. Happy?'

Andy kissed her again. 'Very. Now, as we seem to be attracting some attention, I think it's time to leave,' he said, nodding in the direction of a pair of elderly guests giving them disapproving looks. Turning the car around he drove down the lane. 'How was your mother?' he asked, innocently.

Immediately Charlotte felt her shoulders tense. 'Physically a bit better but as a mother as bad as ever...' she repeated her mother's words and Andy sighed, reaching to clutch her hand.

'Do remember she's been told she might not have long to live. That would make anyone resentful.'

'I accept that, but Mother's resented me since the day I was born! Or so I assume, as obviously I don't remember quite so far back,' she replied, with a faint smile. 'I'm doing my best to help her get through this awful time, but she doesn't seem to acknowledge it. She wouldn't be here if I hadn't suggested it and she's being so well cared for,' she paused to blow her nose, continuing, 'And to add insult to injury I'm footing the bill! Never once has she asked about the cost and offered to pay. Just assumes I'll cover it. Of course I'm happy to do so, but it's not as if she's badly off. Daddy left her well provided for.' She took a deep breath and slowly exhaled.

'Oh! I can see why you're upset. Your mother seems to take it for granted you're happy to pay for her treatments but she still pushes you away as if you don't care. I'd be upset too, if my mother behaved like that. Thankfully, it's not at all likely.'

She flashed him a smile. 'Your mother sounds lovely. I'd like to meet her sometime.'

'You will, but not yet as we can't jeopardise your meeting with Aunt Maud. There can't be seen to be any connection between us,' he said, his forehead creased.

Charlotte nodded, smiling inwardly at how she had distrusted Andy's motives towards her. He obviously had been as keen on her as much as the research. She didn't want anything else to stop her seeing the old woman who might know something about what really happened to Edmund. Although whether or not she would be prepared to share her knowledge was another matter. Settling back in the seat, she told herself to stop worrying and enjoy being with Andy. He was cooking for them that evening and had dropped her at Louisa's before lunch while he shopped. Andy had made it clear he wanted her to spend the night with him again so she had packed a small bag with a change of clothing and toiletries. As she finished Louisa popped her head in.

'There you are! Haven't seen much of you lately. I assume you've been at Andy's?' she said, eyebrows raised.

'Yes, and I'm round there tonight, hence the packing. Sorry I've not been much company since I got back.'

Louisa shook her head. 'No problem. I'm happy you're having...fun,' she said, smirking. 'It works out quite well as Paul is staying over tonight so you won't be playing gooseberry. And we can have an extra-long lie-in.'

Charlotte smiled as she zipped up the bag. 'I'll be back tomorrow night as Andy has an early appointment on Monday. Oh, and by the way, guess who I'm seeing on Monday afternoon?' She told her about Maud and Louisa was suitably pleased and asked if Jim knew about the meeting.

'Oh no, and he mustn't know. Please don't say anything when you next see him, will you?'

'I wouldn't dream of it. And anyway our next appointment isn't for a couple of weeks. He's coming on really well with the physio and Paul's also made up a herbal remedy to ease the inflammation. Seems to be working, too. I've suggested he adds Ayurvedic herbalism to the centre's choice of therapies. We're gradually building a reputation for our treatments as an adjunct to mainstream medicine. And if Gillian does come on board, _'

'Gillian's joining the centre?' Charlotte was surprised.

'Well, it depends. Dad wants her to move in with him, but it's a bit soon. So he suggested she became a kind of consultant for La Folie, working minimal hours and having her own space.' Louisa shuffled her feet. 'If Paul moves in here, his rooms will become free...'

Charlotte laughed. 'You and your father have it all worked out, haven't you? Well, I wish you success with your schemes. I think Gillian will prove to be an asset to the centre but I don't see her as a lady to be pushed.'

'I think Dad's met his match but I do like her so I'm keeping my fingers crossed they end up together.'

The doorbell announced Andy's arrival and after giving Louisa a quick hug, Charlotte ran downstairs to join him.

The next morning Charlotte and Andy enjoyed a leisurely breakfast before setting off from Rue St Pierre to walk through the lanes to the reservoir, something she had not yet visited. The name reservoir, to her, conjured up concrete dams holding back a large, uninteresting area of water and not much else. Andy assured her this reservoir was different, looking more like a lake surrounded by trees and definitely worth a walk around. Willing to be suitably impressed, she hooked her arm in his as they walked along lanes deemed too narrow for the normal speed limit of 35mph and consequently reduced to 15mph. It still meant they had to listen out for traffic coming behind them, but fortunately cars were infrequent. And the occasional tractor was hardly a danger.

The air was mild for October and with no wind it proved enjoyable to weave through the lanes, with sporadic birdsong keeping them company. Andy suggested they compete to guess what kind of birds were singing and Charlotte was able to distinguish between warblers and a mistle thrush while Andy came up trumps with the myriad sea birds. Laughing at their attempts to imitate the cry of a sandpiper, they found themselves on the edge of the reservoir.

This was formed by three 'fingers' of water stretching from the 'wrist' of the dam and they arrived at the tip of the middle 'finger'. Charlotte gasped with pleasure at the sight of the water, dotted with ducks and gulls, and surrounded by thick woodland. Even the concrete dam was picturesque, complete with arches and mini towers, forming a bridge across the water.

'How lovely! I never guessed this was hidden away in the middle of the island. Will it take long for us to walk around?'

'About an hour so we'll back in plenty of time for lunch,' he said, his arm around her shoulders as they admired the view.

'It's so peaceful, isn't it? It has a stillness the sea can never achieve. I imagine it's a great place to come if you wanted to totally get away from it all. Want to think things through.' She stood perfectly still, trying to block everything from her mind, except the fact of standing there with Andy by her side. This felt so right, but...She let out an involuntary sigh, thinking of the barriers to their relationship. Could they be overcome? It would be nice...

Andy pulled her round to face him. 'Are you all right?' he asked, stroking her face.

She forced a smile. 'Of course. I...I was just wondering how it would go with Maud tomorrow, what sort of questions I should ask.' She hated lying to him but it was sort of true.

'Hmm. Shall we chat about it as we walk? Might get some inspiration on the way round.'

Charlotte agreed and they walked on, batting ideas back and forth. She pushed down her concerns about the future – or otherwise – of their relationship.

They arrived back at the cottage energised from their long walk and the abundance of fresh air. Charlotte caught a glimpse of her face in a mirror, noting the pink glow of her cheeks and the sparkle in her eyes. Not one for vanity, she had to admit she looked pretty darn good. Something was definitely agreeing with her. Turning, she saw Andy looking at her, his lips curled up in a warm smile.

'You really are beautiful, Charlotte. And I know we have to change for the lunch, but all I want to do at this moment is make love to you. What do you say?' he asked, softly.

She felt the heat rise up from her neck to her face. 'I think there might be enough time...'

Charlotte had booked lunch at a restaurant recommended by Louisa, The Farmhouse in St Saviours, not far from Andy's part of the island. Not that anywhere was very far, but it did mean they only took ten minutes to get there. Set in lovely gardens with a pool, it offered ideal al fresco dining, but not in October. They were both ravenous after the morning's exertions and chose the traditional three-course Sunday roast. The main dining room, a light and airy space, was separated by a wall of glass doors from the garden, bringing the outside in.

The view was lost on Charlotte and Andy, absorbed as they were in each other. Every time Charlotte looked up she caught Andy gazing at her and this happened so often that when their eyes locked again, they burst out laughing.

'We're behaving like a couple of teenagers, not adults who have been around the block a few times,' Andy said, his eyes crinkled up with laughter.

'Hey! Speak for yourself! I've led a very chaste existence, thank you. Until now,' she said, feeling exactly like a teenager. Andy had brought her alive and made her feel young again. And it seemed she had achieved the same for him.

Andy had just stroked her hand when the waiter arrived to clear away their plates and bring the dessert menu. Releasing her hand he studied the menu as if it was a complex legal document. Charlotte smiled, not at all fooled. By the time they had finished the desserts and coffee, they were in playful mood and instead of going back to the car, wandered around the garden.

He cleared his throat. 'I know we've not known each other very long, but I, I think I'm falling for you. And the thing is, you'll be going home soon and well, I wish you didn't have to.' He pulled her close and kissed her as they stood hidden by a large shrub. Charlotte gave in to the kiss, living in that wonderful moment when all else is of no consequence. As voices floated nearby they drew apart but stayed immobile.

'I...I have feelings for you, too. But it's complicated, isn't it?' she said at last, pushing her hand through her hair and wishing they could stay as they were. 'People do have long-distance relationships and there's no reason why we couldn't. It's only an hour's flight to London so we could meet at weekends...' she trailed off, knowing in her heart it wouldn't work. Or at least not long-term. She would be spending all week looking forward to the weekend and then be in bits when she waved him off on Monday morning.

He kissed the tip of her nose. 'Not sure if it's what either of us wants, is it? We don't have to decide anything now, but I guess I wanted to know how you feel. To see if I have any chance of winning you. For the duration, not just for a few weeks.'

Charlotte took a deep breath. He really wanted a proper relationship! Which would be wonderful if only...

'Let's see how things develop, shall we? There's a lot going on at the moment, what with your family's secrets to resolve and your father's health. And then there's my mother, with her illness...' she said sadly, thinking of the woman to whom she was so close, yet wasn't.

Andy's face fell, registering his disappointment. Charlotte wished she could offer him more, but it wasn't the right time. She could only hope he would wait until she knew exactly what it was she wanted. And what she would be prepared to give up.

chapter twenty-three

Charlotte sat in the kitchen, playing with a bowl of muesli. Her stomach was clenched with nerves and she had to force the food down. The upcoming meeting with Maud was uppermost in her mind and she was surprised to find herself so nervous. She was just an old lady who probably couldn't even remember there had been a war and an invasion. She brought herself up sharp. No, that was wrong, Martin had specifically said she was compos mentis and remembered the past more clearly than the present, like a number of older people. So why was she so afraid of seeing her? Chewing a spoonful of muesli, Charlotte realised she was afraid, not of Mrs Batiste, but of failing Andy and his father. If she messed up this interview it would be the last chance she had of talking to a member of the family. Up to now the research had been impersonal, detached. But Jim's aunt could hardly be labelled 'detached'. Although she and Andy had discussed what to ask, Charlotte had not been convinced by his suggestions. She needed to talk to someone not emotionally involved. It then occurred to her there was someone who could help. Reaching for the phone she tapped in the number.

'Jeanne? How are you? Surviving I hope,' she said, brightly.

'Charlotte! Lovely to hear from you. Yes, all is well chez nous, thanks. Harry's at nursery, which is a godsend, and Freya has just settled down for her nap. How are you getting on with the research for *my* book?' she asked, with a laugh.

'It's that I wanted to talk to you about. I'm seeing Mrs Maud Batiste this afternoon, Andy's great aunt. And I'm worried about what to talk about. How to steer the questions to the family etc. Any ideas?' She explained about the rector having talked to his parishioners.

'That's great news about Maud. But I see your concern. Let me have a think,' Jeanne said, before silence came down the line.

'Right, how about this?' she continued, 'Concentrate on what she'll expect you to ask, that is ask about the farmers in the parish, how they managed short-handed etc. Then you could ask about her role; did she work for anyone in particular or stay at home? Ask about her family. You could then lead the conversation to the Resistance and from there to collaborators and informers. Did she hear anything about it happening in the area? If she's happy to talk you could then bring up Edmund and what happened to him. See what her reaction is. She must have known him as you said she was going out with Harold before he died.'

'Sounds good, thanks. I'm so conscious of scaring her off as, after all, she and Andy are on opposite sides here. She's not likely to say anything to disinherit her grandson, is she?'

'No, but she might let something slip. I think the best way of approaching this is to treat her as if she's not important and relax. It's amazing how much people tell you when they're off guard.' Jeanne chuckled.

'Good idea. At the very least, Jeanne, I hope to give you some helpful background information for your book. The island archives are a mine of information, aren't they?' She went on to talk about what she had researched and Jeanne agreed she would be glad to read her notes when she had finished, together with Madeleine's diary.

Charlotte eventually said goodbye feeling a lot more cheerful about seeing Maud. Now all she had to worry about was Andy and her mother. Not that there was much she could do about either. With regard to her mother, she planned to call her every day or so to see how she was, but not visit unless specifically asked.

The situation with Andy was trickier. Although they had spent the rest of the afternoon and early evening together on Sunday, Charlotte had sensed a slight withdrawal on his part. As if he didn't quite trust her feelings for him. This had been hurtful but she had refused to let him see it, particularly after such a wonderful few days together. Men! Why do they have to be so complicated? Couldn't they see life was never as simple? That sometimes the head vied with the heart where relationships were concerned, she thought, banging her mug on the worktop as she switched on the kettle for another cup of coffee.

Louisa had again lent Charlotte her car for the trip to St Martins, even though she had offered to hire one. The suggestion had been brushed aside, Louisa saying there were far too many cars on the tiny island roads as it was. Thinking it was a pity the weather was too overcast to put the roof down, Charlotte drove slowly down La Route de Jerbourg, keeping an eye out to the right for the sign pointing to La Vielle Manoire. It was hard to miss, a prominent polished granite stone bore the name in gold lettering at the beginning of a lane marked "Private". The narrow lane veered round a bend and she drove for another hundred yards before the house came into view.

Charlotte was confronted with a building looking nothing like a traditional Guernsey farmhouse, but one with a strong resemblance to a French chateau, but not one in the best tradition of such chateaux. It was clear from the result at one time it had been a good sized granite farmhouse but someone – and she did not need to guess who – had added extensions and raised the roof to create a three-storeyed building and then stuccoed the result. Her mouth dropped open as she took in the mismatch of windows, doors and incongruous shutters vainly trying to give an impression of an old, Georgian mansion such as could be seen in Queens Road, St Peter Port.

As she stepped out of the car, her first thought was what would Andy make of it? Heading to the porticoed front door, she could see a swimming pool to one side, set in what was probably once the original farmyard, but was now made to look like a Mediterranean courtyard. It would be funny if it wasn't for the fact the house was rightfully Jim's inheritance, not Harold's, she thought, ringing the bell.

A middle-aged woman dressed in a carer's uniform answered the door.

'Miss Townsend? I'm Sal, please come in, Mrs Batiste is waiting for you in her room.' She ushered Charlotte inside, adding, 'She's having one of her good days today so I've settled her in an armchair near the window. Likes to look outside at the garden, she does. Bless her, it's all she can do these days. Hasn't left her room these two years past,' the woman said, shaking her head and leading the way up the oak staircase which looked as if it had been lifted from another house and shaped to fit in this one.

The dark hall was cluttered with ornate antique furniture. Charlotte shuddered mentally. Her mother had her faults, but at least she had good taste. As Sal bustled along the landing Charlotte asked her what was wrong with Mrs Batiste.

'Old age mainly, but she had a stroke two years ago which took the use of her legs and her left arm.' She then added in a whisper, 'Broken-hearted she is, too. Lost her beloved son Gregory, not that he was much of a son to her, and Harold's not been what you could call a loving husband, either.' Sal tapped her nose and winked, leaving Charlotte to draw her own conclusions.

'Here we are, Maud, your visitor's arrived. Shall I bring up a pot of tea for you both?'

Charlotte walked into the large, stuffy room which was as cluttered as the hall, taking a moment to realise the woman addressed was the tiny figure virtually lost against the cushions in the armchair by the window. She moved closer to see a frail woman, whose wispy white hair framed a gaunt face criss-crossed with wrinkles and bearing a prominent, hooked nose. Rheumy grey eyes stared back at her.

'Would you like tea, Miss Townsend? Or do you prefer coffee?' a voice stronger than she expected asked politely.

'Tea would be lovely, thank you.' Sal nodded to them both and left. Charlotte went to shake the old lady's hand, but realised too late the good hand was twisted out of shape in her lap. 'Oh, I'm sorry–'

'No need. As you can see I can't shake hands, but please sit down. You'll have to pull the chair up close so I can see and hear you properly.' Mrs Batiste nodded towards a chair nearby and Charlotte moved it as near as was feasible. She saw a little gleam of intelligence in the old eyes and felt sorry for her. Something told her this woman had led an unhappy life even before her son died.

'It's very good of you to see me, Mrs Batiste, giving me the opportunity to talk to people like yourself who lived here during the occupation. You must have so many stories to tell,' she said, smiling.

The old lady gave a mirthless chuckle. 'True enough! I agreed to talk to you as I read the first book of Jeanne's, *Recipes for Love*, I think it was called. Thought it was very good.' She sighed. 'My eyes were better then, but now I need Sal to read to me. It's not the same but better than nothing. Anyway, I'm happy to help Jeanne with another book if I can.'

'She's very grateful, I can assure you.' She crossed her fingers as she said this. Although this woman was the "enemy" she hated lying. Even a white lie. 'What a...lovely house you have, Mrs Batiste. Have you lived here long?'

'Thank you. I've lived here since I was married, back in '47, not long before the old man died.' Her face clouded, as if the memory was not a happy one. Whether of the wedding or Neville's death, or both, Charlotte could not be sure. 'Of course, it wasn't like it is now. It was just an ordinary farmhouse with cow sheds and the dairy and not much else.' She sniffed. 'My husband, Harold that is, he wanted to have the biggest, smartest house in the area and he was happy to spend his money on it,' she said, her lips pursed.

Charlotte was saved from replying by the arrival of Sal with the tea tray. After putting it on a side table she said, 'You can be mother, Miss Townsend, can't you?'

She nodded and after making sure Maud needed nothing else, Sal left. Charlotte poured the tea into a china cup for her and a child's beaker for Mrs Batiste, who was able to hold it with her help.

After allowing time for her to have a drink, Charlotte took out her notepad. She went through the list of general questions Jeanne had suggested, before moving on to ask about her own family. Mrs Batiste was happy to answer them all, and Charlotte guessed she appreciated someone taking an interest in her life. Only fifteen when the Germans arrived, Maud had just left school and helped her parents on their small farm, which adjoined that of the Batistes.

'It's how Harold and I knew each other, you see. Not that I saw much of him except when there was a local get together. He went to the Boys Grammar and I went to the Girls so we only met in the holidays. We began courting when we were eighteen, in 1944.'

'Gosh, you have been together a long time, haven't you?' Charlotte said, making notes. She cleared her throat. 'Jeanne is particularly keen to learn anything about the local Resistance. Did you know anyone who was a member?'

'Well, I knew two who were, for sure. Harold and his brother Edmund.'

Charlotte's heart skipped a beat. 'Oh, that is interesting! Do you remember anything they used to do to hamper the Germans?'

'Well, no-one ever told me much about what they did in case I was questioned by the Germans, but I do remember Edmund got into trouble once for giving some food to a Polish POW. The Germans wanted to arrest him but his father talked them round. Paid them off, more like,' she said, with a nod.

'That's odd, I had heard Edmund was an informer and was beaten up and probably killed by a POW.'

Mrs Batiste seemed to shrink into herself. 'He was no informer, not Edmund. But...' She stopped, looking nervously around the room. 'Edmund was a good man, no matter what was said about him.' She lifted her twisted hand as if in emphasis.

'Which is good to hear, Mrs Batiste. It couldn't have been very pleasant for your husband to have his brother accused. And then killed,' she said, gently.

The old lady looked down at her lap, as if mesmerised by her twitching fingers.

'No, I suppose not.' She raised her head and Charlotte noticed tears in her eyes.

'Are you all right? I'm sorry if I've brought back bad memories.'

'It's not your fault, dear. But I am tired and need to rest now. Could you go downstairs and ask Sal to come up, please? It's – it's been nice to meet you.'

Charlotte saw pain as well as grief in her face and felt a frisson of shame for pushing her so hard.

She patted her good arm, saying, 'Thank you again for talking to me, Mrs Batiste. I've really enjoyed meeting you. Do take care.'

Charlotte found Sal in the vast, elaborate kitchen and passed on the message before heading for the front door. Once outside she came face to face with the man who could only be Harold.

chapter twenty-four

Charlotte, in spite of her shock, drew herself up and, with a cool "Good Afternoon", walked past Harold and slipped into Louisa's car before he could say anything. As she turned the car around she saw him standing with his mouth open and his hand raised as if to say, "And who are you?" A tall, heavy man, his beady brown eyes were like currants amongst his jowls and the thin white hair combed back from his forehead reminded her of the Mafia boss from *The Godfather*. The expensive suit and the big Merc parked beside the garage spoke of a man who enjoyed the more expensive things of life. Suppressing a shudder, she drove as fast as she dared down the narrow lane and onto the main road. That was not supposed to happen, she told herself. Harold was not due back for another hour and she could only be grateful she left when she did. And what would Maud say to him when he asked who the visitor was? Trying not to think about it, Charlotte concentrated on driving safely back to Louisa's.

Once home Charlotte put the kettle on for coffee, the image of Maud's anguished face alternating with the surprised face of Harold in her mind. From what she had heard and seen they seemed to be the antithesis of each other, a most unlikely coupling, she thought. Once her coffee was ready she sat down and phoned Andy.

'Hi, it's me, I've just been to see Maud and managed to bump into Harold. Could have been tricky!' She described the interview and her impression of his aunt. 'Something odd happened when I asked about Harold losing his brother, she became quite upset and asked me to leave so she could rest. I definitely touched on a nerve and she also said Edmund was no traitor and a kind man. So, what do think?'

'You're right about it being odd. It might just mean she liked Edmund even though she was Harold's girlfriend. Perfectly normal. Or, she knows something about what happened but won't say.' Andy paused, and she heard his fingers drumming on something. 'Either way, it's interesting stuff and I'm very grateful to you for doing this, Charlotte. What's your take on it?'

'I think she knows something. And if it's to do with Harold then I can see why she'd be reluctant to say more. He looks like a bully and she's so frail and totally dependent on others and couldn't risk angering him.' She sighed. 'Problem is I can't in all conscience suggest we meet again as she answered all my questions pretty thoroughly. We'll have to hope someone else knows something. The rector did say he's still asking around so...' she said, feeling both excited and deflated at the realisation of how close she may have come to the truth.

'Hmm. So you'll stay on for the moment?' His voice was hesitant.

'Of course. I can't leave while Mother's here. She's booked in till the end of the week and I'm not sure if there's a room for her after then. Something to do with a possible cancellation.'

'Does that mean if she leaves at the weekend you'll go back with her?'

Charlotte was torn. Her mother did not actually *need* her at home, having staff around, but it would depend how she was feeling.

'I don't know. I'll think about it once we know what's happening. Would...would you like me to stay?'

'Of course I would!' he cried, 'but you made it clear your life's in London–'

'That's not what I said! I pointed out it was a big decision and something I couldn't rush. And with my mother so ill I can't plan for the short-term, let alone the long-term. We need to spend more time together to see if we have a future as a couple, but with Mother...' She bit her lip, trying hard to sound more composed than she felt.

His voice softened. 'I'm sorry, Charlotte, I'm being unreasonable. But I'm scared if you go back to England you'll forget me and that will be that.'

'It's not likely to happen, Andy. But you're not the one contemplating turning their life upside down.' She felt drained, not sure what she wanted any more. Much as she wanted to be with Andy, his insecurity seemed to equal her own.

'You're right. Look, I'll be busy the next few evenings catching up on work, but if you'd like to go out on Thursday I'd love to see you.'

Charlotte agreed, but thought he could surely have put her before work if she was to return soon to England. Did this show he wasn't as keen about her as he said? Before she had time to dwell on it further, Louisa arrived home wanting to know the outcome of the meeting with Maud Batiste.

On Tuesday morning the rector rang to ask how she had got on with Maud. Charlotte mentioned how Maud had become upset at one point and she hoped it was not as a result of her questions. Martin said he would be calling round to see her and would ask, but he doubted it. 'Mrs Batiste is, as you saw, extremely frail and I've found her quite an emotional lady. I will say you asked after her though. Oh, and the other reason I rang is to pass on the names and numbers of two more parishioners who would be happy to talk about the occupation. Do you have a pen and paper?'

Charlotte wrote down the details, perking up at the chance to continue her research. After saying goodbye to Martin she made the calls, arranging to see a Mrs Falla that afternoon and a Mr Sebire on Wednesday. Then she phoned her mother, and after listening to moans of how bored she was, wished she had not bothered.

'I know there's not an awful lot to do except swim and walk, but the idea is, Mother, for you to *rest*. Giving your body a chance to heal. How are you feeling, physically?'

'A little better, I suppose. Everyone seems pleased with my progress and I admit I'm well looked after and the food is excellent. Did you know the chef's published a book?'

Charlotte sighed. 'Yes, I'm the publisher. And another book will be out soon.'

'Oh! You didn't tell me. Well, he's very good. Mrs Combe could learn a thing or two from him...' Her mother continued in this vein for a few moments until Charlotte interrupted to ask if a room was free for the following week.

'Not as far as I know. Even if there was I might still go home at the end of the week. Gillian and Paul have already said when I leave they will continue supplying me with their remedies.'

Charlotte's heart sank. It looked as if she would have to make the difficult decision of whether or not to play the dutiful daughter. 'In which case, Mother, while you are here, would you like me to take you out for a drive? See a bit more of Guernsey?'

'Thank you for the offer, Charlotte, but I'm not one to play the tourist.'

'Fine. But I think you would like St Peter Port, it has a great selection of shops to explore and I'd be happy to show you around. We could have lunch or something,' Charlotte persisted dutifully.

'It might be diverting, although I'm sure it can't compete with Bond Street. Shall we say Thursday? I have a clear morning I believe.'

They agreed on Thursday morning and Charlotte clicked off the phone with a sigh of exasperation. Wondering why she had let herself in for a morning of trailing round shops – and lunch! – with her mother, she paced around the garden, her arms flailing. Added to which she did not want to return to England yet, it was too soon and she knew her mother would drive her bonkers if they were under the same roof for more than a few hours. And she still needed to make time, when her mind was quiet, for her writing. Would it ever happen? Aargh! What should she do?

Mrs Falla lived in a cottage on the road down to Saints Bay and proved to be a chatty, but not particularly informative, old lady – unless you wanted to hear tales of Mrs Falla's problems with her husband and children, which Charlotte did not. When she went through the list of questions, Mrs Falla managed to digress to other irrelevant subjects and by the time Charlotte left she felt in need of a stiff drink. The thought she might have to repeat the whole experience again the next day was depressing.

That evening Paul joined them for dinner and Charlotte was glad of the chance to talk to him about her mother.

'I spoke to Mother today and it seems she will probably leave this weekend. Will she be all right to go home?'

He gave her a reassuring smile. 'Your mother's in no immediate danger, Charlotte, and is definitely stronger than when she arrived. But even if she were to leave, we can continue with the supplements, herbs and dietary advice, and she could see Gillian in London. Being here does make it easier to keep an eye on her and the physical therapies are a great aid to healing. However, I'm not totally convinced Annette wants to put up a fight, to be honest...' Charlotte felt sick. Why wouldn't her mother want to put up a fight, to live? Surely she hadn't given up? The thought was too awful...

'She's going through the motions but...' he shrugged, 'I'm not sure her heart's in it. I've tried, as has everyone else, but she seems to have closed down and, as you know, your mother is a strong-minded lady and not easily persuaded. I'm sorry,' he said, gripping her hand.

Charlotte, stricken at what his words implied, whispered, 'I wonder why she bothered to come here and – and agree to receive help.'

'For you, Charlotte. She did it for you. Annette comes across as a hard, uncaring lady, and to some extent she is, but I believe she does care about you, although she won't admit it. And I suspect you have mixed feelings about her, don't you?'

She felt his eyes bore into hers and looked down. 'Yes, we've always had a difficult relationship, and I feel guilty for not...loving her enough. I do love her, but I don't like her very much. Such an awful thing to say.' Charlotte felt tears threaten and grabbed a tissue. Louisa, who had been sitting quietly at the table, threw her arms around her. She allowed herself a moment to compose, not wanting to break down in front of them.

'I've wasted everyone's time then, haven't I? You, Gillian, the therapists...'

Paul shook his head. 'Not at all. We've shown Annette there is hope for remission if she wants to continue with the treatments and it's up to her now. And you've proved you care, which is the important thing. Come on, have some more wine, it might help.'

Charlotte took a grateful sip, willing herself to stay in control. She had to face this alone.

Paul went on to ask how her research for Andy was progressing.

Glad to change the subject, Charlotte told him about Mrs Batiste and the mood lightened. Paul was staying over and Charlotte disappeared early to bed. As she lay waiting for sleep to claim her, all she could think about was Paul's words – "she did it for you". Squeezing her eyes tight she forced herself not to cry.

The next morning a cold wind propelled dense, grey clouds across the sky, reflecting the heaviness in Charlotte's heart. It was an effort to shower and dress and she would have preferred to spend the morning snuggled under the duvet, but was due to meet Mr Sebire at eleven. After a double strength coffee she felt better and checked the Perry's guide for his address. It turned out he lived not far from La Bella Luce Hotel and should be easy to find.

Glad of the thick coat she had brought over from London, Charlotte grabbed her bag and ran outside to Louisa's car as the first drops of rain arrived. Once she had located the wipers, she reversed out and headed off to St Martins. Ten minutes later she pulled into the tiny drive of a whitewashed granite cottage with a wooden porch. The door was opened so quickly she guessed Mr Sebire had heard her car. A short, bald man, his bright blue eyes twinkled up at her.

'Miss Townsend, please come in. What a change in the weather! Let me take your coat.' He fussed around her before leading the way into a room so clean and neat it looked unlived in. Taking a seat on a blowsy patterned sofa, Charlotte accepted his offer of tea. He left and returned quickly with a tray burdened with a teapot, two cups and saucers and a plate of biscuits.

Once settled, she asked him about himself, and learnt he was a widower who had lived in the cottage all his life. His grown up children had moved away – one to L'Ancresse and one to Grand Rocque. He managed to make it sound as if they were at the other end of the earth, not on the same small island. Charlotte warmed to the old man who, at nearly 90, was proud to be looking after himself and the cottage unaided. Mr Sebire answered all the general questions without any digression, unlike Mrs Falla.

'We're particularly keen to learn more about the local Resistance, Mr Sebire. Did you get involved yourself, or know anyone who did?'

He grinned mischievously, displaying a row of gaps in his teeth.

'Of course I did! Wanted to give them Jerries what for, I did. Was good fun at first, but towards the end it got nasty, with people being arrested and sent away. Not that it stopped us, mind. We just had to be more careful,' he said, with a wink.

She smiled. 'I've spoken to other islanders and someone mentioned the Batiste brothers, Edmund and Harold as being in the Resistance. Did you know them?'

His face clouded. 'Yes, I knew them. I worked a bit for their father, Neville. Edmund was a nice lad, but that Harold!' He shook his head. 'He were a nasty piece of work. Never trusted him. Something shifty about him, I reckon. Greedy bugger, too. He and his dad dealt on the black market, they did. No wonder he's worth so much now.'

Charlotte leant forward, all ears. 'But I understood it was Edmund who betrayed some neighbours and died violently.'

'He were no traitor! Someone started those rumours about him days before he died. All smelt a bit fishy to me, but I couldn't do anything except tell people not to listen to no rumours. I had my suspicions at the time and I'm convinced now I was right, after what happened.'

Her heart was beating faster as she asked, 'What suspicions?'

Mr Sebire looked her in the eye. 'Why, it was Harold who started those rumours, of course. To protect his own skin.'

chapter twenty-five

Charlotte gasped. 'What! You mean Harold was the informer, not Edmund? But what made you think so?'

'Because a few days before the rumours started I saw Harold talking to a German soldier and he was pointing to a house along the lane, belonging to the Ogiers, a couple of good-hearted folk if ever there were. To be honest, I didn't think much of it at the time, and then shortly after the rumours about Edmund began, he was killed. I didn't want to stir things up for the Batistes, figuring they had enough to worry about so I kept schtum.' He twisted his hands together and his face was full of sorrow as he added, 'Then I heard Mr Ogier had been arrested for hiding an illegal wireless and was sent to prison. Which is when I put two and two together. I've often wished the ol' bugger Harold had got his just deserts instead of lording it over everyone as he has for years.'

Rendered speechless as the full impact of what Mr Sebire said sank in, Charlotte wanted to stand up and do a happy dance. Decorum and caution held her back. As far as the old man was concerned, she was helping Jeanne with her research, not trying to obtain justice for Edmund.

'How utterly fascinating, Mr Sebire, and I'm sure Jeanne could use this kind of thing in her novel. Add a bit of spice to the story, sort of thing. But naturally, no real names would be used.'

'More's the pity! Still, sometimes life has a way of bringing things home to roost, don't you reckon?' The old man looked as if he wasn't too sure if it was true.

'Absolutely. But in the meantime, please don't feel bad about what happened all those years ago. You were not to know how things would turn out. Now, I've taken up enough of your time,' Charlotte said, standing up, 'and I really must go. Thank you again, Mr Sebire,' she said, shaking his hand.

Once in the car she let out a little whoop of joy before starting the engine and driving to La Bella Luce for a celebratory lunch. Before she went inside she had to make a call.

~ ~

Andy was tearing his hair out, metaphorically speaking. He had promised a client a finished set of drawings by the end of the day and it was a close call whether or not he could do it. When his mobile started beeping he was tempted to ignore it, but when a quick glance told him the caller was Charlotte he changed his mind. Their last conversation on Monday had been a bit strained.

'Hi, Charlotte. How are you?'

He listened with mounting excitement as she relayed what Mr Sebire had said, her own elation palpable.

'Brilliant news!' He sprang out of his chair and paced around his office. 'I can't wait to confront Harold with this, show him I know the truth–'

Charlotte cut in, 'Andy, I'm not sure it's wise. Think about it. Do you really want to alert Harold to the fact you're checking up on him? Until we uncover the truth behind Edmund's death and why your father hasn't been accepted as the rightful heir, then wouldn't it be better to keep this to ourselves? I know where you're coming from, but...'

He knew she was right, but for a minute had enjoyed the thought of seeing Harold's face as he told him what he knew.

'Okay. I take your point. But at least now we know Edmund was innocent and I think my father should be told. I don't know how or why, but it might have something to do with him not pushing for his inheritance. Agreed?'

'Hmm. Can't see why it would hurt to tell him, but you'll have to come up with a good reason for how you found out.'

'True. Let me think.' He sat down and idly tapped his fingers on the desk. 'Right, how's this? Dad knows about Jeanne's novel and I can say she has a researcher who's talking to locals about the occupation and suspected collaboration. And someone from St Martins mentioned suspecting Harold was an informer and why, adding his brother Edmund had been falsely accused. Does that sound okay?'

'I think so, as long as you don't mention Mr Sebire by name. He's our secret weapon against Harold.'

'Yes, agreed. What I want is for Dad to open up about why he didn't fight Harold for his inheritance. If he doesn't, I can't see a way forward.' His fingers continued to drum on the desk as he considered calling on his father that evening. Reluctantly, he knew his client took priority. Perhaps tomorrow...

'Are you still there, Andy? You've gone quiet.'

'Sorry, I was thinking about Dad. I'm afraid I've got to crack on, but I'm truly grateful for your help, again. I'll book somewhere nice for tomorrow night as your reward.'

She laughed. 'Everywhere we go here is nice. But I look forward to it. Speak soon.'

As he clicked off the phone he made a mental note to ring his father later to ask if he could pop round first thing the next morning. The sooner he knew about Edmund's innocence, the better.

Andy knocked on the door at nine o'clock, to be greeted by his mother's bright smile.

'*Bon jour, mon ange.* What is it that brings you here? Your father has become intrigued after you called,' she said, leaning forward for a kiss.

'Hello, *Maman*. I'll tell you both once you've made a pot of your excellent coffee. And how is Dad?' he said as they headed into the kitchen, his father nowhere to be seen.

She frowned. 'His back has been better since he is not doing so much the fishing, but his temper is not so good. He is missing the boat and I am missing to have him out of the house!' she said, putting the kettle on. 'But we both hope he can be soon back to normal.' She gave Andy a searching look. 'We both are glad for this help he has received from the centre, but one wonders how long they can be so generous.' Andy shuffled his feet. 'I've been assured the treatments won't stop until Dad's as good as new. So don't worry, *Maman*.'

She pursed her lips but kept quiet.

'Where is the old boy, anyway?'

'Do not let him hear you speak of him this way! He is in the garden, bringing me some vegetables for our soup. Go to him now and tell him I have made coffee.'

Andy let himself out of the back door and followed the path around to the vegetable patch at the bottom of the garden. He could see his father bent over, pulling up a large head of cauliflower and placing it in a trug containing carrots and leeks.

'Hi, Dad. Mum's got the coffee on.' He looked closely at the rows of vegetables. 'The crop looks good this year, better than last year's, I think.'

His father straightened up and nodded. 'Yes, your mother's worked hard on it, laying on plenty of vraic as fertiliser. Right, I think that's enough, we can go in.' He picked up the trug and they walked back along the path to the kitchen, to be greeted by the aroma of fresh coffee. Once everyone was settled in the living room, two pairs of eyes looked at Andy questioningly.

He cleared his throat. 'The thing is, Dad, I've found out something pretty important...' he told them about Harold and waited for the reaction. His father was quiet for a moment, as if absorbing the import of what Andy had said. His mother, however, smiled broadly.

'This is wonderful news, Jim! Your father was innocent, just as your mother always said. Now you may hold your head up high and,' she clicked her fingers, 'to Harold and his family.'

'Dad?'

Jim looked up, a smile hovering around his mouth. 'It's good news, son, thanks for telling me. Something I knew in my heart but couldn't say out loud. Not that it makes much difference. The ol' devil Harold can't be brought to book after all these years and he's still the one with the money.' He took a sip of his coffee as if it was the end of the matter.

Andy was nonplussed. 'But Dad, don't you see? You have every right to the family fortune, always have, regardless of whether or not Edmund was an informer. So if you didn't pursue your inheritance because you thought he was guilty, then now's the time to go for it.'

'Ah, but that wasn't the reason, son. So, as I said, nothing's changed,' Jim replied, not looking Andy in the eye.

'So what was the reason, Dad? Must have been a good one to turn away from millions!' Andy was so annoyed his hand shook, spilling a drop of coffee. His mother grabbed a tissue and blotted it, tutting as she did so.

His father lifted his eyes and Andy saw the pain in them.

'I can't tell you. It's not something to be discussed. Just accept there was good reason for me to waive any claim on the property and money.' He banged his cup on the table, stood up and marched out of the house. Andy and his mother were left staring at each other, wide-eyed with astonishment.

~ ~

Charlotte, using Louisa's car, picked up her mother from La Folie at 11 am. Annette was waiting in the hall, elaborately dressed in a Chanel suit and Armani coat, topped with a toning bow-trimmed fedora. Charlotte forced herself to smile as she ushered her mother outside. St Peter Port was in for a treat. She knew Guernsey had its fair share of stylish, wealthy women, but had never seen anyone quite so dressed-up for a quick shopping trip and lunch. Thank goodness she had booked a table at La Fregate, highly recommended by Louisa, for their meal. Which at least would be up to Annette's standard, she hoped. Charlotte herself was immaculately turned out in smart trousers, a leather jacket and neat ankle boots. No hat.

'How are you, Mother? You have more colour in your cheeks than when I last saw you.'

'That's probably the make-up. But I do feel somewhat better, thank you, I've been able to go out for walks around the garden and the cliffs. The air's so bracing by the sea, don't you think?'

'Oh, yes, I love it, particularly after being in London.' She started the car and drove down the lane, while her mother described a woman she had met at dinner the previous evening. Apparently they had attended the same boarding school, although not at the same time, and they had spent a pleasant time comparing notes. Charlotte made appropriate comments as and when required, glad her mother was being sociable with someone.

In spite of her mother's obsession with designer labels, she did seem to enjoy browsing the small boutiques and the only department store, Creaseys. Charlotte, knowing how much Annette loved shoes, also took her down the front to a pretty shoe shop where she tried on various styles, coming away with three pairs. Her mother, never the easiest customer, was more mellow than usual and actually thanked the staff for their help. Charlotte could only think it was the illness or the treatment which was having this effect.

By the time they returned to the car they were both ready for lunch. Although the restaurant was in Town, it was perched atop a steep hill and Louisa had advised her to drive in case the walk was too much for Annette.

The restaurant had magnificent views, looking down over St Peter Port, the harbour and out to the islands and Annette looked gratifyingly impressed as they were escorted to a window table. The maître d' bowed deeply as he pulled out their chairs and Annette gave him a gracious smile.

Charlotte ordered drinks and they concentrated on their menus.

'Louisa tells me her father, Malcolm, who owns La Folie, comes here regularly and says the food is excellent,' she said, glancing across at her mother.

Annette's eyelids snapped up.

'Oh, did I not tell you? I met him the other day when he was at the centre. A charming man I thought, and so devoted to Gillian. He told me about having been a successful hotelier in Canada and how he set up La Folie. Any recommendation from him is not to be ignored.'

'I hadn't realised you'd met, I saw quite a bit of him when Louisa and I became friends and liked him from the start,' Charlotte replied, putting down her menu. 'Are you ready to order, Mother? I am.'

Their order given, the women focussed once more on the view and silence settled around them. Charlotte's eyes swept over the harbour and out to Herm, remembering the wonderful day she had spent there with Andy. Only a few weeks ago, but so much had happened since. A mixture of good and bad. The thought caused her to peek at her mother, whose face was a frozen mask as she gazed out of the window. What's going through her mind? How does anyone told they have a terminal illness deal with such news? As if she knew she was being observed, her mother turned her head.

'It is beautiful, is it not? I understand why you like coming here, although I would have thought the business would keep you fully occupied. It certainly did with your father. He was rarely home, as I'm sure you remember.' Her face twitched as if at a painful memory.

Charlotte played with her glass, unsure how to answer. 'Daddy loved the publishing world and was jolly good at what he did. He enjoyed all the socialising, too. There were always parties going on at one publishing house or another. I...I thought I loved it as much, but came to realise I wanted more from life. It's why I've handed over most of the running to Tony while I write and, and do other things. Find what I truly want, I suppose.'

Her mother's eyebrows lifted and she stared at Charlotte with the scathing look which used to drain her confidence when a child. And even as a young woman.

'In my day we did not have the luxury of looking for what we "truly wanted". Unless we had a particular career in mind, and I did not, then a woman sought a good marriage. In that I was fortunate, although I was not blessed with–'

'The son you wanted, Mother?' Charlotte's voice was sharp.

'I was going to say long marriage, losing your father when I did. He was only in his sixties, after all. And although I admit I wanted a son, I was not unhappy to have a daughter,' her mother said, coolly.

Before Charlotte could reply a waiter arrived with their starters, giving both of them time to assess the direction of the conversation. The last thing Charlotte wanted was a fight, aware how inappropriate it was at such a time. And what would be the point? Her mother was hardly likely to admit to being an uncaring parent and metamorphose into the kind of mother she had always longed for. Deciding discretion was the better part of valour, she changed the subject.

'Have you definitely decided to leave La Folie on Saturday? I understand there's a room available and the rest would do you good, Mother.'

Annette pursed her lips. 'I have already said I wish to return home and there's no point in asking me to change my mind. Not only am I anxious about the garden but I have various...commitments which I cannot ignore. There will be plenty of time for me to rest once I've satisfied myself all is as it should be.'

Charlotte was mystified as to the commitments, but thought it best not to pursue it. 'In which case, would you like me to come back with you so I can be of use in some way?'

'Oh, there's no need for you to do that, Charlotte, I can manage.' She paused for a split second, adding, 'Thank you for your offer. It was kind of you.' Annette's face was touched by the glimmer of a smile and Charlotte nodded in acknowledgement. And guilty relief. 'Oh, and by the way, this seafood cocktail is one of the best I have ever tasted. Malcolm was absolutely right about this restaurant.' The smile still hovered.

'Good, I'm pleased. Would you like another drink? Perhaps some wine?'

The focus returned to the meal and Charlotte did her best to be a considerate hostess, keen to make sure her mother had no complaints. The conversation was a little stilted, with Charlotte talking about her friends in Guernsey and Annette about the WI. By tacit, unspoken agreement, the subject of Annette's illness was never mentioned. As they returned to the car, her face slightly flushed, Annette said how much she had enjoyed both the shopping and the lunch. Charlotte smiled, saying it had been a pleasure and drove her back to La Folie thinking it had turned out better than expected. But she still felt guilty about letting her mother return home alone.

chapter twenty-six

That evening Charlotte allowed herself to daydream while soaking in the bath. It wasn't something she encouraged, being by nature more of a realist, but thoughts of love and romance persisted in taking over her mind. Luxuriating in the heady perfume of the aromatic oils she had swished into the water, she knew she wanted more from life than what her mother referred to as a "good marriage". The phrase spoke volumes, confirming as it did Annette had married for security rather than love. She experienced a pang of sadness for her parents, wishing they could have had a happy, loving relationship instead. Acknowledging her own foray into marriage had not been entirely successful, she had at least thought herself in love with Richard and he with her. Looking back, Charlotte conceded it was nothing like the intense emotion she now felt towards Andy.

The thought of perhaps spending the rest of her life with him was intoxicating but...there was always a "but", wasn't there? If she was a character in a romance novel, all obstacles would magically dissolve away and she and her lover would live happily ever after. But she wasn't: she was a flesh and blood woman who was falling in love with a flesh and blood man – with issues. Although he seemed to be saying he loved her and wanted to be with her, she sensed his reticence about the difference in their backgrounds. And if he were to meet her mother, his fears would be confirmed. But she wasn't her mother and not as hung up on class and money. The problem was as she saw it, Andy, in spite of his own successful career, viewed himself as the son of a poor fisherman, albeit one deprived of his inheritance. And, deep down, she knew she was not completely sure herself. Holding her breath, she submerged her head, hoping to clear her mind. It didn't work.

Andy arrived at seven, looking particularly suave, she thought, in a pale grey suit and open-neck cream shirt. He barely gave her time to say hello before cupping her face in his hands and giving her a lingering, ardent kiss. Releasing her, he smiled and said, 'I've been looking forward to that all day. How about you?'

'Me too,' she murmured in his ear, and dropped a light kiss on his cheek. The scent of lime cologne lingered in the air. He took her hand, leading her to the car and opened the passenger door with a bow. Laughing, she slid into the seat and he walked round to the other side, and slipped in.

'I've booked a table at a seafood restaurant, Le Nautique, overlooking the harbour. As you love fish,' he said, touching her hand.

'Lovely. I always feel as if I'm being particularly good when I eat fish and won't put on weight.' She patted her stomach, laughing.

'You have a gorgeous figure, please don't diet. Can't abide stick thin women.'

'There's no fear of it happening to me! Love my food too much.'

Their eyes locked for a moment before Andy turned his head and started the ignition. Charlotte's stomach, only slightly rounded, was full of butterflies. It promised to be a fun evening.

Two hours later Charlotte sank contentedly back into the car, having enjoyed great food and good company. Andy had been attentive and flirtatious and she began to hope they could resolve their mutual reservations about a long-term relationship. They were en route to his cottage for coffee and, hopefully, a sleepover.

During the evening Andy had told her about Jim's reaction to the news about Harold and how he had refused to say why he would not contest the inheritance. As he spoke Andy raked his hands through his hair in frustration. She had grabbed his hands to calm him down, saying his father must have a good reason and he had to be patient. Charlotte agreed it was odd, but there was nothing to be done by getting angry. Thankfully, he had let the subject drop and she went on to describe the outing with her mother. By this time both of them were moaning about their respective parents being stubborn and hard to understand, and the irony of it made them burst out laughing.

Back at the cottage Andy put the kettle on and measured out the coffee while Charlotte set out mugs and milk.

'Fancy a nightcap with the coffee?' Andy asked, holding up a bottle of single malt.

'Please.' Charlotte carried a tray into the sitting room and placed it on the table in front of the sofa before closing the curtains and switching on lamps. With the ceiling lights off the room was cosy; soft pools of light illuminating the pictures on the walls. She kicked off her shoes and curled her legs on the sofa, whisky in hand. Andy brought in the coffee, picked up his glass and joined her.

'Warm enough?' he asked, pulling her close.

'Mm, yes thanks. Thank goodness for central heating!' She sipped her drink, enjoying the peaty taste of the whisky in her mouth. Andy tipped back his glass, sighed contentedly and, taking her glass, put both of them on the tray. He leant close again, tracing the outline of her mouth with his finger before kissing her gently on the lips.

'Would you like to stay tonight?' he asked, between kisses.

'Yes, love to. I...I'd like to talk about something,' she replied, when he sat back.

'Sure, go ahead. I'll pour the coffee.' He filled their mugs and leaned back on the sofa, his eyes on her face.

Charlotte flicked her hair back as she gathered her thoughts. 'It's about my mother and, and everything. Us. Guernsey. London. What to do.' She stopped and took a sip of her coffee.

'I see. Or rather, I don't see, not yet anyway. But I get the drift. Why don't you tell me more?' He smiled reassuringly.

Emboldened, she continued, 'As I told you, Mother's returning home on Saturday and I feel guilty about letting her go alone. Not that there's much I can do her staff can't, but still...So, I thought perhaps I could go to London, catch up with the business, do some writing which I absolutely must do soon, and then invite Mother to stay for a night or two. I can keep an eye on her, make sure she's not getting worse. All things which I can't do if I stay here,' she said, pushing the words out quickly.

Andy's forehead creased into fine lines. He picked up his mug. 'Are you saying you *want* to go back to London or think you *should*? And where do I come into it?'

She sighed. 'That's the question I can't answer. It's your call, Andy. I feel I should go back, though not necessarily immediately, but part of me wants to stay here because – because of you. But we both need to be clear what we feel for each other –'

The kiss took her by surprise. His lips held hers so firmly she threw her arms around him and gave into the pleasure coursing through her body.

'Have I answered your question? I want there to be a future for us, but I understand it's not going to be easy. There's your mother, your home, your business – it's a big deal,' he said, grasping her hands.

Charlotte smiled her relief. If they could find a compromise it could work.

'Neither of us can make any promises yet, we haven't known each other very long, have we? Could we agree to see as much of each other as possible and see...how it goes? No expectations, no commitments. Just getting to know each other better.'

Andy nodded. 'I'd go along with that. Our lifestyles are so different so we have to make adjustments. I can't offer you what you've been used to and, frankly, it probably wouldn't appeal to me. Grand houses, busy social whirl...'

'I don't give a fig about my old lifestyle. I admit I've been spoilt by having people look after me but I can learn how to cook and clean and...' for a moment the thought of having to clean a house herself caused her to panic, but surely she could have a cleaner? She could easily afford it. Clearing her throat she went on, 'do all the usual household things. To keep an eye on the business I would need to visit London regularly, but it's not an issue. The real problem is my mother and being there for her while she...she's still around.' Her voice shook as she said the painful words.

He stroked her face, wiping away a stray tear. 'Please don't cry. According to the doctor nothing bad's going to happen for months and if your mother does persist with Gillian's treatment she could pull through and go into remission.' He held her tight for a moment and Charlotte relaxed into his arms. Perhaps something could be worked out with regard to her mother. The woman who had made it clear she did not need Charlotte's help. Or at least not yet.

She was woken the next morning by a smiling Andy bearing a mug of steaming coffee.

'Come on, sleepyhead. You'll have to get a move on if you want a lift,' he murmured in her ear then dropped a kiss on her nose. Showered and dressed he presented a complete contrast to the man she remembered making love to her the previous night. Summoning a sleepy smile, she pushed the hair out of her eyes and sat up.

'Thanks. You're looking remarkably cheerful this morning. Any particular reason?' she asked, already knowing the answer.

He sat on the bed and handed over the mug. 'You know why!' he said aiming a mock punch at her arm. 'I'm happy because you've agreed to spend a little longer here before rushing back to London. Here meaning in my home – and my bed.'

Now fully awake, Charlotte's lips curled up at the memory of their discussion last night. Andy had been persuasive in his argument about there being no need for her to leave immediately and by staying here, in his house, for a couple of weeks, they could become better acquainted, as he put it. Remembering their passionate lovemaking brought a warmth to her cheeks. They were fast becoming *extremely* well acquainted!

'And I'm happy too. Will I get coffee in bed every morning once I move in?' she asked, tilting her head.

'Huh! We'll see. But as it's the one skill you've managed to learn, perhaps it should be you bringing me coffee. The next step will be teaching you how to cook so I can enjoy a cooked breakfast in bed,' he said, grinning.

Charlotte giggled. 'You might have to wait a while for that pleasure. Perhaps I should sign up for cookery classes and receive professional tuition.' She managed to duck in time to avoid the pillow Andy threw at her and swung her legs out of bed to head for the shower, still laughing. Andy grabbed a quick kiss before returning downstairs.

After a rushed breakfast of juice and toast, they set off in the car for St Peter Port. Andy dropped her at Louisa's before continuing to his office in Clifton, off College Street. Charlotte walked into the kitchen to find her friend munching on a bowl of muesli.

'Morning. Another good night?' Louisa asked, with a mischievous smile.

'Good morning. Yes, it was and I've something to tell you...'

By the time Charlotte had explained her plans Louisa was flinging her arms around her, smiling broadly.

'I'm so pleased. I'd love to see you make a go of it with Andy, particularly if it means you'll live in Guernsey.' She stood back and looked enquiringly at Charlotte. 'You do plan to move here, don't you?'

'If it works out, I suppose so. For the moment I've said I'll stay a couple of weeks or so, see how we get on. But like you, I'm keeping my London house whatever happens. It's a good idea to have a backup plan, I think.' She helped herself to coffee and sat down at the table. 'We're not making a fuss about it and I won't tell Mother yet. Andy isn't saying anything to his parents either. Especially not until this business of Harold and the inheritance is sorted. In case he learns I've been talking to people, particularly Maud.'

'Don't worry, I'll only tell Paul. Are you leaving today?'

They continued to chat until Louisa departed for work, with Charlotte promising not to leave until she returned at teatime. Once on her own she rang the car hire company Andy had suggested and arranged for a car to be brought round later, to be hired by the week. Andy's cottage was a bit out in the sticks and she would definitely need transport. At the moment Charlotte was not sure how she would fill her days, except for making a proper start on her novel, well overdue. The novels bought in Frome had been engrossing and provided valuable pointers for her own book. Now was an ideal opportunity while she had no other commitments. No excuses, she told herself, going upstairs to change.

That evening Charlotte pulled into Andy's drive and parked next to his car. Excitement and nervousness warred within her, creating a feeling of light-headedness as she manoeuvred her case from the boot. A deep breath and she wheeled the case to the front door. Before she could ring the bell, Andy flung the door open and pulled her into his arms.

What seemed like hours later, but was only seconds, Charlotte released herself and smiled. 'That was some welcome! May I come in now, please? It's a little chilly out here.'

Andy grinned and grabbed her case while she walked down the hall and into the kitchen. Leaving the case at the bottom of the stairs, he joined her, pulling out a bottle of champagne from the fridge. As he turned round Charlotte spotted the label bearing the name *Krug* and burst out laughing.

'How did you know?' she asked a puzzled looking Andy.

'Know what? I was told by the wine merchant it's one of the best, but if you don't like it–'

'It's a fabulous champagne! My grandmother was a distant cousin of the head of the Krug family and I'm using the pen name of Louisa Krug for my writing. I wondered if Louisa had told you,' she said, taking off her coat.

'No, she didn't, it was a fluke. And now I hear my girlfriend is not only the owner of a publishing company but is related to the Krug family. Any more I should know?' he asked, looking unhappy at the thought. He reached for a couple of champagne glasses.

'I don't think so. And I am only a very distant relation. Actually, Krug's my favourite champagne and I'd have told you about the connection at some point. Are we toasting something in particular?' she asked, hoping to defuse his concern.

'Yes, you staying with me. I know we only agreed it'll be for two weeks, but I'd like to think it might be for longer. So,' he said, popping the cork and pouring the wine, 'here's to us!'

'To us!' she repeated as they clinked glasses. A few sips of the creamy bubbles and Charlotte began to relax. It had dawned on her how little they both knew about each other and actually staying in his house was very different to the occasional sleepover. Andy had thought to provide some nibbles to soak up the wine and she took a handful before they moved into the sitting room.

'I thought we'd chill out tonight and order a takeaway. All right with you? We have a choice of Indian or Chinese, whichever Madam prefers,' he said, as they snuggled together on the sofa.

'Indian would be lovely, thanks. Have you any plans for the weekend?'

'Not really. The good news is I don't need to do any work so can concentrate on entertaining my house guest,' he said, kissing her cheek.

'Good. I do have to take Mother to the airport late morning, but it won't take long. I'll say I'm staying on at Louisa's for a bit longer, and I doubt if she'll query it.'

'Right, let's order the food.'

Charlotte arrived at La Folie to find her mother listening to Paul and Gillian, who appeared to be reminding her what she should and should not do to look after herself. Charlotte held back until they had finished and then joined them. Her mother turned round. 'Ah, Charlotte, there you are. We were saying our goodbyes.' She directed her attention back to Paul and Gillian, graciously thanking them for their assistance. Charlotte could not help thinking her mother treated them more like her staff than medical professionals, and was mortified. However, neither Paul nor Gillian seemed to take offence and hugged her as they said goodbye.

'I'd like to add my thanks, too. I appreciate all your hard work and, as I'm staying on for the moment, hope to see you again soon. And Malcolm,' she added, smiling at Gillian.

'Yes, that's a good idea, I'll talk to Malcolm. Perhaps a meal one evening,' Gillian said, as they kissed.

Doug arrived with Annette's case and the three of them walked out to the car. Once her mother and the luggage were safely installed, Charlotte slipped behind the wheel.

'Are you okay? Looking forward to going home?' she asked, glancing at Annette.

'I am quite all right, thank you. And I shall be pleased to be home, although they have been very good to me here.' Her mother said, not bothering to face her. Charlotte sighed inwardly and started the engine, grateful she wouldn't be accompanying her mother home. What would be the point if you're barely acknowledged?

At the airport Annette insisted she did not come in and wait with her, so Charlotte gave her a brief hug as they said goodbye.

'I'll be returning to London in a couple of weeks, Mother, although I may not stay long. Would you like to come and stay for a day or two?'

'If it fits in with my next appointment at the clinic, then yes, thank you.' A brief nod and she was gone.

As Charlotte began the drive back to Andy's, not far down the road, her spirits lifted. At least her love life was something to celebrate, she thought, anticipating a blissful weekend ahead.

chapter twenty-seven

On Monday morning Charlotte kissed Andy goodbye as he left for work, the big smile on both their faces testament to how the weekend had panned out. She stretched languorously as she headed upstairs to shower and dress. Andy had proved to be quite the romantic, suggesting they went to the cinema on Saturday evening to watch a romcom, *Couples Retreat*. A tale of four long-married couples who needed to re-invigorate their relationships, it had been both fun and thought-provoking. Charlotte had appreciated Andy's willingness to see a film many men would have avoided. They had joked together in the bistro afterwards as they enjoyed a meal and a bottle of wine, arriving home in a relaxed and amorous mood.

Sunday had seen them touring the island by car, stopping off at the west coast beaches for bracing walks while the wind fashioned white caps on the waves. Wrapped up in warm jackets and scarves, they ran along the golden sands and peered into rock pools teeming with tiny life. Andy introduced Charlotte to the tucked away bays of the north-west, complete with small boats bobbing about on the swirling sea. Grabbing her hand, he pulled her along the sand and over rocks and by the time they arrived back at the car, their faces were flushed from both the exercise and sheer *joie de vivre*. Charlotte felt as if transported to another life – as if she had stepped out of her own skin and into someone else's. Her heart thumped with exhilaration at the chance of a fresh start, and in such a beautiful place as Guernsey. And with this gorgeous man who kept smiling at her with his soft brown eyes.

The memories whirled in her brain as Charlotte readied herself for the day. Skipping about the bedroom to the sounds of Island FM on the radio, she slipped into jeans and sweater while wondering how best to spend the day. She decided to phone Jeanne and ask if she could call round to her house in Perelle, not far away.

Jeanne was happy to agree, suggesting late morning while Freya had a nap. Charlotte collected her research together before tidying the kitchen and bedroom. Some plumping of cushions on the sofa and the cottage looked neat and tidy. She had watched and learnt from Louisa over the past few weeks, picking up the basics of housework. It had never been an issue previously, as she had never considered not having cleaners and housekeepers. In the long-term she knew she would not want to be without at least a cleaner, but was happy to manage for a little while. Perhaps it was time to let go the "daughter of the manor" persona. Not completely convinced, she closed the front door.

Charlotte had not been to Jeanne's before and kept an eye out for the lane off Route De La Perelle. A hundred yards along on the left and she pulled into the drive of Le Petit Chêne, a double fronted cottage to the side of which she spotted an old-fashioned orchard. Sniffing the air, Charlotte was assailed by the invigorating scent of the sea, and thought how wonderful it must be to live yards from the beach. She knocked softly and Jeanne appeared within seconds.

'Charlotte! Great to see you again. Please come in.'

Jeanne's blue eyes sparkled and her long dark hair was tied back in a ponytail, giving her the appearance of a teenager rather than the thirty-five-year-old Charlotte knew her to be. Marriage and babies obviously suited her. Jeanne led the way into the kitchen, asking if she would like tea or coffee.

'Coffee, please. What a lovely room, Jeanne. And so homely, with a clever mix of old and new,' she said gazing around at the butter-cream painted units, old pine table and enormous dresser displaying blue and white china.

'This was your grandmother's cottage, I believe, yes? And Andy said you renovated it yourself. I'm impressed!'

Jeanne laughed. 'With the aid of a great team of builders! I chose everything, though, and did some of the decorating. Nick came into my life about then and when we got together he made loads of stuff,' she said, pouring hot water into a cafetière. 'Let's go into the sitting room, we can relax on the sofa.'

Charlotte followed her across the hall into a bright, warm room with chairs and sofas nestled around a log-burning fire in the inglenook fireplace. Bright rugs covered the oak floor. Jeanne placed the tray on a low table and Charlotte sat down, sinking into feather-cushioned softness. Once Jeanne had poured the coffee she joined her on the sofa.

'Well, this is nice. I don't often get anyone popping in these days, people think I'll either be walking around like a zombie or trying to soothe a screaming baby,' Jeanne said, passing her a mug.

'I must say you look wonderful and not at all like a zombie! Freya must be about two months old now, is she sleeping through the night?'

'Yes, for the past couple of weeks. Bliss! And she's so good during the day, a little angel. I've been very lucky,' Jeanne said, curling her feet under her legs. 'How are things with you? A little bird told me you and Andy were an item. Is it true?'

Charlotte admitted it was and told Jeanne she was staying with him until she returned to England in two weeks. And she might be back after catching up with her business. Jeanne said she hoped to see her return and they went on to discuss the research. Charlotte handed over copies of her notes and conclusions together with Madeleine's diary.

'Thanks. I plan to start my book soon so this is a godsend. What about yours? Have you been inspired to get back to it?'

'Yes I have and with nothing else to distract me, I can use the next two weeks to write.' They went on to discuss the writing process and Jeanne shared what worked for her. Charlotte lapped up the chance to talk to a fellow writer. Their conversation was finally brought to a halt by a thin wail emanating from the baby monitor in the kitchen. Jeanne leapt up, saying she would be right back.

The cry became a gurgle and Charlotte heard Jeanne soothing her daughter before she returned downstairs.

'Here she is, Charlotte, I don't think you two have met. May I introduce Miss Freya Mauger.'

Deep blue eyes surveyed her from under a mop of dark hair and Charlotte smiled, reaching out her finger which was promptly grabbed in the tiny fist. Freya smiled and she was smitten.

'Isn't she adorable? I haven't had much experience of babies, but would love to hold her if she'd let me.'

Jeanne laughed. 'Only for a moment as she's anxious for her feed. Here, as long as you support her head she'll be fine.' She handed over the baby, wearing a miniature-sized top over leggings, and Charlotte held her like she would a precious antique, with ultimate care. Freya wriggled in her arms, bringing her head up level with Charlotte's. She watched a big toothless smile appear before a fist reached out to grab her hair. 'Ouch!' she cried, gently releasing the tiny fingers.

'That's why I keep my hair tied back most of the time,' Jeanne said, with a grin. 'She's just started to smile so you're honoured to receive one.'

Freya's face crumpled and she let out a piteous cry, prompting Jeanne to take her back.

'Time for her feed. You don't mind do you, but I'm breastfeeding.'

'Absolutely not. Unless you'd rather I left?'

'Don't be silly. Let me get comfortable and we can carry on chatting.' Jeanne settled into an armchair and Freya must have realised lunch was on the way as she stopped crying and nuzzled into her mother. Once she was feeding happily, Jeanne continued their earlier conversation, all the while stroking Freya's downy hair. Charlotte was mesmerised by the baby and when Jeanne turned her round to feed off the other breast, caught a glimpse of a contented smile. Although immersed in their tête-à-tête, a part of her mind was diverted once more by the idea of what it would be like to have her own child. Could it be possible? With she and Andy becoming closer, it might. Her worry about not having maternal instincts began to recede as, touching and holding baby Freya had tugged at something in her psyche. And heart.

Her inner soul-searching was brought to a halt when Jeanne unplugged Freya from her breast and lifted her onto her shoulder to rub her back. Charlotte, glancing at the clock, realised she had been there for nearly two hours and it was time to leave the little family in peace.

Standing up, she said, 'Thanks for the coffee and chat, but I must be going.'

'It was lovely to see you and you must pop round again. Freya seems to have taken a shine to you,' Jeanne said, getting out of the chair. As they reached Charlotte's side, the baby's head swivelled round and she smiled and gurgled. The women hugged and Charlotte dropped a kiss on Freya's head as she said goodbye.

Once in the car, she waved at a smiling mother and daughter before turning round and heading back to the main road and home. She fizzed with excitement at the thought of actually starting her book, revved up by Jeanne's genuine support. In her head Charlotte started mapping out the initial chapters, now clear about the starting point of the novel. Part of her was not yet convinced her writing would be any good, but Jeanne had pointed out it was normal for even successful authors to write several drafts before they were happy. But intruding into these plans was the image of a baby girl with big blue eyes and an infectious smile. Did Andy want children? She had no idea. It would be safer to concentrate on her writing.

The first time Charlotte sat down and typed "Chapter One", she froze. It was if all the words had deserted her. Then, slowly they came back and, whether it was rubbish or not, she continued typing more freely. The next few days passed in a pleasant routine of writing interspersed with an occasional walk or drive to clear her head. Andy remained the chef but Charlotte helped with preparation and shopping. She dug around in his collection of cookery books and found one for beginners by Delia Smith and began to read it secretly, wanting to surprise Andy with a meal when she felt more confident – and competent. She started with the proverbial boiled egg for lunch one day and soon progressed to a cheese omelette, which, although not by any means looking like the ones she had been served in restaurants, tasted fine.

The evenings were spent cosying up on the sofa after supper, listening to music or watching television. Fortunately they shared similar tastes in both: listening to a mix of classical pop artists like the Stones and Queen and younger stars like Amy Winehouse and Coldplay and watching dramas and comedy. It was fun exploring each other's interests and tastes and Charlotte began to feel as if she had known Andy for far longer than the actual six weeks it had been. She attributed the improved, easy flow of her writing to the effect of being in a loving relationship and hoped it would continue. Not just the writing, but the wonderful closeness with Andy; something she had never experienced with Richard.

On Friday morning, as Andy was leaving for work, Charlotte announced she would be cooking dinner that evening.

His eyebrows shot up. 'Wow! You mean actual cooking, not a bring-to-life in the microwave affair?' he said, grinning.

'Yes real cooking, if you don't mind. I've been reading a how to book and think I can manage to cook a simple meal now,' she said, suddenly not so sure of herself.

'I'm sure it'll be fine and I look forward to this evening. But don't stress about it as we can always go out if necessary,' he said, giving her a kiss.

Once Andy had left she pulled out her faithful Delia. Although Charlotte had thought it would be complicated, she realised an easy option would be roast chicken, requiring little input from the cook once it was in the oven. Delia had made it sound simple and, to be sure, Charlotte phoned La Folie's chef, Chris.

Initially they discussed his latest book, which he was about to send for editing. Then she mentioned her desire to cook a meal and, once he was over the shock, he confirmed her choice was a good one and suggested she bought a ready-stuffed, basted chicken to make it easier. And a ready-made gravy. Heartened by this advice, she completed her shopping list and set off for the M&S Food Hall in St Martins.

After her groceries were packed away, Charlotte settled back to her writing, losing herself in the story as it appeared as if by magic on her laptop screen. Such a contrast to how it had been a few months ago. She took a brief break for lunch, a homemade tuna salad, and continued tapping away through the afternoon until, with a shock, she realised Andy would be home in little more than an hour. Within twenty minutes the chicken was in the oven and the potatoes were ready to follow shortly. She had bought ready prepared vegetables to save time and was planning to steam them later. Pleased with her efforts, she opened a bottle of wine ready to greet Andy on his return. It was the weekend and they could relax.

He arrived minutes later, sniffing the air as he entered the hall.

'Something smells good. All under control?' he asked, pulling her into his arms. She let her head fall onto his chest, her hands settling on his lower back. Andy seemed to enjoy it.

'Of course,' she replied at last. 'Dinner will be served in about thirty minutes and the kitchen's out of bounds till then. You'll find wine and glasses in the sitting room and I'll be with you in a minute.' A quick check all was well and Charlotte joined him on the sofa. Andy had poured two glasses of wine and raised his saying, 'To your first meal!' She laughed and touched glasses before taking a well-deserved sip.

'Lovely. How was your day?' she asked, curled up beside him.

His face clouded. 'That no-good cousin of mine has really done it this time. He'd only been out of prison for a few days after the last punch up, when he got high on booze and drugs and got into a fight with a guy a lot smaller than him. Upshot was, the other man ended up seriously hurt and is in hospital with a fractured skull and smashed up face. He might even lose the sight in one eye,' he said, sighing.

'Oh, how awful! The poor man! And what about Dave? What's happening to him?'

'He was arrested and charged with GBH and has been sent to Les Nicolles, our local prison, for two years. In the past he's got away with heavy fines or a few weeks banged up. It makes me embarrassed to be a Batiste.'

'It's not your fault, Andy. Perhaps it's a good thing your side of the family is not accepted by Harold's side, means you can remain distant to what happens with them.' She thought back to her meeting with Maud. 'I bet his grandmother will be upset. Despite her being married to Harold, she came across as quite a decent old lady. What's his mother like?'

'Cath? I don't know her that well. I occasionally see her out shopping and we nod, but don't speak. Looks like someone beaten down by life, in spite of being fairly well off. I understand Harold settled something on her when

Uncle Gregory died. Explains why Dave's turned out as he has. His mother bails him out when he's in trouble and he still lives at home – at twenty-nine!' He shook his head in disbelief.

'Cheer up, don't let it stop us enjoying ourselves. I'll finish the cooking and will give you a shout when it's ready,' she said, dropping a kiss on his head as she stood up. Taking her glass with her she disappeared in to the kitchen. The vegetables were arranged in the steamer and the chicken taken out to rest. All looked – and smelled – good, and Charlotte sipped her wine while wondering how to carve a chicken. Thinking it might be a man's job, she asked Andy if he would mind doing it while she served up the accompaniments.

'This looks wonderful. And you've done it all yourself? I'm impressed,' he said, grabbing the carving knife and fork. Minutes later the food was set out on the dining table and Charlotte beamed with pleasure, her face flushed from the heat of the kitchen. She held her breath as Andy took his first bite.

'Delicious!' he cried, leaning over to kiss her. 'For someone who'd never even boiled an egg, you've cooked a great meal. My first attempt was spag bol, and I used a ready-made sauce.'

Her face grew hotter as she basked in his praise, sending silent thanks to Chef Chris for his useful advice. Perhaps this cooking lark was not as difficult as she had imagined – although this early success wasn't likely to induce her to spend too many hours in the kitchen. She much preferred to write now it was flowing at last.

Later, as they sat together on the sofa, Andy said, 'Work was good today. Not only did I finally win the planners round about the old farm redevelopment which has been dragging on, but I also managed to convince them my design for a big house extension's in keeping with the area. They're such dinosaurs! It's taken months to get permission even for the extension and I was worried my client would go elsewhere. Still,' he said, kissing her nose, 'it's sorted now and he's over the moon.'

'Well done, so we have something else to celebrate. To your extension!' she said, giggling.

He wasn't able to resist her deep laugh and it wasn't long before they were rolling about on the sofa in helpless laughter, having placed the glasses out of harm's way. Charlotte was pleased they could forget about his family problems for a while, knowing Andy was still upset with Jim over his reluctance to explain why he hadn't claimed his inheritance.

After a lazy day on Saturday, Charlotte and Andy joined Malcolm, Gillian, Louisa and Paul at Le Fregate as Malcolm's dinner guests. Gillian had phoned during the week to invite them and Charlotte was delighted to accept as part of an acknowledged couple. The conversation and wine flowed freely and, together with excellent food, made for an enjoyable evening. It looked to her as if Gillian and Malcolm were as loved up as ever and wondered how long it would be before he popped the question. Which would mean Gillian facing the same choices as she was over Andy. Life was never simple, she thought, as they said their goodbyes.

Andy was keen to go for a long cliff walk on Sunday and they started out from Petit Bôt Bay planning to walk to Jerbourg before having lunch at L'Auberge restaurant, a few metres inland. He had said he wanted to show her something after lunch. Charlotte was intrigued and when she asked what it was about, he refused to say. As they walked along the exposed cliff tops a strong, chill wind buffeted them, trying to force its way through the layers of jackets, sweaters and scarves. Once around Icart Point and dropping towards Saint's Bay they enjoyed much needed shelter until they hit Moulin Huet Bay when again they did battle with the wind. It was only when they reached the wooded valley did it became still and they stopped for a break, looking down at the bay with its sprinkling of rocks. The tide was out, exposing a patch of golden sand.

'Pretty, isn't it? Louisa and I walked along here in the spring but I haven't been around in the summer to see it at its best.'

Andy cupped her face in his hands. 'I hope you'll be here next summer, and the next and the next...' he said, dropping kisses on her lips, cheeks and forehead. She let out a long breath.

'It's what I hope too,' she murmured, licking off the salt from his kisses.

'Good, and in the meantime we've still nearly a week to enjoy together. And I, for one, mean to enjoy every moment I can. Are you ready to press on? My stomach's telling me it's lunchtime,' he said, accompanied by an audible rumble.

'Let's go.'

The walk up and along the cliffs overlooking Moulin Huet was hard work, but rewarded by the views back along the coast to Saint's Bay and Icart. As they stood for a moment to catch their breath, Charlotte said, 'I can understand what attracted Renoir to this bay. It's got craggy rocks of all shapes and sizes and lovely stretches of golden sand. No wonder he painted it so much!' She spotted a distinctive crocodile shape of rocks seeming to swim out to sea. Pointing, she asked, 'Do those rocks have a name?'

He followed the line of her finger. 'Yes, the Pea Stacks, although I've no idea how they got it. There's so many rocks around here, making it pretty treacherous for boats. You have to keep your distance when sailing round from Jerbourg. Dad sometimes fishes here but he knows the waters like the back of his hand. Come on,' he said, grabbing her hand, 'you can have a good look on the way back. I'm hungry!'

Andy led the way from the cliff path, heading inland towards, among other places, L'Auberge restaurant on the other side of La Route de Jerbourg. Charlotte was glad of the chance to refuel and rest. Her legs ached and they still had to walk back to the car at Petit Bôt. With a grateful sigh she slid into a chair, her eyes drawn to the outline of Herm, partly hidden in cloud.

'I've been to Jerbourg before, with Louisa, and we thought the views were fantastic. It was such a clear, sunny day we even saw Jersey.'

'Yep, it's one of the best spots for island watching. When we've finished our meal we'll walk down to the Point,' Andy said, picking up the menu.

'Sure, anything, as long as I can rest my legs for a while,' she said, smiling at him.

Forty-five minutes later, after a filling Sunday roast and a glass of wine, they headed outside, walking along the narrow road past the Jerbourg Hotel and through the car park. Andy caught her hand and walked carefully towards the edge of the small bay, stopping above a natural finger-shaped causeway pointing out to sea. A white squat building perched at its tip. Some kind of lighthouse, she guessed.

Andy flung out his arm. 'Here's where it happened. Where my grandfather was killed.'

chapter twenty-eight

'Oh! I knew it must be in the area around Jerbourg from reading Madeleine's diary and the police report but...' Charlotte said, giving him a hug. She gazed down at the rocks and shuddered, remembering Madeleine's words *"I've seen his poor battered body with my own eyes"*.

'Seeing the actual spot brings home the awfulness of what happened,' she whispered. The sea, whipped up by the wind, crashed angrily against the rocks which had once held Edmund's broken body.

Andy's jaw tightened and she could sense the anger below the surface. They simply *had* to find out what happened if he was to let it go. Turning, he pulled her away from the edge and said, 'You might think it strange, but ever since I was a boy, I've known it was up to me to solve this mystery. It's gnawed away at me for years, getting worse since I've seen Mum and Dad struggling to survive. But now, thanks to you,' he said, a smile playing around his mouth, 'I think I'm nearly there. This puzzle will be solved, and soon.'

Charlotte nodded, a lump forming in her throat as she wondered how it could be achieved.

The walk back along the cliffs restored the earlier happy mood and they arrived back at the cottage looking forward to a quiet evening in, eating supper in front of the television.

The next morning Charlotte woke late, to find Andy sitting on the bed fully dressed and with a mug of coffee in his hand. For her. 'Oh, you should have woken me. I was going to make breakfast...'

'No problem. You looked so peaceful, I hadn't the heart to wake you. Any plans for the day?'

'I'll ring Mother to make sure she's okay and then crack on with my writing. But I might be glad of a break so could we meet for lunch?' she asked, sitting up to relieve Andy of the mug.

'Yeh, I'd like to, but it will have to be a quick sandwich in Town, as I have a deadline to meet.' They agreed a time and place before Andy kissed her and left. Charlotte sipped her coffee, trying not to dwell on the fact she had only a few days left to spend with him. They had talked about the future again last night, agreeing they wanted to continue their relationship, even if it was long-distance for the foreseeable future. So much depended on her mother...Thinking of her now prompted Charlotte to finish her coffee before heading for the shower. She could have phoned her mother while still in bed, but it jarred. You did not phone someone such as Lady Annette Townsend, a stickler for proprieties, while sitting naked in a man's bed. Even more so if he wasn't your husband.

Half an hour later Charlotte cleared away the remains of breakfast before picking up her phone.

'Good morning, Mother. How are you?'

'I'm quite well, thank you. I made an appointment to see Dr Rowlands last Friday and told him about my new treatments. He seemed surprised and, I think, shocked about this, and still wanted me to undergo further chemotherapy as originally agreed.'

Charlotte bit her lip. This had been expected but Paul and Gillian had been adamant chemo could do more harm than good. 'So, what did you say to him?'

'That I didn't see any reason to have more chemo, which would undoubtedly make me feel worse, if it can't cure the cancer. He did, in all fairness, admit he could not guarantee any further treatment would prolong my life.'

'Well said, Mother! Does it mean you're continuing with the natural alternatives prescribed by Paul and Gillian?'

There was a silence on the line and Charlotte waited impatiently for her mother's answer.

'For the moment, yes. I do admit I've been feeling a little better since taking the herbs and supplements, so it would be foolish to stop. And Mrs Combe has been zealous at providing fresh, organic food without animal protein, as prescribed by Gillian. However, Dr Rowlands wasn't happy about my decision and we did not part on good terms.'

Relief flooded through Charlotte and she went on to say she would be back in London on the coming Saturday, and again invited Annette to come and stay if she wished. Her mother thanked her and said she might do so as Gillian wanted to see her about a new treatment and would be back in London for a few days. Charlotte finished the call feeling she had at last made a breakthrough with her mother. This was the first time she had ever taken notice of something she, Charlotte, had suggested. Definitely a result! And with her relationship with Andy growing stronger, life was looking up.

Cheered, she settled down with her laptop to add a few thousand words to her *opus magnus*. The quick sandwich with Andy turned into a slightly longer and much tastier moules frites, accompanied by a small glass of wine and followed by coffee. They had reassured each other they needed quality time together, asking what difference would half an hour extra make. Back home, Charlotte happily wrote another thousand words before the warbling of her phone broke the flow. Annoyed, she picked it up meaning to switch it off, but saw it was Martin Kite's number. The thought he might have another parishioner eager to talk changed her mind.

'Hello, Charlotte. You haven't left Guernsey yet, have you? Only I remember you saying you might be leaving soon.'

'No, still here for a few more days. Is something the matter?' she asked, picking up a note of anxiety in his voice.

'I'm not entirely sure. I called in on Maud Batiste at the weekend, as usual, and she was quite distressed. She wanted me to ask if you could visit her again, saying it was important. Do you know what it could be about?'

Charlotte thought back to their meeting. Maud had become upset when she mentioned Edmund's death, but surely, two weeks later, she wouldn't still be distraught? Pangs of guilt knotted her stomach at the unwelcome thought.

'Not really. I can only think she's remembered something she thinks would be useful for Jeanne's book. Although why this would distress her...'

'Perhaps I shouldn't say this, but under the circumstances I think you should know Mrs Batiste may not have long to live. You must have seen how frail she is and her doctor's confided in me it could be anytime. I believe she knows this, but I agree it seems strange she needs to see you urgently.' He sighed and Charlotte wondered again how someone like Martin coped with the dying. She knew she would be utterly hopeless. 'It might not be anything after all, but if you could spare the time to see her I'd be grateful, Charlotte.'

'Of course I'll see her. Has she said when?'

'Yes, Wednesday afternoon, at three. Again she wants it to be when her husband is out. You know,' he added, reflectively, 'I do wonder if she's afraid of him, which is sad.'

'Mm, it is. Anyway, Wednesday's fine with me, Martin. Bye.'

Intrigued by the request, she took a few moments to get back into the head of her characters, but once achieved managed to finish the chapter feeling pleased with her progress. Perhaps writing a novel wasn't going to be as hard as she had previously found, which was a relief. Jeanne's encouragement had made her see the process in a different light and she so wanted the chance to be a published author like her. Recognised for her own creation.

As Andy listened to Charlotte explain about Maud's request, he became more and more excited, waving his arms around while they prepared supper.

'Whatever it is she wants to say, I don't suppose it will help much. But I can't help feeling intrigued. I only wish I could be there, but it would put the cat among the pigeons, for sure,' he said, pouring them glasses of wine.

'I'm only glad I'm still here. By the sound of it, the old lady might not survive much longer and we would never have learnt what it is she has to say. Which reminds me, I had a chat with Mother and she's continuing with the natural treatments.' Charlotte explained how Annette was now putting her faith in the combined efforts of Gillian and Paul and would stay clear of chemo.

'We all know there's no guarantees, but apparently some new protocols have had good results on liver tumours and Gillian wants Mother to take part.'

'I'm so pleased.' He gave her a keen look. 'Will this have any bearing on what you decide about moving here?'

She sipped her wine, knowing he was likely to ask. 'If Mother continues to make good progress, then I'd feel happier about leaving England. But I doubt we'll know anything more concrete for a few months so...' she shrugged.

Putting his glass down, he then flung his arms around her. 'That's okay, as long as you continue to spend more time here with me, then we can make it work, can't we?' he said, adding emphasis with an ardent kiss. For a moment she wished she could just cut loose from her old life and move in with Andy. But it wasn't the right time.

'Yes, of course we can make it work. But in the meantime, perhaps we should concentrate on getting supper ready. All the writing I did today has made me hungry.'

Charlotte was on a roll. Her writing flowed and she began to look forward to sitting at her laptop each day. She could now empathise with the writers signed to her publishing company. Although their work was non-fiction rather than fiction, they had told her of the joy of seeing their word count build up and the buzz when the ideas flowed. Even if her novel was not successful, she could not imagine returning to being solely an editor. She would *need* to write.

It was with some reluctance Charlotte switched off the laptop on Wednesday afternoon, ready to go and see Maud. Her head hummed with the sounds and smells of eighteenth century Naples as the new Lady Emma Hamilton, wife of the British envoy, awaited the arrival of Horatio Nelson, her future lover. A far cry from twenty-first century Guernsey.

Charlotte picked up her notebook and pen, pushing them in her handbag, before grabbing her keys and leaving. The drive along winding lanes brought her back to the present with a bump, with the need to concentrate and avoid hedges, walls and other vehicles. She arrived at La Vielle Manoire unscathed and five minutes early.

Sal opened the door.

'Afternoon, Miss Townsend. I'm glad you could come as Mrs Batiste's been in a bad way these past few days. Really upset about something, she is. Let's go up, shall we?' She started for the stairs and Charlotte followed.

'I bumped into Mr Batiste last time I was here, did he say anything to you?'

'He asked who you were and I said a friend of the rector's, thought it was for the best. He doesn't generally like visitors, doesn't Mr Batiste. Hope that was all right?'

'Of course, thank you.' Charlotte breathed a sigh of relief. Harold could hardly have made a fuss about someone connected to the rector.

Sal stopped outside Maud's bedroom and before opening the door, whispered, 'She's worse than when you last came, so you might have problems hearing her.' Charlotte nodded and followed her into the room. This time Maud was in the hospital-style bed; one which could be levered up and down and with safety rails to keep her from rolling out. Propped up on several pillows, she looked even more wizened than last time and her eyes were closed. A sweet, musty smell hung in the air. Charlotte's heart sank.

'Maud? Your visitor's here. That Miss Townsend you've been expecting.' Sal gently touched the right arm resting on the bed cover.

The old lady's eyes opened slowly and she turned her head towards Sal. 'She's here? Good. Bring a...chair round...could you, please,' she said, in a voice so quiet Charlotte strained to hear the words. Sal set a chair right by the head of the bed and motioned Charlotte to sit down.

'Would you like any tea? Maud can only drink cold drinks at present and there's a beaker of water by the bed if she needs it.'

'I'm all right, thank you.'

Sal left and Charlotte turned to face Maud. 'How are you, Mrs Batiste? I'm sorry to see you're not able to sit in the chair.'

Maud grimaced. 'I don't think...I've long...to go, dear. The doctor's been visiting...more this past week than...for months. And I want...need...to tell the truth,' she said, her rheumy eyes staring at Charlotte. Her twisted hand twitched on the bed.

'I'm so sorry to hear that. But are you sure it's me you want to talk to? Not the rector or someone?'

The old lady's head nodded slowly. 'Yes, I have to...tell someone who's not...involved...not know the family. And I like you...feel I can trust you.' Charlotte sucked in her breath as Maud went on, 'It's too late to make things...right. That wretched grandson of mine...he shouldn't be inheriting everything. Should have been...Edmund's son.' She tossed her head side to side, her mouth twisted in despair.

Charlotte felt a pang of guilt; she was hardly "not involved" with the family. Likening herself to the proverbial Trojan Horse, she said, 'Please, Mrs Batiste, don't upset yourself. It was a horrible thing which happened to Edmund but it was hardly your fault–'

'There's the rub. It *was* my fault. In a way. I could have...stopped him. But...I was afraid. Afraid he would hurt me, too.'

Charlotte's heart thumped hard in her chest. Was she saying what she thought she was?

'I don't understand. Who could you have stopped? Who was being hurt?'

Maud took a deep breath. 'I should have...stopped Harold hitting...Edmund. Killing him.'

chapter twenty-nine

'What? You saw Harold kill Edmund?' Charlotte was stunned. This was the last thing she had expected to hear. But if it were true...

Maud tried to clutch her arm and Charlotte gently gripped the twisted fingers.

'Yes. God forgive me, but I did. They didn't...know I was there. It was dark and I was...on my way to see...Harold at the farm from my parents' house...at Jerbourg.' She coughed and Charlotte held the beaker of water to her lips, letting her take a long drink. 'Thank...you,' she said. Taking a deep breath she continued, 'I saw them facing each other near...the edge of the cliff and I...hid behind some shrubs. They were...shouting. Edmund said something about...Harold spreading rumours that he, Edmund, was an informer when they...both knew it was Harold. Edmund said when he...confronted Harold about it he had promised to stop...but Edmund said he knew he hadn't. Said he was going to...report him to the...Resistance. Harold said he wouldn't...dare, they were family. Got angry and starting punching...Edmund in the head...Harold was a big man. Edmund fell down...didn't get up.' Maud gasped and mouthed "water" so Charlotte again held the beaker for her. Her head was spinning with what she had heard and she wished she had asked for tea after all.

Maud went on, her voice sunk even lower, 'Before I realised what...he was going to do, Harold dragged Edmund...to the edge and...pushed him off.' Tears glistened in her eyes and her face crumpled in misery. Charlotte gently wiped Maud's eyes with a tissue, feeling sorry for the old lady who had held such a terrible secret for so many years. Although she did wonder how she could have borne to marry a man she saw kill his brother...

'To this day I don't know...if Edmund was still alive when...when Harold threw him off the cliff.' She gazed at Charlotte through wet eyes. 'I've never told a soul. Not even Harold knows I...I saw him that night.'

Charlotte cleared her throat. 'May I ask why you didn't tell him?'

'I was afraid to. And...and I was in love with him. Or at least I thought...I was,' she added, a bitter note creeping in. 'Barely twenty, I was besotted. He had a...swagger, a way of talking, you knew he...would be somebody. There was a war on...the Germans...lack of food. I wanted someone to protect...me.' She turned her head away, saying, 'I never wanted Edmund...dead, he was a good...man, but after...I realised Harold would...inherit and if we married I'd be secure.'

She watched as Maud's face dissolved into a spasm of self-disgust. Again she wondered how she could have lived with herself, but looking at her now she realised she hadn't. Her ravaged body was the result of what Paul referred to as karma. As for the killer himself...her hands gripped into fists at the thought of him not only getting away scot-free, but of inheriting someone else's fortune.

'Have you thought of telling the police? To get justice for Edmund and his family?'

Still with her head turned away, Maud said, 'I couldn't face the shame and, and I have no money...of my own. But when I'm...gone, it won't matter. Want to stop Dave...inheriting, he's no good. *You* could tell the police.' Slowly Maud turned her head and her eyes seemed to be pleading with her.

'It's not that simple. Without evidence the police could do nothing.' Charlotte thought for a moment. 'Would you be prepared to sign a statement of what happened?'

'If you promised...it wouldn't be given to the...police until after I died.'

As it looked as if the poor woman wouldn't live much longer, she quickly agreed. 'I can write it all down now, if you wish. And we can ask Sal to witness your signature. She doesn't need to see what you're signing.'

Maud nodded her agreement and Charlotte took out her notepad and wrote what she dictated. She then read it back to make sure Maud was happy with it before calling Sal upstairs. Covering what she had written, she asked Sal to witness Maud signing it.

Sal frowned. 'I'm not sure I should if I don't know what she's signing. Could be something harmful to her.'

'It isn't, I assure you, Sal, but I respect your decision. Thank you, I'll sort something out.'

Sal, with a worried look at Maud, left.

The old lady blinked rapidly. 'Does that mean what I said isn't...going to count for anything?'

Charlotte had an idea. 'Not necessarily. What if I asked the rector to witness you signing it? I'm sure he'd be willing to help and wouldn't tell the police until...'

'I suppose so, if there's no other way. Hadn't wanted him to know...ashamed, but if no choice...'

'Good. I'll contact him and he can get in touch with you. By the way, you said something about Edmund's son. Surely he should have inherited instead of Harold?'

'By rights, yes. No-one knew he...had a son back then, his widow disappeared to France. It was a big...shock when he...turned up years later! Harold nearly had a heart attack,' Maud said, looking puzzled. 'He...came here to see us and...Harold took him off somewhere...to talk. Next thing I knew the...man left, looking as white as a...sheet. Harold told me they'd come to an...arrangement and we were...to keep everything. Thought it was odd, but was glad...my son.'

'I understand. It would have been a big upset to lose your home and land.' Charlotte was disappointed Maud didn't know more, had hoped to solve the mystery, for

Andy's sake if nothing else. 'I think I'd better leave you to rest now, Mrs Batiste. Do take care.'

She patted her arm and the old lady nodded before closing her eyes. Charlotte put the statement in her bag and returned downstairs to find Sal hovering in the hall, looking unhappy.

'I didn't mean to imply you were doing anything wrong, Miss Townsend, but Maud hardly knows you and–'

'It's all right, Sal, you were right to be cautious. We're going to ask the rector to be a witness instead.'

The woman's face cleared. 'Oh, that's a relief. If he thinks it's okay, then I needn't worry.'

'There's just one thing, Mrs Batiste would rather her husband didn't know about this, so if you'd keep it to yourself please?'

Sal smiled. 'No problem. I won't breathe a word.'

'Thank you. Bye for now,' Charlotte said, keen to get away. As Sal opened the front door she was relieved to see Harold's car was not outside and after jumping into her own, sped down the drive. At the bottom she halted, then made a sudden decision to turn right towards Jerbourg. Once in the car park she phoned the rector. Luckily he was at home and she asked to call round to see him, saying it was urgent. He said to give him thirty minutes and she agreed. Her hands shaking with excitement she called Andy.

'Hi, I've got something incredible to tell you...'

Charlotte pulled into the rectory drive, a multitude of butterflies flapping around her stomach. The rector *had* to agree! Or else...she didn't want to think about that and rang the bell with gusto. Martin opened the door, eyebrows raised. 'I know you said it was urgent, but–'

'Sorry! Forgive me, Martin, but once I explain I hope you'll understand.'

Once settled in his study, Charlotte told him about Maud's confession and her request concerning the police. Martin's eyes widened in surprise as he listened.

'I hadn't been aware of this man Edmund until now. I'd assumed Harold had inherited as the only son. It's quite a sorry tale, isn't it? And Edmund had a son who should have been the heir?' He shook his head, frowning.

'Yes, apparently. Look, I have her statement here,' she said, handing it over. 'It's not signed, of course, but if you were willing to witness Mrs Batiste signing it, then it would be evidence against Harold, wouldn't it?'

'I suppose so. It does explain a lot about why she seems afraid of him, doesn't it?'

Charlotte nodded. She wanted to hurry Martin on, but realised as she wasn't supposed to have any connection to the family, it might look odd. 'Are you happy to witness it? Mrs Batiste was happy to have you there and no-one else. Because of confidentiality.'

'I don't see why not. If it eases her conscience and brings justice to the poor man's family. Although it will be up to the courts to decide.' He sighed. 'I had no idea what a can of worms we'd open when I put you in touch with her. Still, you weren't to know either. Must have been quite a shock,' he said, gazing at her.

'Yes it, er, was. But perhaps some good will come out of it, as you say. I'm a great one for justice,' she said, squirming in her chair.

'Right, well thank you, Charlotte. I'll go round tomorrow as time seems to be running out for the old lady. Am I supposed to hold on to her statement until...later?'

She hadn't thought about that. She knew Andy would have liked it in his own hands but couldn't think of a valid reason to ask for it back. But if you couldn't trust a man of God, who could you trust?

'Please. And would you let me know when you've been to see her? So I can feel at ease.'

'Of course. It sounds as if you two built up quite a rapport for Mrs Batiste to trust you with something so, so momentous. I'm glad, as I don't think she had many friends.'

Charlotte left feeling a little calmer but still anxious. Afraid Maud would not live until the rector witnessed her sign the all-important document. One which would at last guarantee Jim's inheritance.

chapter thirty

By the time Charlotte arrived home it was after five and she found Andy drinking coffee in the kitchen. He jumped up as she came in, asking, 'What happened with the rector?'

'He's agreed to go round tomorrow morning to see Maud and witness her signature. And he'll ring me when he's been. All we can do is hope she's well enough to sign,' she said, giving him a kiss.

Andy frowned. 'Maud's that ill? Hmm, it'd be sod's law if she died before he got there.' He pushed a hand through his hair as he paced around. Suddenly he stopped and grabbed her. 'Whatever happens, I now know the truth and can tell Dad who killed Edmund. Which is something. And it's down to you, the most clever, beautiful woman I've ever known. Thank you.' He kissed her hungrily on the mouth and she melted into his arms, all the excitement and worry pushed aside as the heat rose in her body. Whispering, 'Come on, let's go upstairs,' Andy led the way to the bedroom.

Later, languid from their lovemaking, they lay in each other's arms as they talked about the possible repercussions of Maud's shock confession.

Andy stroked her cheek as he said, 'If, and I know it's a big if, but if we get a signed statement and then Maud dies, then Martin or whoever, is free to report it to the police, right?'

She nodded, almost asleep under his touch.

'So, assuming Harold's arrested, and by God I'd do my best to make sure he was, then Dad would be acknowledged as Edmund's heir. Agreed?'

'Yes, but something still doesn't add up. Even without Harold being proved to be the killer, your father's the natural heir and always has been. But he hasn't pursued it for some reason. I wonder what really happened when he met Harold? And whether or not Harold's guilt changes that?'

Andy fell onto his back and stared at the ceiling. 'I don't know and can only hope when he knows the truth about Harold he'll change his mind. Perhaps he's had a misguided sense of loyalty to Harold for working on the farm over the years and didn't want to deprive him of his livelihood. It beats me! But once Harold *is* charged I'll encourage Dad to make a claim. Surely he couldn't want that bloody cousin of mine to inherit!' he said, banging his fists together in anger.

Charlotte reached over and kissed him. 'Hey, stay calm. I'm sure it will all be resolved. It might take some time, but I have a feeling in my bones–'

'Oh, do you? Well, please tell me more,' he teased, taking her in his arms again and dropping kisses on her breasts. As her own body responded all thoughts of explaining anything disappeared and she gave herself up to his lovemaking.

Andy left the next morning looking, Charlotte thought, like the proverbial cat on a hot tin roof. She didn't blame him, she felt on edge herself and it wasn't her family's skeletons coming out of the cupboard. Wondering briefly if there were any in the Townsend dynasty, and deciding she couldn't cope with any more angst, she tried to focus on her writing. It took a while for her to pick up where she had left off the previous day, but the words finally made a reluctant appearance on the screen, absorbing all her attention. Charlotte stopped only to make a coffee late morning and was tapping away happily when her mobile rang.

'Hello, Charlotte. It's Martin. Just to let you know I've been round to see Mrs Batiste and she's signed the statement and I acted as witness.'

Relief flooded through her and she punched the air silently. 'Thanks for letting me know, I can relax knowing it's what she wanted. How – how was Mrs Batiste?'

'Worse, I'm afraid. But oddly, she seemed relieved, more peaceful. I think telling someone what happened has freed her in some way. She has my word nothing will be made public while she lives and is now ready to accept the inevitable.'

'Do you know how long...?'

'Her doctor arrived while I was on the way out and said he thinks it's a matter of days, a week at the most.'

'Oh dear. Well, again thank you for phoning, Martin. I'm leaving on Saturday so may not see Mrs Batiste again, but I do plan on coming back soon.' They said their goodbyes and Charlotte immediately rang a delighted Andy. It was now only a question of time...

~ ~

After receiving Charlotte's call Andy let out a whoop. Fortunately he was alone in the office, his client having left moments before. Pushing his hands through his hair he stood up and did a circuit of the small space between the desks. He found it hard to take in. After more than sixty years Edmund's name was about to be cleared. He could no longer be made to feel ashamed of his grandfather. Not that he had for one moment accepted his guilt, but others had. In his mind it was what others thought of him and his family that mattered, though Andy was aware it was stupid. His father had been perceived as the "poor relation", the "outcast", and Andy's short fuse had been lit too often by snide remarks from other boys at school. In a small island like Guernsey even an old scandal like Edmund's had not been allowed to die completely. Thinking about it now, Andy wondered if Harold had kept the embers burning over the years, determined to paint a black picture of James Batiste, son of the traitor Edmund.

Sitting down again, Andy phoned his father to ask if he could come round and see them both. Jim sounded surprised but said they were in for the rest of the day. Thinking there was no time like the present, Andy grabbed his keys and left.

His mother answered the door and smiled.

'It is lovely to see you, *mon chér*. There is something wrong, no?' she asked, the smile replaced by a frown.

'No, *Maman*, there's – there's something important I need to tell you both.'

Yvette's eyebrows rose. 'You are making a mystery. Let us go into the sitting room, your father is reading the paper.'

'Hi, Dad. How are you? Back okay now?' he said, sinking into the sofa.

Jim folded up the copy of the *Guernsey Evening Press* and studied his son. 'I'm okay, lad. That nice physio lady, Louisa, says I can start doing a bit more fishing as long as I don't spend too much time out in the boat. Did I hear you tell your mother you've something important to say? If so, you'd better spit it out because you look as if you're about to burst.'

Andy took a deep breath. 'Remember I told you Jeanne was writing a book set in the occupation?' His parents nodded. 'Well, she...asked a friend to do some research, which included talking to people who were here at the time and one of those who came forward was Maud Batiste,' he said, seeing his father's head jerk in surprise.

'Old Maud? But she's bed bound, so I heard. How could she have–'

'The researcher had apparently requested the help of the vicar to find old parishioners willing to talk. The rector of St Martins visits Maud regularly, so I understand, and how it came about she interviewed Maud at home.' Andy felt his palms moisten at the white lies but believed it was justified.

Jim nodded. 'Go on.'

'It turns out Maud had something on her conscience and called the woman back a second time to...to confide in her.' He noticed his mother lean forward and clasp his father's hand. Jim's face was inscrutable. 'What she told her was to be kept confidential until after her death, which is likely to be within days according to her doctor.'

'So how do you know about it then?' Jim butted in.

'I'll explain later, Dad. What it boils down to is this. She saw Harold fight and kill Edmund and has kept it a secret until now.'

Yvette gasped, her hand flying to her mouth and Jim's eyes widened in horror.

'You're telling me Harold killed his brother? I know he's a bully and a cheat but...to kill his own brother! I find that hard to believe. Couldn't she have made it up?'

'Why would she? Maud doesn't come out of this at all well. She witnessed a murder and did nothing about it. Even went on to marry the bastard. But it's been on her conscience all this time and she wants Harold to get his just deserts.'

Yvette, looking dazed, asked, 'Did she not say why he killed Edmund?'

'Yes, she heard them arguing. And this is crucial, Dad,' he said, 'Edmund knew Harold was an informer and told him he knew, so Harold started the rumour it was Edmund. Your father found out Harold was still playing dirty and was going to report him. It's why Harold killed him.' Andy sat back on the sofa, feeling drained.

'So the ol' bugger really did it, did he? Can't say I'd be sorry to see him banged up. He could share a cell with his no-good grandson of his. That's assuming the police can prove it, which I doubt after all this time,' Jim said, stroking his chin.

'Maud signed a witnessed statement describing what happened, and we...I think it should be enough to convict him. At the very least, Dad, it means he'd be stripped of everything he owns – the house, land, various properties and cash – and *you'd* be entitled to them. You'd be a wealthy man, Dad,' he said, leaning forward.

Yvette gasped. 'Wealthy! Us! Oh, that would be–'

'Impossible! I'm not the heir and never was. So forget about me inheriting anything,' Jim said, red-faced.

Andy couldn't believe it. 'Not the heir? But of course you are, Dad, you're Edmund's son–'

Jim, his shoulders sagging as if bearing a heavy weight, shook his head. 'No, that's where you're wrong, lad. I'm not Edmund's son. My mother...had an affair. I...was illegitimate.'

chapter thirty-one

It was if he had been punched hard in the solar plexus. For a moment Andy felt the breath leave his body and he couldn't speak. His parents were hazy figures in the room and he could hear sounds emanating from their mouths but couldn't make out the words. What had his father said? Not Edmund's son? It couldn't be true! It would be too cruel now...

'Andy? Sorry, lad. It's been a bit of a shock for you, I know. Was for me, too.'

His eyes cleared and he saw his father leaning towards him and gripping his arm. Behind Jim his mother's pale face hovered into view.

'Dad, please tell me. What makes you so sure your mother had an affair and you were the result?'

'Well, he told me when I first met him, that I wasn't Edmund's son,' Jim said, fidgeting in his chair.

'Who's "he", Dad? Your mother's lover?' Andy was shocked. Surely this was a nightmare and he'd wake up soon...

'No, no I never met him. He was dead, so I was told. It was Harold who told me...' A look of uncertainty flitted across his father's face.

Andy began to relax. 'You're telling me Harold said Madeleine had an affair and you believed him? Did he have any proof? What did your mother say?'

Jim coughed, keeping his head down. 'He said it was well known she was seeing one of the neighbours, shortly before Edmund died. Said maybe Edmund had found out and challenged the man and that's why he'd ended up dead.'

'Dad, I understand why you might have been...misled at the time, but now you know what really happened to Edmund, do you still believe what Harold told you?'

His father's face crumpled in misery and Andy stood up and hugged him. Yvette, mouthing "coffee", disappeared to the kitchen, while Andy continued to hold his father. That bloody bastard Harold! He wanted to kill him for what he'd done to his family. Pity they no longer hanged murderers, though hanging was too good for someone like Harold.

'Did you ever ask Grandma about this?' he asked eventually.

'God no! You can't ask your mother something like that. But she rarely talked about the time of Edmund's death, said it was too painful and it made me wonder if what he said could be true. Harold threatened to take me to court if I pursued a claim and said he'd testify my mother was having an affair and bring more scandal down on our heads. And remember there was no DNA testing back then.' Andy saw the tears in his eyes. 'I couldn't risk it, son. I couldn't blacken our name further and hadn't the money for advocates. And at the time, back in the 60s, the house didn't look much and the land wasn't worth an awful lot. Not like now.'

'I understand, Dad. I'm not blaming you, I'm angry with that...that bastard Harold, and his pack of lies. Please say you no longer believe him.'

Jim shook his head. 'No, I don't.'

Yvette arrived with a pot of coffee and handed round cups before sitting next to Jim.

Looking from her husband to Andy, she said, 'Is everything all right, now? Is it true we will be wealthy?'

Andy grinned. 'It looks like it, *Maman*. Although it might take a while.'

'Oh, I can wait. But it would be nice to make a holiday somewhere warm this winter. It would do your father's joints a lot of good.'

The men looked at each other and smiled.

After sipping his coffee, Jim asked, 'How did you find out about this? You said it was confidential.'

Andy shifted uncomfortably. 'Charlotte, the researcher, is a friend of Jeanne's and we met and...became friends. Somewhere along the line I mentioned our family and the story about Edmund so when she heard Maud's story, she passed it on to me, in confidence. At least until after Maud's death.'

His mother gave him a sharp look.

'Friends you said. But I sense you are more than that, yes?'

'Well, yes we are. We've been seeing each other quite a bit, but she's English and has to go back tomorrow for a while. Her mother's...not well and she also has a business in London.'

This time it was the parents who looked at each other.

'Is it serious with this Charlotte? You have not spoken of anyone for years!' Yvette said, her eyes shining.

'I think so, but there's a lot to sort out first. But when she comes back I'll introduce you. Promise.'

His mother nodded, looking pleased. The look of a mother keen to see her only child settled with the right partner.

Andy finished his coffee and glanced at his watch. He had a meeting scheduled in thirty minutes.

'I have to go, but are you clear about what I've told you? Remember we can't say anything to anybody until Maud dies and her statement is given to the police.'

They both nodded their agreement.

'Where's this statement now, son?'

'The rector of St Martins has it. He witnessed her signature. So it's quite safe. And if you're at all unsure about being Edmund's son, Dad, we could insist on a DNA test. That would scupper Harold's lies.'

'There shouldn't be any need for a test, in the eyes of the law I'm Edmund's son. It says so on my birth certificate.' Jim flashed a smile at him.

'Good.' Andy stood up. 'How about we go out fishing on Sunday, Dad? See who can catch the most again, eh?'

Jim laughingly agreed and his parents followed him to the front door, exchanging hugs before he left. Andy sank behind the wheel feeling both drained and exhilarated. He had hated fibbing to his parents but told himself he'd set the record straight one day. But he was also fired up by the thought his father now saw himself as the rightful heir. With a shock he realised one day *he* would inherit too. Shaking his head at the thought, he switched on the engine and drove as fast as he dared to Town, singing a slightly off-key version of Queen's 'We are the Champions'. It felt good.

~ ~

Charlotte was relieved when Andy phoned to say he'd been to see his parents and told them everything. Or rather, a censored version. Telling her he'd explain more later, he also said his father was now prepared to claim the family estate. She couldn't resist performing a little dance around the room before checking the contents of the fridge. Nothing much shouted 'celebration meal' so she phoned La Bella Luce and booked a table for that evening. Only a matter of yards from Edmund's modest grave, it seemed a little inappropriate, and she hoped the family would now install a more fitting headstone. If the evening's weren't so dark she would have suggested they took flowers there tonight. Perhaps another time. Making a determined effort to stop her mind drifting, Charlotte sat down in front of her laptop and continued with her writing.

When she heard Andy open the front door she rushed into the hall and flung her arms around his neck. Andy dropped his messenger bag and lifted her in his arms. They both laughed as he swung her around before easing her gently down, then kissing her. Charlotte managed to say she had booked a table for dinner at eight before Andy caught her hand and pulled her, laughing, up the stairs. Well, she thought, tumbling onto the bed, this is one way to celebrate.

Charlotte waved Andy off the next morning aware of the chunk of lead settled in her stomach. This was to be her last full day in Guernsey and even though she reminded herself she planned to return soon, she wished she wasn't going away. It seemed unfair – her efforts on Andy's behalf had finally borne fruit, and she was leaving. If it wasn't for her mother she would have stayed but...she shook her head. Her mother had to come first. At least she had something to look forward to that day as Louisa had suggested they meet for lunch at La Folie. They had not seen each other for nearly two weeks, but had kept in touch by phone. Determined to be more cheerful, Charlotte opened her laptop and lost herself in eighteenth century Naples for a few hours.

Louisa was waiting in the dining room, having bagged a table tucked away at the back.

'My, you're positively blooming. Looks as if being with Andy suits you,' Louisa said, embracing her.

Charlotte felt her face flush. 'Yes, methinks it does. And you seem particularly loved-up yourself.' Louisa's face glowed with happiness and the lines of worry had disappeared, making her look ten years younger. She was glad for her friend. It was about time she experienced happiness after the trauma of losing her mother. But knowing her own mother's life might be cut short increased the leaden feeling in her gut.

After ordering their meals, they settled down to the serious business of catching up.

'So, when are you two making it official?'

Louisa fiddled with her cutlery. 'It's up to Paul. Although we've moved in together sooner than planned, we still need time to be absolutely sure. And I think Paul's not completely happy about the cliché of marrying the boss's daughter. He's too sensitive for his own good, that's the trouble.' She sighed.

'I'm absolutely convinced you two were made for each other, so don't worry. You could always get Malcolm to threaten him with a shotgun if he doesn't make an honest woman of you!' Charlotte said, giggling.

Louisa joined in and the mood lightened just as their food arrived. All was quiet while they made inroads into their salads. Charlotte, after checking there was no-one in earshot, shared her news about Maud and Harold. Louisa sat transfixed, food balanced on her fork.

'Wow! It's like something out of a book or a film. Andy must be over the moon. And Jim. He does know, I presume?'

'Yes, Andy told his parents yesterday. But there was a hitch...' She went on to tell her about Harold's threats to Jim and Louisa's eyes opened even wider.

'How awful! Poor Jim. No-one could understand why he hadn't pushed his claim and now it all makes sense.' She looked thoughtful as she chewed on a mouthful of salmon.

'It does. The only problem is nothing will happen until after Maud dies and then it's up to the police what happens about Harold. Jim's not lodging his claim yet, to avoid stirring up problems for the old lady. Oh, and Andy told his parents about me.'

The women carried on chatting as they ate and Charlotte was glad they'd found time to meet. One thing she didn't have in London was a close girlfriend and she and Louisa got on so well. It was ironic, she thought, although they were both living in the city at the same time, they actually did not meet until both were in Guernsey, at La Folie. And now it looked as if they were both planning to live permanently in the island. Funny how life turns out.

It was Halloween on Saturday and the ubiquitous hollowed out pumpkin lanterns glowed in house windows as Andy drove Charlotte to the airport that evening.

Anxious parents shepherded their small offspring, carrying buckets and dressed up as witches, vampires or devils as they went from house to house trick or treating. Charlotte watched them, her eyes moist as she wondered again whether or not she would one day be a mother. She had not broached the subject with Andy yet, feeling it might be too soon. He had said nothing to indicate his views either way, and she resolved to say something when she returned.

'You look thoughtful. Anything you want to share?'

She turned to face him and smiled. 'No, I was only watching the children in their outfits. Quite scary some of them, aren't they?'

Andy peered out of the window and nodded. 'Yep, they must have spent ages putting on their face paint.' Turning back to her he added, 'Are you okay? You've been very quiet today.'

Her mouth twisted. 'There's been a lot to think about. But I'm okay, thanks.'

'Good.' He squeezed her hand. 'I'll phone you every day so you won't feel lonely in that mansion of yours,' he said, with a grin.

'Hardly a mansion! But it is a bit big for one person, I admit. Although there's Mrs Thomas and her flat takes up the top floor.'

'I rest my case! I look forward to seeing it one day.'

'As soon as things settle down we'll have a weekend in London together. It'll be fun,' she said, wondering how long it would take. There was her mother and the situation with Maud and Harold to contend with...

Andy pulled into the airport and drove into the car park. Charlotte walked alongside holding his free hand while he wheeled her case to departures. Once she was checked in they took the stairs to the café where he ordered a glass of wine for her and a lager for himself. There was plenty of time as her flight was delayed by half an hour.

'So much has happened since I arrived in September. It's hard to believe it's only been a couple of months,' she said, swirling her glass of Merlot.

He clutched her hand. 'They've been the best weeks of my life, so far. And here's to many more!' he said, touching her glass with his. She returned the toast, thinking if anyone had told her two months ago what lay in store for her, she wouldn't have believed them.

'And you're soon to become heir to a valuable estate. Life's definitely on the up for you,' she said, tilting her head on one side.

'Haven't given it much thought. Despite his back, Dad's pretty fit and could last for many years yet so I don't think I'll get to play the part of wealthy playboy,' he said, his mouth pulled down.

'Hey! Playboy indeed! Apart from anything else it would be a waste of your talents as an architect. Wouldn't you prefer to be remembered as the man who designed such and such a building rather than the man who blew a fortune on fast cars and women?' she said, punching his arm.

'Ouch! Okay, I'll settle for being the successful architect lucky enough to have captured the most wonderful, beautiful woman as his wife. What do you think?' He gazed into her eyes and she blinked.

'Have...have you just proposed? Or...?' she found it difficult to breathe, not wanting him to say he was teasing.

Andy knelt beside her, holding out the ring-pull from his can of lager.

'Charlotte, beautiful Charlotte. Would you do me the great honour of becoming my wife?'

chapter thirty-two

S he burst out laughing. She knew she shouldn't, but the sight of Andy on one knee holding out the ring-pull was too much.

'If you really mean it, then yes, I'd be honoured to be your wife. Now, please get up before anyone notices,' she said, allowing him to fit the 'ring' on her finger. Glancing around she caught a few people giving them funny looks.

'Thank God for that, I didn't want to look a prat only to get turned down,' he said, kissing her before regaining his chair. A huge smile filled his face and she smiled in return, her heart thumping with excitement and love.

'I hadn't planned to ask you yet, hence the lack of a ring. But having to say goodbye yet again, brought it home to me how much I love you and didn't want to lose you.' Andy picked up her hands and kissed her fingers one by one, avoiding the piece of metal on her ring finger. His eyes locked onto hers as he went on, 'Since learning the truth about Harold and...and everything, I've gained more self-respect. I needed to be worthy of you and now I feel I am.'

'But Andy, you were always worthy of me. You're a wonderful, clever, loving man and any woman would be proud to call you hers. I'm just glad you chose me,' she said, still shell-shocked.

Before he could say any more the tannoy interrupted, announcing the departure of her flight. They scrambled downstairs and Andy stood by while she headed towards security.

'We'll choose a ring when you get back!' he shouted, waving. She smiled and waved her left hand, remembering to remove the ring-pull before going through the metal detector. 'My engagement ring,' she explained to a puzzled looking security guard as she binned it. Once through she ran to the gate where she was the last passenger to arrive. Even a frown from the check-in girl couldn't burst her bubble of happiness as she followed the other passengers out to the plane.

After take-off the drinks trolley was wheeled out and Charlotte ordered champagne. Although the norm would be to share it with her new fiancé, this wasn't possible so she raised her plastic glass in a silent toast to Andy – cheers!

On Sunday morning Charlotte woke up momentarily disorientated. A grey light filtered through the curtains and as her eyes adjusted she realised she was in her own bedroom in London and not in Andy's. The pang of disappointment was soon replaced with the memory of his proposal. She lay on her back and stretched, luxuriating in the knowledge of her engagement, albeit unofficial while *sans* ring and *sans* fiancé.

They had talked for what seemed like hours the previous night after she arrived home. It was agreed neither would say anything to their respective parents until they were together again and had bought a ring. This meant Andy would need to fly over to England to meet her mother, something Charlotte was, at this time, not entirely happy about. Still, it could hardly be avoided, she told herself. But Annette could be charming when she wanted to be, particularly if the man concerned was shortly to become heir to an estate.

Reluctant to get up and face the first day on her own for weeks, Charlotte padded barefoot across the Aubusson carpet to the window and drew the curtains. The first day of November lived up to its poor reputation with fog swirling around the square, obscuring the central private garden. Not much of a welcome home, she thought, frowning. She tried to conjure up the image of the view from La Folie on a bright, spring day and failed.

All she saw was grey fog enveloping the grey figures of those brave enough to venture out.

Turning back into the room Charlotte decided the only thing to do was to enjoy a long soak in the bath, enveloped in the scent of exotic oils. Her en suite was spacious enough to accommodate the swinging of a family of cats, and as she turned on the tap over the voluminous bath tub, wished Andy was there to share it. While waiting for it to fill, she called Mrs Thomas on the house phone to ask for a pot of coffee. Once the oils were added to the steaming water, a fragrant mist filled the room and Charlotte felt more cheerful. Mrs Thomas arrived with the coffee, placing the tray on a small table beside the bath. After she left, Charlotte sank into the bath with a sigh of contentment.

Then the doubts crept in. This house – her house – was a stunning, Georgian house immaculately and expensively furnished. Complete with the most efficient housekeeper Charlotte had ever known. And she was planning to give it up for a charming, but comparatively small cottage in Guernsey, minus any help. Could she do it? She loved Andy to bits and wanted to spend her life with him, but it would be at a high cost. Money wasn't an issue. She had loads and Andy was successful in his work, so not exactly broke. But financially not in her league. She couldn't imagine him letting her pay for everything, he had his male pride. And he was not likely to inherit from Jim for many years so...How could she suggest a compromise without either hurting or angering him? No solution popped into her head. Oh, hell, why can't life be simple? She sank under the bubbles, thinking she would have to speak to Andy about it. Soon.

Later that morning, Andy phoned and after a few moments of catching up, Charlotte brought up what was on her mind.

'Andy, everything has happened so fast and we haven't had time to discuss where we'll live and how we'll pool our resources. Both quite important issues, don't you think?' She held her breath.

'I assumed we'd live in the cottage or is it not grand enough for you?' He sounded hurt.

Oh dear. This wasn't going to be easy. 'I neither want nor need grand. But it's not exactly large, is it? And I'm happy to help with buying something bigger–'

'I don't need your money! And I've put so much of myself into the cottage–'

'I know you have. Let's talk about it later shall we? When I get back,' she said hurriedly, not wanting to have a row only hours after becoming engaged.

'All right, if we have to.'

Charlotte rang off, feeling frustrated. Why did Andy have to be so pig-headed about money and property? Richard had been only too happy to accept her not inconsiderable financial contributions after their marriage. And she couldn't help but see the irony in Andy shortly becoming heir to wealth in his own right.

After giving herself a few minutes to calm down, she phoned her mother. Annette confirmed she would be arriving on Monday at lunchtime and planned to stay for two or three nights, but would be out most of the time. This suited Charlotte as she needed to spend time at the office catching up with Tony. With the weather so grim she could not face leaving the house and made herself comfortable in what had been her father's library, now housing a desktop computer on the Victorian partners' desk. Looking around at the serried ranks of books safely stored behind the glazed doors of the floor to ceiling bookshelves, Charlotte had a brief vision of her father, content in the old leather armchair, a book in his hands and a glass of wine or brandy on a table by his side. On occasion a cigar was lit, but more often than not, would burn itself out in the ashtray if her father became engrossed in his book. Closing her eyes now, she could discern the faint smell of cigar smoke which had permeated the fabric of the room. Her chest tightened with the pain of her grief and tears seeped down her cheeks.

Oh, why did he have to go and leave her? She needed him *now*, wanted him to say her mother would be fine, there was nothing to worry about. Just as he had said many times when she was a child and something had upset her. She whispered to the empty room, 'Daddy, I've met this amazing man and...and we're engaged. Richard left last year so I'm free to start again and Andy makes me feel happy and...loved. Though there are some problems...I'd like your blessing, please, and wish you could meet him.' Brushing away the tears, she continued, 'Mother's ill again, and we don't know if she'll pull through. Can you help? I'm not sure how, but–' she broke off as her mobile trilled into life. She blew her nose and answered it, not checking the caller.

'Charlotte? Martin Kite. Hope I haven't disturbed you?'

'Not at all, Martin. Has...has something happened?' Her pulse quickened in anticipation.

'Yes, I'm afraid Mrs Batiste passed away last night and I thought you might like to know.'

'Of course, thank you. Were you with her?'

'I was. Sal had phoned to say the doctor thought it was imminent and I sat with her. It was peaceful, which is always a blessing in these circumstances,' he said, sombrely.

'Was...her husband there?'

'Actually, he wasn't. He had gone out earlier in the evening to have dinner with some friends, I believe, but hadn't left a contact number with Sal.' Charlotte heard him sniff.

'Oh. I don't suppose there's a date arranged for the funeral? I'd quite like to attend if I can make it.'

'Not yet, no, but it's likely to be the week after this. I can let you know.'

'Thanks.' She cleared her throat. 'Mm, what will you do about the statement, Martin?'

'Ah, yes. It's been very much on my mind these past few days. I spoke to an old friend here who happens to be a retired policeman and sounded him out. He said I should arrange to see the Chief Officer and has offered to go with me, as they worked together. Naturally, I didn't mention any names to John, but now Mrs Batiste is no longer with us, it doesn't matter. I shall go along tomorrow but will request no action is taken until after the funeral. A reasonable compromise, I thought. Do you agree?'

She did and as they finished the call, was left experiencing a mix of sadness and relief. As she scrolled to Andy's number on her mobile the thought crossed her mind the 'John' Martin referred to might be John Ferguson, the retired inspector who helped Louisa track down her mother's killer. If it was, then she thought Maud's statement would be in safe hands. And now she had good news for Andy.

The fog lifted on Monday and with it Charlotte's spirits. She made an early start and was in the office by eight thirty, much to the surprise of the receptionist who, judging by her flustered appearance, had only just arrived herself. Charlotte smiled and after exchanging greetings, headed to her office. The Georgian building, minutes away from her house in the heart of Bloomsbury, had been divided into three and Townsend Publishers occupied the entire first floor. The rooms were light and airy, enjoying high, elaborate ceilings and original marble fireplaces. Charlotte's father always referred to it as "a home from home" and she could see why. It was like a cosy club, with panelled rooms leading off the central staircase. Charlotte had just settled at her desk when Tony appeared.

He grinned at her. 'The grapevine announced your arrival and it's good to see you here, Charlotte. How's things?'

'Fine, thanks. You'd better sit down, Tony, we've a lot to discuss. First of all, can we talk about Chris's books?'

Once they had discussed those books and others in the pipeline, Charlotte explained about her ideas for the future and her intended move to Guernsey. Tony was surprised and pleased she had met someone and confirmed he would be happy to take on a bigger role within the company.

The walk back to the house took five minutes and Charlotte dawdled, keen to enjoy some fresh air after a morning in the office. The deciduous trees in the square were shadows of their former selves, stark against their evergreen neighbours. The overcast sky emphasised the bleaching of colour from the area, leaving only white, grey and splashes of green. Charlotte felt as if the city was telling her to move on, find somewhere with more light and colour. As she approached her house, a taxi drew up outside, depositing her mother on the pavement. The driver carried the case up the short flight of steps before leaving.

'Hello, Mother. Did you have a good journey?' Charlotte asked, kissing her cheek before opening the front door.

'Yes thank you. For once the train was on time and the heating worked.' Annette was muffled up in a heavy wool coat, scarf and gloves as if venturing to the arctic rather than London in November. Charlotte left the case in the hall and went in search of Mrs Thomas while her mother unwrapped herself. She came back to find her in the sitting room, rubbing her hands by the fire.

'Lunch will be ready in fifteen minutes, Mother.' She went and stood by her, trying to examine her face as she warmed her own hands. The dark shadows had gone and it looked as if her mother had put on some weight. Good. 'You're looking well. How's it going with the treatments?'

'Quite well, I believe. It's why I'm here as Gillian wants to run some tests to check my progress. Are you free to take me this afternoon? I have an appointment at four.'

'Of course. Will you be seeing her again this week?'

'On Wednesday or Thursday, depending when the results are ready. Then we're to discuss the new protocol she's excited about and wants me to consider.' Annette turned to face her. 'What are your plans, Charlotte? Are you back for good?'

'Not exactly. I'm happy to stay if you need my help with anything and I've things to sort out here, but I might need to return to Guernsey next week. A funeral,' she added, thinking at least that was true.

Her mother's eyebrows shot up. 'A funeral! But surely you haven't lost a friend so soon?'

'No, no, it's...a friend's aunt, and they would like my support. But it's not important, if you–'

Annette waved her hand. 'I don't *need* you to be here, Charlotte. Go and be with your friend if you wish, I'm sure she would appreciate your thoughtfulness.'

Charlotte felt her cheeks redden but didn't correct her mother's assumption. But one day there'd be a lot of explaining to do...

Mrs Thomas came to announce lunch was ready and they moved to the morning room at the back of the house. They were greeted by the enticing aroma of home-made vegetable soup, accompanied by plates of salad and glasses of freshly made juices, Mrs Thomas having been advised of Annette's strict diet. Once settled at the table conversation was desultory, consisting mainly of observations on the weather and what the local WI had planned for the winter months.

Later Charlotte drove her mother to Richmond and waited while she was with Gillian. She was pleased to see them come out smiling from the consulting room.

'Your mother's doing really well, Charlotte, and assuming the blood tests are good, I think we can say the programme's working,' Gillian said, patting Annette's arm. 'It might mean Annette spends some further time at La Folie and I'm sure a room could be found, if it suits you both?'

'It's fine by me, if Mother's happy to go back,' Charlotte said, giving Annette a quizzical look.

'I can hardly refuse to go if it's improving my chances of recovery, can I?'

'Good. I'll see you on Wednesday afternoon and we can go over the results and confirm the ongoing treatment,' Gillian said, guiding them to the front door. After exchanging goodbyes, they left.

Once in the car Charlotte asked her mother if Gillian had said when she would need to return to Guernsey. Annette replied the following week had been suggested, subject to room availability. Charlotte nodded, thinking it could work out well with her own plan to return for Maud's funeral. And she and Andy could announce their engagement to both sets of parents at the same time. Perfect!

The next morning Annette disappeared to meet up with a fellow WI chairwoman, saying she would be out for lunch. Charlotte was happy to return to the library and her writing, glad to be relieved of chauffeur duties. She had not made much progress when she received a call from the rector. He started off by saying the funeral was arranged for the following Monday at 2 pm, if she still wished to attend.

'It looks as if I might be coming back next weekend anyway, Martin, so that's fine. How...how did it go with the police?' she asked, keeping her fingers crossed.

'The Chief Officer was, to put it mildly, astonished to be presented with evidence relating to a crime which took place more than sixty years ago, but he agreed it would be pursued. Mr Batiste will be taken in for questioning after the funeral as I'd suggested and, in the meantime, the police will dig out the old files. I'm glad my friend John was with me as apparently he solved another war-time case, which meant the Chief took it seriously. Right, I'd better get on and I hope to see you next week,' he said, briskly, before ending the call.

Charlotte immediately rang Andy with the news and he, in turn, said he'd pass it on to his father. They had arranged to see an advocate later in the week to discuss Jim's claim to the estate. She heard the excitement in his voice as the time was fast approaching for Harold's downfall.

'I only wish I could be there when he's arrested but guess I'll have to settle for reading it in the *Guernsey Evening Press*. Dad's still not taken it in, but once we've seen the advocate, it should become more real. Mum's already looking at holiday brochures!' he said, laughing.

'Good for her! They deserve it. Perhaps they should consider a world cruise, it would give them a chance to enjoy some well-earned pampering while seeing the sights. You said they haven't travelled much.'

'No, they couldn't afford it. A cruise sounds a good idea, I'll suggest it. But as it could take ages for the legal stuff to get sorted, I'd better tell Mum to hang fire for the moment.'

Once Charlotte had said goodbye she returned to her writing powered up by the phone calls and looking forward to seeing Andy, trying not to think of their own unresolved issue. And as long as her mother's blood test results were good it wouldn't be long before they were back together.

chapter thirty-three

Charlotte paced up and down Gillian's waiting room, a pretty little sitting room decorated in soft tones and furnished with linen-covered sofas. Intriguing artefacts from around the world lined the shelves. It was a room exuding calm and peace, but Charlotte was not seduced. She wanted to know what was happening in the adjoining consulting room.

Finally she heard the sound of voices as the door opened and Gillian preceded her mother into the room. Her smile said it all and she sagged with relief.

'The tests look good, in fact better than I expected, and I've contacted La Folie about a room for Annette and she can arrive on Sunday,' Gillian said, standing between them. 'I'll be spending more time in Guernsey myself while I wind down this practice. Malcolm wants me to be a consultant naturopathic doctor for the clinic.'

Charlotte's eyebrows rose. 'That's good news, on both counts.' She turned to her mother who, dressed immaculately in Armani, looked as if she'd been invited for afternoon tea rather than to receive vital test results. 'I'm so happy for you, Mother.'

Annette nodded, a brief smile touching her lips.

The women said their goodbyes and left. Charlotte's heart was singing. Not only was the prognosis looking better for her mother, but she could now plan her return to Guernsey. Annette was booked on an evening train to Somerset, having refused Charlotte's offer of a lift, saying she was quite capable of travelling on her own. During the drive back to Bloomsbury, Charlotte said she would book her own flight for the next day and would keep in touch when they were both in Guernsey. Her mother made no comment and for once Charlotte was glad she showed a lack of interest in her life.

'Did Gillian say whether or not your cancer can be...cured?' she asked, tentatively.

A shadow crossed her mother's face. 'Hmm. No-one talks about a cure, only remission, particularly with liver cancer. However, she's having good results with other patients and thinks I have a good chance of long-term remission myself. So in theory I could become cancer-free,' she said, her voice wobbling.

'Oh, Mother! I do hope so. I'm glad you're at least giving yourself this chance to beat it,' she said, gripping her mother's hand. Unusually, Annette did not shrug it off. Charlotte had to let go to steer the car, but for a moment felt they were a little closer. With an inward sigh, she joined the line of traffic heading into central London.

Charlotte's gaze swept over the waiting crowd and when her eyes caught those of Andy, her pulse raced as she ran into his arms and kissed him.

'Hey, have you missed me so much? It's only been a few days,' he said, laughing.

'Seems longer. So much has happened this week...' She clung onto his arm as he steered her outside to his car. After stowing her case in the boot he took the driving seat, leaning over for a quick kiss before starting the engine.

'I've given myself the afternoon off, thinking we could go shopping after lunch.'

Charlotte was puzzled. Andy, like many men, avoided shopping as much as possible.

'Shopping? What for, groceries?'

'No, silly. Don't we need to choose something sparkly?' he said, his eyes crinkled up in amusement.

'Oh! A ring. I hadn't expected you to buy it so soon.' Her heart thumped with excitement at the thought and she leant across and kissed him.

'I take it that's a yes?' he said, pulling away from the kerb. She nodded in agreement and settled back in the seat, looking forward to what promised to be a fabulous afternoon.

On Friday morning Andy left early to collect his father for their appointment with the advocate, leaving Charlotte to catch up with her writing. In theory. In practice she gazed dreamily at her ring, which caught the light while she attempted to type. Her first engagement ring, a traditional ruby and diamond, had been chosen by her ex-husband and she had never liked it, whereas both she and Andy had fallen in love with this ring, a pear-shaped emerald, surrounded by diamonds. Andy, saying the emeralds matched her eyes, had insisted on buying her matching earrings. She was touched by his thoughtfulness and generosity and planned to buy him an engagement present, once she had found something suitable. Giving up on her writing, she leant back in the chair and found herself thinking about the previous evening.

Andy had cooked supper and afterwards they had cuddled up together on the sofa, drinking wine and planning the future. Charlotte knew she had to say something, albeit belatedly, about the pretty important topic of children. The conversation about where they were to live would have to wait.

'Andy, we haven't really discussed whether or not we want children. What...what are your thoughts? Do *you* want children?' she said, avoiding his gaze as the mass of butterflies once again filled her stomach.

He reached up and tilted her face towards him. 'I'd always hoped to be a father one day, but I appreciate neither of us are as young as we were. If you're happy to try it's fine by me. But if you'd rather not, that's okay too. I want to spend the rest of my life with you, darling, with or without children. Okay?'

The butterflies flew away and Charlotte smiled at her gorgeous, generous hearted man.

'In which case, I'd like us to try for a baby, before we both become old and shrivelled.'

'Great, from now on we can forget the, er, safety barrier and see what happens, shall we? And there's no time like the present,' he said, putting their glasses of wine out of harm's way. She laughed and began to unbutton his shirt...

The memory of their passionate lovemaking brought a flush to her cheeks and Charlotte got up and went to make a coffee. It was going to be difficult to concentrate on the antics of Lady Emma Hamilton today, she thought, although there were similarities. She daydreamed instead about what it would be like to be a mother. Scary – and wonderful. She was sure Andy would make a brilliant father and for a moment felt the loss of her own. Her child – if she had one – would be deprived of a lovely grandfather and she would have loved her father to be around to dote on it, as he had her.

Twisting her ring around her finger, she thought of the potential grandparents she had yet to meet. Charlotte thought they sounded lovely and she and Andy had agreed they would visit them together on Saturday with their news. On Sunday she would introduce Andy to her mother, relieving them of the need for secrecy. Except where the 'other' Batistes were concerned. She would go alone to Maud's funeral and slip away unnoticed after the service. Harold would find out soon enough who she really was.

~ ~

Andy was jubilant as he and his father left the advocate's office, but his father looked pensive.

'What's the matter, Dad? I know he said it could take months to sort out the legal stuff, but at least he was convinced your case is watertight and Harold should never have tried to bamboozle you the way he did. You and Mum will be able to buy whatever you need,' he said, glancing at his father's frowning face.

Jim turned towards him, saying, 'I'm not too sure about this DNA lark, son. If we do need to use one as proof, how are we going to get Harold or Dave to agree? Don't think I would, in their shoes.'

'Oh, that's what's bothering you! I shouldn't worry, Dave's DNA will be on file thanks to his police record, and once Harold's arrested the police could take his DNA. In any event, the advocate was sure it wouldn't come to it. Trust me, Dad, it'll be fine. Why don't you and Mum start looking for a cruise, sometime next year? Do you good to travel a bit,' Andy said, opening the car door for Jim.

His father's face lightened. 'Well, if you think we could. I've always wanted to visit the Mediterranean countries, somewhere warm for my old bones. I suppose we should be able to afford it.'

Andy, slipping into his seat, burst out laughing. 'Afford it? Dad, the estate's worth millions, and I'd guess there's a pretty penny in the bank too. You could afford to cruise around the world for the rest of your lives if you wished.'

'Now that does sound like a good idea! Your mother wouldn't need to cook or clean and we could live like lords,' Jim said, chuckling. 'I'll tell you one thing, son, I don't want to live in his big house. Wouldn't feel comfortable. How about I give it to you?'

Andy gasped. 'What? Very generous of you, Dad, but I wouldn't want it either. You could put it up for sale and buy something more to your taste, and still have money over. Unless you do decide to spend your life at sea, then you won't need a house.'

Jim grinned and they drove back to St Sampson to tell Yvette the good news.

Half an hour later, Andy left his parents happily discussing cruises versus land-based holidays and drove back to his office. His own reason for celebration bubbled away inside, and he could hardly contain his happiness, wanting to shout it to the world. Another twenty-four hours and he could proudly present his beautiful fiancée to his parents. Now that would be a shock for them. Andy knew his mother was anxious for him to settle down and give her grandchildren, which he fervently wanted himself. He had not dared to hope Charlotte would want a family, after all she was thirty-nine and had her business to run. When she said she would like to try he was over the moon, wanting it to happen as soon as possible. But he had been truthful when he said he wanted her even if there couldn't be children. He counted himself a lucky man to have won her love.

Then he recalled they still hadn't discussed the thorny subject of where they lived. Not something he was keen to bring up. He had thought he would live in his cottage forever, had done much of the work himself. And he didn't want Charlotte throwing her money around, either. Gripping the steering wheel, he wondered how they were going to resolve it. All he knew was he didn't want to lose her.

~ ~

Charlotte twisted and turned, checking her reflection in the mirror. She had decided a skirt and jacket would be the better option for meeting her future in-laws, a more feminine look, and more likely to be approved of by the French Yvette. She didn't realise how nervous she was until Andy came into the room unexpectedly and she jumped.

He looked amused. 'I don't know why you're so anxious about creating the right impression, I'm the one you're marrying and anyway, they'll love you on sight. Just like me,' he said, grabbing her and giving her a kiss.

'It's all very well for you to say, but you wait until you have to face *my* mother tomorrow and then we'll see who's nervous,' she teased.

'You're right, I am scared of facing your mother, the Lady Annette Townsend no less, and telling her I'm marrying her daughter. She doesn't sound the type to be impressed by a mere architect,' he replied, widening his eyes in mock fear.

Charlotte laughed. 'I don't think my mother's bothered who I marry and if a mere architect is good enough for me, then it's all that matters. Now, be serious and tell me if I look okay?' She swirled round and he gave her the thumbs up.

'Come on or we'll be late and Mum hates people being late for a meal. I'm hoping she's cooked one of her French specials in honour of *le petite amie*. God knows what she'd serve up if she knew you're my fiancée!'

She grabbed her bag and followed him downstairs, picking up the bouquet of flowers she had bought earlier. Andy collected a bottle of Krug from the fridge before locking up. Charlotte, glancing at the heavy grey clouds, hoped the threatened rain would hold off for the afternoon, any moisture would turn her smooth waves to frizz in seconds. She fiddled with the ring under her glove while Andy drove through the middle of the island towards St Sampson, along roads new to her. The car was soon filled with the perfume of the oriental lilies in the bouquet, reminding Charlotte of her mother's hothouse at home. Although her passion was roses, Annette liked to grow a few exotic flowers in her hothouse, often filled with an almost overpowering mix of scents from the result of her efforts. Or, to be more exact, those of the gardener.

Thinking of her now, Charlotte wondered how tomorrow's lunch would pan out, not feeling quite as confident as she had sounded earlier. Deciding it was silly to worry now, she focused instead on the music playing on the CD and was soon carried along by Amy Winehouse, accompanied by an off-key Andy. Minutes later he pulled into the small drive of a semi-detached cottage in a lane not far from St Sampson Harbour, or the Bridge as the locals called it. As Charlotte stepped out of the car she saw a curtain twitch and smiled at Andy.

'Someone's checking me out.'

Taking her hand he led her to the front door, which opened before he could ring the bell.

The slim, attractive woman, wearing a mid-length skirt and silky blouse, received a kiss from Andy, then turned and smiled at her. 'Hello, you must be Charlotte. I'm Yvette, please, do come in,' she said, opening the door wide.

'Pleased to meet you...Yvette. These are for you,' she said, thrusting the bouquet into her arms.

'Oh, they are beautiful, thank you.' They exchanged kisses. 'Come, my husband is in here.' She pointed to the sitting room and Andy, still holding her hand, went in. Yvette disappeared, presumably to put the flowers in water. As Charlotte entered, a thin grey-haired man with smiling brown eyes, stood up slowly and shook her hand. The skin of his hand felt rough and calloused but the grip was firm. She liked him immediately.

'Charlotte, that's a nice name. Mine's Jim. Please sit down, Yvette will be back in a minute.'

She sat on the sofa next to Andy, who had nodded at his father before sitting down. She hoped Yvette would return soon, feeling awkward sitting there with her gloves on. Andy had just opened his mouth when Yvette bustled in to join them.

'*Alors*, how lovely it is to meet a friend of Andy's. Is it a long time you have known each other?'

Andy cleared his throat. 'A few months. Actually, *Maman*, I...we've got something to tell you both. Charlotte and I are engaged.' He lifted her hand, removing the glove to display the sparkling stones.

Yvette's hand flew to her mouth and Jim's jaw dropped. For a moment both were speechless and then Yvette reached over to embrace first Charlotte and then Andy, saying, 'I am so happy for you both. But such a surprise. Andy, such a bad boy you are to say nothing!' She tapped his arm.

Jim offered his congratulations, his face split in a wide smile. Andy reached into the bag at his feet and pulled out the Krug. 'Shall we have a glass to celebrate? Or is lunch ready, *Maman*?'

'Oh, lunch will wait! *S'il vous plait* Andy, fetch the glasses and we will have an aperitif, *non*?' Yvette's face was flushed with pleasure and Charlotte hoped her own mother would be as happy with the news. After they had raised their glasses in a toast, Andy told his parents how he and Charlotte had become close over the weeks. Even Jim's eyes misted over while Andy talked and Yvette had to dab at the occasional tear. The story continued once lunch – coq au vin – was served and by the time she and Andy left, Charlotte was left in no doubt she was a welcome addition to the family. Hugs and kisses, accompanied by cries of 'come again soon', enveloped her as she stood at the front door. Andy gently propelled her out and into the car, returning the waves of his excited parents as they drove away.

'Phew! Sorry about that, hope you didn't find them too much. But Mum is French so...' he shrugged.

'I thought they were lovely and you're lucky to have such loving parents. You might find meeting my mother will be rather different. And,' she said laughing, 'I suspect it won't be long before Yvette will be asking you if there's likely to be any *petit enfants* on the horizon.'

'Well, we're working on that, aren't we?' he said, stroking her thigh. 'Perhaps we shouldn't delay the wedding, just in case.'

'Mm, fine by me, as long as my mother's stable I'd be happy to make it soon. Let's see how she is tomorrow and we can start making plans.' She squeezed his hand, her heart thumping at the ever-closer prospect of shortly becoming Mrs Andy Batiste. Having met his parents and seen for herself their modest lifestyle and the tiny home where he had grown up, she did again wonder about the issue of their future home.

The Family Divided

'Andy, I think we need to talk when we get home.'

chapter thirty-four

Back at the cottage Charlotte made a pot of coffee before joining a wary looking Andy in the sitting room. She poured out two mugs, handed Andy his coffee and sat down beside him.

'What's the matter? It's not my parents is it? I know they were a bit full on but –' He reached out to stroke her hair.

'No, it's nothing to do with them. It's – it's about what I said when I was in London. About where we will live and our lifestyle.' His face took on a shuttered look but she had to press on. It was crucial to their future. 'I know you love your cottage, and quite rightly so. But, to be frank, it's not where I would see us living as a couple. And possibly with children. We...they would need more space. I'm used to having my own study and you need yours, and I have a lot of things I'd like to bring over from London...' She stopped, wanting him to say something.

'I know my house can't compete with a London mansion, but I put a lot of work into it. I'm proud of what I've done here,' he said, waving his arm. His face still inscrutable.

'Yes, and you have every right to be. It's lovely. But it's–'

'Too small for Madam?' He looked solemn.

Her heart sank. He was cross and she might have known it would all end in tears...She took a deep breath, determined to speak her mind.

'This is the twenty-first century, Andy, and I would want us to be equal partners in our relationship. You know my background and you fell in love with me in spite of it. We've had different upbringings, which doesn't bother me. And I would want to put my money into our home. Not a mansion but something...elegant and I'd like a cleaner or housekeeper.' She gripped her mug tight and watched for his reaction.

'Well, I hate to admit this, but you're right to say we would need something bigger if we had children. So perhaps we can consider moving, as long as we can find something we both like. And a cleaner should be okay as long as they don't live in. I hate the idea of servants which is what they would look like to me.' He smiled for the first time since they had returned home.

'You really don't mind? But...what about the cost? Would you let me put my money towards it? I know how expensive houses are over here.'

'Yes, but I have to sell this place first so let's wait until then before buying a new one. Agreed?'

Relief flooded through her. She guessed how hard it must have been for Andy to agree and her heart was filled with love for this wonderful, understanding man. 'I've been so worried you would think me stuck up–'

He kissed her hard on the mouth. 'I do think you're stuck up, but I still love you.'

Annette was flying in late morning and Charlotte had arranged to pick her up at one and take her out for lunch, saying she wanted her to meet someone. She and Andy had agreed he would wait for them at Le Fregate while she collected Annette in her hire car. The chilly weather again made the wearing of gloves seem unremarkable.

As Charlotte entered La Folie she spotted her mother talking to Gillian by the reception desk and walked over to join them. Annette allowed herself to be hugged and Gillian smiled warmly.

'I hadn't realised you were returning so soon, Gillian. Are you staying long?'

'Two weeks this time, and then we'll see.' She turned to Annette saying they would catch up later and said goodbye to Charlotte before leaving them alone. Charlotte shepherded her mother to the car, asking if she had had a good flight. Annette said it had been comfortable and settled into the passenger seat. Driving down the lane Charlotte asked if any specific treatments had been arranged by Gillian.

'I shall continue on the current programme until I've had a scan tomorrow. Gillian wants to see if the tumours are shrinking before changing anything.'

'Oh, right. Fingers crossed, then,' she said, glancing at her mother's inscrutable face. She was tempted to delay telling her mother about the engagement until after the scan, but if the news was bad it would be even harder to say anything. How do you share your own good news with someone who's seriously ill? At least they were not having a party to celebrate.

Not much more was said on the journey and Charlotte pulled into the restaurant car park feeling in need of a stiff drink. Thankful she and Andy had resolved the issue of homes and money, she was happier than she had been only the day before. All she wanted now was for her mother to accept Andy as her fiancé. As they walked into the bar, she smiled at the sight of Andy at a nearby table and ushered her mother towards him. He stood up and extended his hand.

'How do you do, Lady Townsend? I'm Andy Batiste, a friend of Charlotte's.' Dressed in an immaculate suit, shirt and tie, he looked the epitome of eligibility, Charlotte thought, her heart swelling with pride.

Annette allowed him to shake her hand and a smile hovered around her mouth. 'Pleased to meet you, Andy. I'm afraid Charlotte has told me nothing about you, so you may have the advantage of me.'

He pulled out a chair for her and Charlotte sat on Andy's other side, leaving him between the women.

'Mother, there's something important I need to tell you...'

Annette sat quite still while Charlotte explained about the engagement, offering her hand as confirmation. Her mother's eyebrows rose as she admired the ring, offering her congratulations to them both, accompanied by a warm smile. Charlotte was stunned. And Andy looked the same.

Her mother must have registered the look on Charlotte's face as she said, 'I'm not stupid, Charlotte. I have long since thought you must have met someone here, I've noticed the change in you. I was simply waiting for you to tell me.' She looked from one to the other. 'However, I must admit I was not expecting to be informed you were engaged. It does seem rather hasty after your recent...divorce,' she said, her eyebrows raised.

'We, er, didn't see any point in waiting, Mother. But I do hope you're happy for me and will welcome Andy as your son-in-law.'

'Of course I'm happy for you. And once I get to know Andy better, I'm sure I shall like him.' She then surprised them by calling over the waiter and asking for a bottle of champagne. Charlotte's eyes widened.

Annette smiled. 'I can hardly not toast my only child's engagement, can I?'

Charlotte and Andy exchanged a quick glance.

Moments later the waiter arrived with the chilled bottle and poured out three glasses.

They each lifted their flutes. 'To Charlotte and Andy, may you be very happy together,' Annette said, touching glasses.

Charlotte, dazed, sipped her champagne, wondering if her mother's treatment also included something for improving maternal feelings. Whatever had caused the change, she could only be grateful. Catching Andy's eye he gave her an imperceptible wink. It seemed she need not have worried about her mother's reaction after all...

In the car on the way back to La Folie Annette brought up the subject of the wedding, asking if she had made any plans.

'Not yet, but we were thinking of sooner rather than later.'

'Very sensible. You're not getting any younger and I assume you'd like children? Or are you already pregnant?'

Charlotte's face reddened. 'No, I'm not. But, yes, we would like children, although it may not be easy at my age.'

Her mother pursed her lips. 'True, but women older than you have conceived, some more than once. And I would quite like to be a grandmother.'

She was so surprised she nearly lost control of the car. 'I...never thought you were bothered. When I was married to Richard–'

'Oh, but I knew there was no question of a family with him. Most of my friends are now grandparents and they seem to think it's the most marvellous thing. I may not have been a loving mother but I think I could be a doting grandmother. Assuming I'm still around,' she said, biting her lip.

Charlotte patted her mother's hand, fear tightening her stomach. 'I'm sure you will be. Gillian and Paul seem confident they can help you and Gillian's very experienced.'

Annette nodded. 'They will do their best, I'm sure. And I'm very grateful to you for suggesting I seek alternative advice. At least now I have a fighting chance,' she said, smiling at her.

Again Charlotte was taken aback, this time for being thanked. Her mother was definitely changing.

'I'm glad for you, Mother. It's what we all want.'

The weather on Monday morning set the mood for the day of the funeral – cold, dull and wet. Charlotte shivered as she gazed out of the cottage window at the rain bouncing off the car. Turning her back on the dismal scene, she filled the kettle for another cup of coffee. After all the excitement of the past few days, today she felt a bit low at the thought of the funeral ahead and hoped the caffeine hit would help. Apart from the weather and the funeral there was nothing to make her feel like she did and she was annoyed with herself. Winter had never been her favourite time of year and she wondered if the SAD syndrome could be at the root of the problem. She needed sun and warmth, not rain and cold. As she made her coffee her mind drifted back to the conversation with Andy the previous evening. They were discussing the wedding.

'How about next month? Before the Christmas madness descends on us all. Business is quiet around then and I could take a couple of weeks off,' Andy said, kissing her as he joined her on the sofa.

'It's a bit soon! Not sure if I could arrange everything so quickly.'

'What's to arrange? I thought we both wanted a quiet do, just family and close friends.'

She asked herself why she was panicking. Andy was right, a few guests and an intimate party after the ceremony. How long could that take to plan? On her side there was her mother and possibly a couple of friends from uni and Andy only had his parents and a few close friends, including mutual ones like Louisa and Paul.

'You're right, it could be done. What about the venue?'

'The only option is the Greffe for the wedding itself, but we can have our party anywhere. Only about sixteen guests can come to the service but we're not looking at any more, are we?'

'No, that's fine. All we'll need is a restaurant with a private room.' She snuggled up to him. 'What about the honeymoon? I'd like somewhere hot and secluded,' she said, nibbling his ear.

'Then hot and secluded it is.'

Charlotte, her hands wrapped around the coffee mug, smiled at the thought of "hot and secluded". They had decided to ask Glenn, the owner of Louisa's travel agency, what he could come up with and Andy was to check out the Greffe for possible dates for the wedding. With the need to give sixteen days' notice there was no time to lose for early December. The happy thoughts of weddings and honeymoons finally pushed away the earlier mood and Charlotte finished her coffee before sitting down to write a list of potential wedding guests. She and Andy were going around to Louisa's that evening to break the news of their engagement. It looked as if they might be receiving an early wedding invitation as well.

She arrived at the church ten minutes before two o'clock. The rector was at the door greeting a straggle of mourners keen to get out of the rain. He smiled as she approached and as they shook hands, said he was pleased she had been able to come.

'I wanted to pay my respects, Vicar, but I'll disappear once the service is over.' She turned to check they were alone and whispered, 'The police aren't going to turn up here, are they?'

'No, certainly not. I believe they will call round tomorrow morning–' he broke off as the hearse arrived.

'I'll leave you to it,' she said, vanishing into the church, keen to avoid coming face to face with Harold. The pews were decently full of mourners, probably acquaintances of Harold rather than Maud, Charlotte thought, slipping into a space at the back. The only person she recognised was Sal, the carer, seated a couple of rows ahead. A blast from the organ announced the arrival of the cortège and everyone rose to their feet. Charlotte kept her head down, but took a quick peep as the coffin drew level. Harold was the sole mourner pacing behind, sombre in black. She hugged to herself the knowledge such an evil man was soon to reap his just deserts, and shivered slightly as he passed.

Without warning the image of her mother intruded into her thoughts. With the results of the scan only days away, the thought of whether or not the news would be good was never far from her mind. But here, in the church, her eyes following the progress of Maud's coffin towards the altar, it seemed an omen. She had to grip onto the back of the pew in front to stop herself sagging. No, no she couldn't accept it. Her mother must not die! The organ sprang into life again as the congregation sang the first hymn and Charlotte forced herself to join in. It helped to soothe her and she was able to sit down feeling calmer as the rector read out a brief eulogy, explaining Maud's widower was too upset to read it himself.

'Humbug!' she muttered under her breath, causing a neighbour to glance in her direction. As she listened to a fulsome description of "a paragon of virtue, wonderful wife and mother", Charlotte relived the time she had spent with Maud and decided it was a load of hogwash. She wouldn't allow herself to wonder what she could say about her mother if...Forcing her mind back to the service, thinking although Maud had been no saint, she was not as black as her husband. And Charlotte respected her for wanting to put things right for Jim and was present solely for that reason.

The service was concluded and the journey of the coffin reversed and as it passed her Charlotte looked up to find Harold's baleful eyes on her. A look of puzzled recognition crossed his face and she immediately looked away, her heart racing. He was obliged to walk on and Charlotte waited until the church had emptied before leaving. She watched from the porch as the hearse and mourners' cars left for the interment in the cemetery and then retrieved her car. Even though she knew Harold could not harm her, she was glad to get in the car and drive away. And the service had brought up things she couldn't bear to think about.

The Family Divided

The evening with Louisa and Paul washed away the darkness of the funeral. Charlotte and Andy were welcomed warmly by their friends and as soon as Louisa spotted her ring, she let out a joyful cry.

'I can't believe it! You two haven't wasted any time, have you? But I'm so, so pleased for you both.' Hugs and kisses were exchanged again and Andy brought out another bottle of Krug, causing Louisa to have a fit of the giggles, shortly joined by Charlotte.

Paul raised his eyebrows, but was grinning as he opened the bottle. After the requisite toast to the newly engaged couple, they sat down to catch up on the events of the past few days. By the time they were leaving, Charlotte noticed Louisa was looking pensive.

'Everything all right?' she whispered as they stood apart from the men.

'Yeees. But now you're engaged and getting married next month, I'm hoping Paul won't be long popping the question. I'm always worried–'

'Hey! Don't be silly. He adores you, just give him time. Not everyone rushes full-speed ahead like us. He might even propose at our wedding, he's such a romantic at heart,' Charlotte said, giving her a hug.

Louisa's face brightened and she agreed it was a possibility. Andy grabbed Charlotte's hand and as she shouted goodbye, she hoped she was right. It would be lovely to have a double celebration.

The next couple of days passed slowly and Charlotte struggled to focus on her writing. Her mind continually wandered off to her mother's scan and the all-important results due on Wednesday, and also to Harold and his longed-for arrest. By Wednesday afternoon Charlotte could wait no longer and rang her mother at La Folie.

'Hello, Mother. Have you had the results yet?'

'Ah, Charlotte, I was going to ring you. Yes, Gillian's just informed me the scan shows the tumours have shrunk a little, which is good news.'

'It certainly is! Oh, I'm so pleased. What does Gillian say?' She felt the lead dissolve and she smiled.

'I'm to start on the new treatment we discussed and will be monitored regularly, and she says it looks promising for a remission.' She paused. 'Now, tell me if there's any news about the wedding.'

'We can book the Greffe for the 12th December and we think we've got somewhere for the party. I'm just waiting to hear from the travel agent about the honeymoon, and then it's full steam ahead.'

Her mother wanted to know all the details and Charlotte, surprised but pleased by her interest, was happy to oblige. The call ended with her saying she would call round to see Annette the next day. Change was definitely in the air.

Andy arrived home from work waving a copy of the *Guernsey Evening Press*.

'It's in the paper!' he cried, swinging her around the hall.

'What is? Oh, is it about Harold?' she asked, her own excitement matching his.

'Yep, front page too. Look,' he said, handing it over.

Charlotte scanned the headline "Wealthy land-owner charged with murder and fraud", underneath which a photo showed a scowling Harold, his arm raised as if to ward off the photographer. She read on for the details. Looking up she saw the gleam in Andy's eyes and kissed him.

'It's all come right, darling. There will be justice for your family at last.'

COMING NEXT

Echoes of Time

The Guernsey Novels Book 5

Natalie Ogier returns to Guernsey to escape an abusive ex-boyfriend and buys a beautiful cottage built on the site of a derelict and secluded farm. Her only immediate neighbour is Stuart, a descendant of the original owners.

Not long after she moves in, Natalie experiences disturbing dreams and is also troubled by unexplained noises. The atmosphere grows increasingly chilling and unfriendly and she feels afraid in her new home.

Natalie is wary of Stuart, suspecting him of being responsible for what is happening in the cottage. But after he rescues her from potential harm, she learns to trust him and together they seek out the truth. Tales of betrayal, injustice – and ultimately revenge – echo down the years...